DRAWN TO DEATH

KAT SHEHATA

In loving memory of JoJo
Thanks for the inspiration, Mom

PROLOGUE

SYDNEY REYNOLDS

The handle on the bathroom door rattled.

I removed my cucumber eye mask and stared at the door, thinking maybe I had imagined it.

"Vaughn?" I called my husband's name. "Is that you?"

No answer. The floorboards creaked in the hallway. Someone was out there.

"Honey?" Vaughn left for the hospital an hour ago to check on a patient. I couldn't imagine he'd returned home. My client, Evelyn Sinclair, had an art show that evening. Since Vaughn had been called to work, we agreed to go separately and meet at the gallery.

Maybe there's been a change in plans.

I drained the sudsy water from the bath, clicked off the spa music, and reached for a towel. Spa-scented bubbles clung to my body as I stepped out of the tub. The aromatherapy candles on the counter flickered when I tossed my towel in the hamper and replaced it with my fuzzy pink robe.

I searched the room for my phone to check my messages, then realized I'd left it on the nightstand in our bedroom. I turned on the lights, killing my atmospheric mood lighting, and moved to the bathroom door. I held my breath and listened for signs of life. No footsteps. No movement in the hallway.

The house was quiet except for the pitter-patter of raindrops beating against the windows.

Vaughn always changed his clothes and showered when he came home. Maybe he didn't want to disturb my spa time and decided to use the guest bathroom to clean up.

Or maybe it isn't him trying to open the bathroom door?

I shook off the thought. I wasn't usually so paranoid, but I'd received a string of disturbing phone calls and texts from an unknown caller over the past few weeks that had my senses on high alert.

I had initially believed the calls to my cell were random. They were infrequent. Nothing more than the sound of a man breathing. But this morning, a gift box was on my desk when I got to work. A card was tucked into the ribbon with my name scrolled across the center.

I opened the envelope and read the note. *"Wear this for me tonight, Sydney."*

No signature. Just a hand-drawn heart. My husband was a cardiovascular surgeon, so it wasn't off the mark to draw a heart to hint that it was from him.

But when I opened the present, I was surprised to find a skimpy negligee and thigh-high silk stockings. I gasped from the shock and checked around the room to see if any of my coworkers had noticed. Thankfully, no one had. Naturally, my first thought was that my husband had sent the gift.

But it wasn't like Vaughn to send something risqué that would embarrass me at work. A dozen beautiful roses, yes. But he never bought me kinky lingerie.

As I processed the boldness of the gift, I suspected my husband was not the sender. I had the uncomfortable feeling the raunchy gift and disturbing calls were related. I planned to discuss the matter with Vaughn that evening and then decide if the harassment warranted a call to Chicago PD.

Wear this for me tonight, Sydney.

My mind raced with disturbing thoughts. Did the unknown caller break into our home while I was bathing?

Do you seriously believe an intruder would be so kind as to wait for you to finish your "me time" before he attacked you, Sydney?

The idea was ridiculous. I had to be reasonable. Once I got to my bedroom and retrieved my phone, I would text Vaughn. He was never too busy to step away and return my call.

I unlocked the door and twisted the lock. As the door creaked open, I peeked into the hallway. I placed my hand on my chest and laughed with relief. An adorable teddy bear was holding a red satin heart, leaning against the wall.

Red and white rose petals were scattered along the floor like bread crumbs leading the way to our bedroom door. This was undeniably Vaughn's romantic gesture.

Red roses for the passion that burns in my heart. White for the pureness of our eternal love.

Instrumental jazz music played, and the soft glow of a salt lamp created the romantic ambience that was the work of my sweet, handsome and very romantic husband.

I felt foolish for letting my imagination run away with wild ideas about an intruder.

I lifted the bear off the floor and cuddled him in my arms, smiling as I pictured my handsome husband strolling into the hospital's gift shop and purchasing a cartoonish stuffed animal.

He often spoke of the sweet senior citizen volunteers who

ran the gift shop, teasing me that one or two or all of them had a massive crush on him, the handsome heart surgeon who visited them daily for his chocolate bar and peppermints fix to satisfy his sweet tooth.

"I'm sure the ladies teased him when he bought you," I whispered playfully to the bear.

As I headed toward our bedroom, butterflies of excitement fluttered in my stomach. I felt a rush of gratitude that I had married the kindest and most thoughtful man I had ever known. Vaughn was everything. I couldn't wait to see what other surprises awaited in our bedroom.

I hope this means he's no longer upset with me.

After we'd made love last weekend, I had hinted to him about spicing things up with some naughty play toys. He seemed insulted that I would prefer an instrument to take the place of his magical touch.

I hadn't meant to insinuate that I needed more, just something different. He had a healthy ego, and after I'd suggested it, I felt guilty because I'd hurt his feelings. Vaughn hadn't explicitly said as much, but he'd acted moody afterward, and we hadn't made love since.

Surgery days wiped him out, and he rarely had the time or energy during the week to indulge in romantic encounters. I hoped to reward his thoughtful gesture with the pleasurable kind of kisses that drove him wild, along with a fantastic evening under the sheets.

I pushed open our bedroom door and glanced around to find my husband. More rose petals were scattered on the bed and all over the room, but he wasn't there. Instead, there was a bottle of bubbly in an ice bucket, two champagne flutes, chocolates, and juicy strawberries—and the skimpy lingerie I'd received at work spread out across the bed.

This is wrong. I tossed the gift box into the dumpster behind our office and stuffed the skimpy contents of the gift into the bottom of my computer bag. Had Vaughn searched my personal belongings?

Was he angry I wasn't more receptive to his gift? Maybe he had come up with another way to spice up our love life without the sex toys. Did he think I wanted to wear this?

I glanced at the nightstand. The honeymoon picture of us on Captiva Island had been turned facedown—

The electricity went out. The room fell dark. Heavy footsteps thundered up the stairs.

Oh, God! I'd fallen into a trap. I fumbled through the darkness, desperate to reach my phone. The only light in the room came from flashes of lightning from the storm looming over the Windy City.

Crash! A heavy body tackled me and slammed me down on the bed. Instead of falling on a pillow to soften the blow, my head banged against the wooden headboard, knocking me nearly unconscious.

While I struggled to reorient myself, a man straddled my body and covered my mouth with a gloved hand to muffle my screams.

"You're mine now, Sydney. He can't have you anymore." He pushed against me and moaned, aroused by my helplessness and fear.

A lightning bolt struck, followed by a rumble of thunder that shook the windows. While the room was illuminated for a split second, I saw my attacker's face. He was wearing a ski mask.

I couldn't make out his features, but something about his voice and his body's familiar shape alerted me that the man shoving a gag into my mouth and securing my wrists with zip ties was someone I knew.

He tied a bandanna around my eyes to serve as a blindfold and secured my ankles with rope.

I screamed for help, but the gag prevented the sound

from escaping my lips. I tried to fight him off and struggle free, but he was too strong.

I reverted to survival mode and remembered the lessons I'd learned from a self-defense class I'd taken with my girl-friends over the summer.

"If an attacker threatens you, fight for your life. Never let him take you to a second location. The place where detectives find corpses, not survivors, is Location B."

Once my assailant had me subdued and silenced, he tossed me over his shoulder and lumbered down the stairs. I was disoriented from being upside down, and I'd hit my head so hard that I was sure I was suffering from a severe head injury.

I couldn't see and relied on my other senses to navigate my nightmare.

The back door of our townhome opened and closed, then I recognized the sound of a heavy van door sliding open. My attacker dumped me on a pile of musty blankets. He slapped a handcuff on my wrist that was attached to a chain.

Oh, God. It's him.

A new level of fear overcame me when I knew beyond a shadow of a doubt the identity of my attacker. I writhed and kicked my bound legs in a desperate attempt to save myself from the horror that awaited at the hands of my abductor.

I cried out for my husband. "Vaughn!"

The door slammed shut. The engine revved. The van sped off toward Location *B*.

BONES—EVELYN

THREE MONTHS EARLIER...

"I saved the best for last," Sydney said.

When my real estate agent rolled up to an old brick building on Halsted Street with a torn red awning and security bars on the first-floor windows, I thought she was playing a cruel prank.

"This is the place?" I pointed to the historic commercial building in Chicago's famed arts district. The old warhorse had power lines zigzagging overhead and a battalion of street-smart pigeons ready to open fire on passersby.

"*This* is it, Evelyn." Sydney slung her Louis tote over her shoulder and led the way to the entrance.

I treaded lightly under the tattered awning that proudly announced "Chez Arte" and tiptoed around the bird-crap splatters that littered the entryway. The droppings were so expressive and heavily layered that they held the spirit of a Jackson Pollock painting.

Once inside, I covered my mouth to stifle a scream. Inlaid tile floors, exposed brick, vast open spaces, and huge picture windows caked with no less than six inches of city grime.

"What do you think of her bones?" Sydney asked.

I slowly turned, taking it all in. "I'll need to refinish the floors, replace some fixtures, power wash everything, rehome the vermin." I pointed to a trail of rodent droppings along the wall.

I didn't see the space for what it was. I was excited about what she could be. I imagined portable room dividers for our artists to hang their art and create gallery space for each individual. The wall on the far side of the room had enough space for a small stage and seating area for thoughtful presentations and conversations with the artists.

"What are you thinking, Evelyn?"

"This is in my budget?" I glanced up at an antique brass chandelier needing a good polishing. I flipped the light switch. Dead.

"It's on the lower end of what we discussed, which gives you extra room to budget in the remodel. If you want to consider properties outside of Halsted—"

"No way. Location is nonnegotiable. The gallery must be on Halsted."

"Right. Let's continue the tour."

When we reached the second floor, I pulled back the dingy curtains to let in the light. I saw a row of trees lining the sidewalk out the window. There was a bike rack in front of the building and another art gallery a block away. Perfect for cross-promoting with my fellow artists.

I've been a part of the highly publicized Final Friday Gallery Walks since I moved to the city as an artist and art lover. The idea that I would be a gallery owner and have a studio in the famed art district was my wildest dream come to life.

While I mentally tallied the remodeling bill, an unending wave of emergency vehicles roared down the street. Hearing sirens from police cars and frantic honking from firetrucks was as natural to the city as pigeons cooing over discarded hot dog buns.

But this was different.

I moved to the front window that faced the street to get a better look at the action. "Someone must've died to get this much attention."

Sydney moved to the window and tapped on the glass, pointing out a line of law enforcement vehicles. "Murdered," she said. "You don't get that many cops if you have a heart attack."

I nodded, acknowledging the native Chicagoan's keen observation. I was from a small town in Ohio and had only lived in the city for a short time. I wasn't naive. I knew Chicago was dangerous. I had stopped watching the evening news because the crimes were too disturbing.

In my short time in Chi-Town, I experienced city life's positive side. An active social scene, museums, tourist attractions, Portillo's hot dogs, the White Sox, the Bulls, the Bears, the Cubs, the Blackhawks, the Bean, the beluga whales at the Shedd Aquarium...

"Did you know it was going to happen?" Sydney asked. "The accident, I mean. Did you have a feeling you were going to die?"

I was absorbed in my thoughts and hadn't noticed Sydney's demeanor had changed. Her eyes glistened with tears, and she looked rattled. Her question had thrown me off. I had never mentioned my near-death experience and wondered what had prompted her to ask me about it.

Sydney must've read my bewilderment and elaborated. "I checked out your website. I wanted to find the perfect building for your gallery, and I did my research. Your survival story is amazing." Sydney waved off her rush of emotions as if dismissing the conversation.

"What's wrong?"

"Nothing. Everything is perfect. That's what scares me." Sydney pulled a tissue out of her purse, dabbed her eyes, and blotted her tears without smearing her makeup. "I just got married. I've never been happier. I'm afraid the bubble is going to burst."

Sydney smiled softly and shook her head, chastising herself for getting too personal with a client. "Enough about me."

"No way," I said. "I need to see a pic of your *bubble*."

Sydney lifted her phone and shared a series of wedding shots and candid selfies with her incredibly handsome blond-haired, blue-eyed husband. "This is Vaughn. We met six months ago. Love at first sight," Sydney beamed. "He proposed after we'd known each other for two weeks. Every-thing happened so quickly. I haven't had a moment to settle into my new life."

I was happy for Sydney. Truly. Seeing her cuddled in the arms of her new husband was a subtle reminder that I had neglected my personal life. "You two are adorable. Full disclosure, I'm a little jealous. I haven't been on a date since I moved here. Where did you meet this handsome guy?"

"Through an executive dating service. I've been so busy with my career that I never meet anyone outside of work. The idea of hooking up with a guy at a bar or through a dating app wasn't my scene, so I researched and found a boutique matchmaker service."

Sydney lifted a business card out of her purse and pressed it into my palm. "The Armstrong Agency. You are their ideal candidate, Evelyn. Smart, successful, financially well-off, talented, and gorgeous. I'll call the owner and give you a glowing referral."

I shook my head, embarrassed by her flattery. I opened my mouth to argue, but I couldn't think of one reason why I wouldn't take Sydney up on her offer. I had been consumed by my artistic ambitions and moving to a new city caused me to fail miserably in the dating department.

I gave Sydney an appreciative smile and thanked her for the referral. "And the answer to your earlier question is *no*. I never saw it coming. The day I died was as normal as any other day. No premonitions of death. No vultures circling the lake. No little voice inside my head warned me not to get into the water. Zero awareness. I was blindsided."

"Alright." Sydney shook off her anxiety. "Enough about death and hot guys. Let's talk art galleries." Sydney and I had only met a few times to discuss my real estate needs, but we had an instant rapport. We were around the same age, mid-twenties, career driven, and shared the same passion for fixer-uppers.

Sydney moved to the staircase and ran her fingers along the mahogany railing. "Does this under-market-value diamond in the rough put off an Evelyn Sinclair Gallery vibe?"

The emergency sirens had trailed off, leaving the omnipresent hustle of street noise. The city's pulse ebbed and flowed with the movements and moods of the people who lived and worked in the Windy City.

Every town has its share of crime. Everything will be fine as long as I'm careful.

"She's perfect." I may have been out of my mind to invest in the ghost of an old art gallery, but it seemed a thousand percent crazier—and sadder—not to follow my dreams.

"Wonderful," Sydney said. "Since you'll be paying cash, we'll be able to close as soon as the paperwork is in order. Let's go back to my office and talk offers."

DRAWN TO HIM—EVELYN

I PULLED BACK THE CURTAINS IN MY STUDIO AND WELCOMED the warmth of the fall sunshine. I cracked open the window to invite fresh air into my artist's loft but got a whiff of dumpster trash from the alley behind my building.

While the stench of cigarette smoke and rotten garbage was unpleasant, I found Chicago's energetic buzz and chatter a refreshing change from my previous small-town life. My debut collection of paintings was complete for the opening, and I needed to take a mental break and draw something for pleasure.

I closed my eyes and listened to the sounds of the bustling city. Honking horns, bursts of laughter. Pigeons cooing, sirens blaring. Beeps from the crosswalk signal, dogs barking at passersby. The collective energy of my new home energized my creativity.

I'd been so consumed with remodeling my new gallery, working on marketing for the opening, and settling into my new life that I had neglected my artistic soul. I packed my art supplies and headed into the city to hunt down my inspiration.

The divine scent of freshly brewed coffee and sweet treats welcomed me as I entered Taboo, my favorite local café. The quaint local business was stocked with people engrossed with their phones, loners tapping on their Macs, and the usual coffee-loving crowd getting their early morning buzz on.

I ordered a macchiato and found a table in a corner. I slurped the foam off the top of my drink and savored the sweet cream and caramel drizzled over the top as I scanned the room, searching for my next victim.

I pulled my sketch pad and pencil out of my purse, then held my hand in a ready position as I sized up my prey. College kids, retired couples, uptight business pros…

There you are.

A handsome man with thick, dark hair seated by the exit door caught my attention. He was drinking a healthy green smoothie and tapping on his phone. He probably wouldn't notice if I snuck a couple of glances at him while I sketched his portrait. I started with a faint outline of his face and broad shoulders, then filled in the details.

The shearling collar of his thick coat was flipped asymmetrically—one side up, one side down—giving an edge of irony to his impeccable style and physical perfection.

When I peeked up for another glance, he busted me staring. My heart pounded as he held my gaze for an uncomfortable few seconds. The allure of his golden-brown eyes held my attention until I forced myself to turn away.

Jeez. That was awkward. I sank my teeth into a jumbo-sized bear claw and shifted in my chair to signal my surrender from our staring match. Sketching strangers was something I did all the time. I rarely got busted.

Now that I was thoroughly embarrassed, I drew blindly and let memory serve as my guide. It was impossible to forget his face; even if I didn't capture all his features perfectly, his eyes were unforgettable.

When I'd turned my attention away from him, I could still feel the heat of his stare. My sixth sense alerted me that I was engaged in a dangerous game. I was in Chicago, covertly spying and sketching a handsome Italian man.

I hated to thrust a stereotype on a guy I knew nothing about, but what if he was *connected*? I glanced up to see if the handsome stranger wanted to play another round, but he had disappeared. As an artist, I owned the idea that I had a fantastic imagination. Life would be dull without 1,001 *what-if* scenarios playing out in my head all the time.

I smiled as I processed the handsome man's reaction to my not-so-covert staring.

What do you have to hide, big guy?

Going with the connected mob guy fantasy, I sketched edgy, dark lines and shadows around his features and drew a jagged scar across his neck like someone had sliced his throat but failed to finish the job.

Judging by his size and bulging muscles, I pegged him as an enforcer on *The Outfit's* org chart. The menace to society that solves problems and cleans up the messes to keep the higher-ups out of trouble. I took some artistic liberties and added a thick gold chain with a blingy cross pendant and some edgy neck tattoos—

"Mind if I join you?"

I let out a yelp as the stranger pulled out the empty chair at my table and slid into the seat across from me. The intensity of his glare was sharp enough to slice me in half.

The stranger fixed his gaze on mine as he awaited my response.

What the hell does he want me to say?

I glanced down at my drawing and winced. It was one thing to sketch a portrait of a random guy in a coffee shop.

But it was a new level of fucked up to add scars, unholy tattoos, and religious symbols.

"I was just leaving." I flipped my sketch pad over to hide my horrid drawing, hoping that was the end of the awkwardness.

"You're a talented artist. Are you a professional?" The stranger leaned back in the chair and crossed his leg, making it clear our conversation wasn't over.

I wanted to grab my purse and bolt, but the stranger had positioned himself between me and the door. He had a commanding vibe, and I sensed he went on a mental reconnaissance mission every time he entered a room.

"No, drawing is just a hobby," I lied. My art gallery was a couple blocks away, with my self-portrait visible from the street. If Eagle Eye wanted to know who I was, all he had to do was look out the window.

The stranger leaned back in the chair like a cool and casual jaguar, lounging on a low tree limb, swishing his tail as he basked in his predatorial glory. "You think drawing strange men in a coffee shop is a good idea?"

The answer, of course, was no. I had made a mistake, and he called me out for it, but he didn't need to treat me like a criminal for drawing his picture. Instead of allowing him to art shame me, I ended the conversation on my terms.

"Obviously not." I flipped over my sketchbook, giving him a full view of my masterpiece. "Let's make a deal." I leaned forward and locked my gaze on his to let him know he wasn't the only big cat in the concrete jungle.

"How about I give you the drawing, and we'll forget this little incident ever happened." I tapped my pointy, black-painted fingernail over his portrait. "Deal?"

With a nod and a prideful smirk, he accepted my offer.

The big guy may have thought his intimidation technique had frazzled me into submission. Still, as he savored his false victory, I had already constructed my retaliation plan. Instead of handing over my work—I never gave out my drawings for free—I ripped out the page and tore it into a million pieces.

I swiped his half-empty green smoothie, littered the shreds into his cup, and stirred the paper into the mix with his straw. I slid the cup back in front of him and blinked innocently like the helpless prey he believed me to be.

"Oh, sorry. Did you want me to sign it first?" I cracked up at my lame attempt at humor. How could anyone seriously be mad at me for drawing a picture?

The guy grinned at my good-natured attempt at defusing an awkward situation. "No problem. I made copies." He slid his phone out of his pocket and turned it around so I could see the screen.

There were a series of photos of me drawing his picture. Another round from his vantage point at the table where I'd first seen him, then several more from behind my back when I thought he had left.

While I sat there, staring at the photos in bewilderment, I sensed my innocent sketch had been perceived as a mortal sin by the enforcer who had inserted himself into my personal space. He wasn't messing around. He was seriously pissed. Maybe my connected mob guy theory wasn't that crazy after all.

"I wish you hadn't torn up the original," he said. "I was going to ask you if I could give it to my mother. She's always nagging me to get some neck tattoos." The guy picked up his smoothie cup and squinted at the remains of his portrait, oozing with green slime and clinging to life against the clear plastic cup.

I laughed more robustly than I'd intended. I hadn't realized I was holding my breath. I'd made the regrettable mistake of letting my eyes wander. My gaze zoomed on his thick arms and broad chest, then skidded into dangerous territory as I admired the muscular shape of his rocking body.

My cheeks warmed with embarrassment when he busted me checking him out. His eyes were wild with amusement, and I sensed the attraction was mutual.

The handsome stranger held my gaze, enjoying his effect on me. "What's your name?"

"Evelyn."

"Evelyn, *what*?"

I made a flat line motion with my hand. "Just Evelyn." Even though he seemed to share my dry sense of humor, I wasn't ready to trust him and give up my last name.

He grinned and offered his hand as a truce. "Nice to meet you, *Just* Evelyn. I'm *Just* Leo."

I accepted his peace offering and grasped his hand. His skin was warm, and his grip firm. His alpha male vibe pulsed, *"Don't fuck with me... Don't fuck with me... Don't fuck with me..."*

The stranger's phone beeped, momentarily stealing his attention. His eyes sharpened as he read a text. His expression intensified while he scrolled through whatever information had landed on his phone. Clearly, the news wasn't good.

While Leo tapped out a response, I took the hint that our impromptu meeting had run its course. This was an intriguing guy, but I needed to get to work. I gathered my art supplies, shoved them back into my purse, and gave him a friendly wave goodbye as I headed out.

Leo tore his gaze away from his phone and was on my heels in a hot second. As we headed toward the door, a long line of emergency vehicles raced past the coffee shop, sirens screaming. A sound that was sadly becoming normal.

"Which direction are you headed?" Leo tossed his cup into the recycling bin. Then he opened the door and touched the small of my back as he ushered me out of the café. A warm wave of attraction washed over me from his gentlemanly gesture.

I had taken Sydney's advice and signed up with the Armstrong Agency—the matchmaking service. I had been on about a dozen dates with an array of handsome, successful, and intelligent men—but I hadn't found any of them as intriguing or sexy as Leo.

"That way." I pointed in the direction of my gallery. The same direction the emergency vehicles were racing off to.

"I'm headed that way, too. I'll walk you back."

I squinted into the sun peeking over the skyline, shining her spotlight on the Windy City. Despite the city's dark side, there was always light at the end of the Loop. Maybe my *light* was the dangerously handsome man walking beside me.

DEATH POSE—LEO

THERE WERE THREE REASONS WHY I WAS ESCORTING MY NEW friend to work. The first was the most obvious. The streets were dangerous. Evelyn should never walk alone. She was a living, breathing invitation to would-be criminals.

She wasn't paying attention to her surroundings. She had no personal safety device in hand. In a hot second, a sexual predator could roll up beside her, snatch her off the sidewalk, and shove her into the trunk of his car before she could even dream of screaming for help.

"Do you work around here, too?" Evelyn looked up at me and offered a gentle smile. The air was frigid in the early morning hours. She looped a gauzy cotton scarf around her neck as she shook off a chill.

At first glance, the design appeared to be an abstract of fall colors. On closer inspection, I recognized the image of a person—or an ape—or however one would classify Bigfoot. The wild yeti had some wicked little watercolor friends with big teeth and devil horns running amuck in their fabled forest habitat.

Evelyn's bold fashion sense starkly contrasted with her calm, quiet beauty. Even with the crazy scarf, tall boots, and gorgeous long hair, her bright-blue eyes were her most striking characteristic.

"Yeah, today I'll be working in this area." Small talk wasn't my style, and I never gave up personal information without running a background check first. This led me to the second reason I was walking the artist to work—I wanted to know more about her.

"What do you do for a living?" she asked.

"I was about to ask you the same thing."

Her lips curled into a devilish grin. "You'll see."

Evelyn had a fun-loving attitude and approachable charm that sucked me into wanting to spend more time with her. If it hadn't been for the body of a missing person that required my attention, I would've wanted to spend the rest of the day with her.

Evelyn stopped in front of a newly remodeled building and pulled a clunky set of keys out of her bag. A spotlight shone on a single painting displayed in the window while the rest of the glass was covered with brown paper to hide the contents inside.

The painting was a portrait of the beautiful woman beside me—but the artist had taken some liberties with the state of her condition. Evelyn had portrayed herself as a ghost.

Her gorgeous hair cascaded down her breasts in long, loose waves. Her skin was translucent and radiated an eerie shade of blue. She wore a billowy cream-colored gown with a row of tiny blue flowers painted along the bustline and a tight corset accentuating her hourglass figure.

I didn't know much about art, but I knew a hell of a lot about dead bodies. The artist had a keen eye for macabre details. She had smudged the paint to create postmortem discoloration around the fingers to give the viewer an approximate time of death. No bloating. No insects. No decay.

The subject—*Evelyn*—had not been dead for long.

Aside from the fact that Evelyn had drawn herself as a corpse, the most haunting part of her portrayal was her death pose. Evelyn aimed her finger at me, the viewer, as if blaming the audience for her murder.

Her expression was frozen in an agonizing scream that echoed off the bent trees and withered landscape that melted in her wake. Coming from the sky, a devilish creature with black-tipped wings and talons for feet ascended upon the subject and was a moment away from capturing Evelyn's tortured soul.

Wherever the angel of death planned on taking her—she wasn't going without a fight.

I tore my gaze away from Evelyn's death portrait and shot the living artist an accusatory glare. I tried to form an intelligent response to her gory painting, but I went with my gut and said the first thing that came to mind. "Damn."

Evelyn laughed at my one-word assessment of the painting she had obviously thrown her heart and soul into creating. "Yeah, my style isn't for everyone. I had to block the windows to hide the rest of my collection. I didn't want to frighten the neighborhood children."

I shook my head, worried I had insulted her. "I didn't mean to insinuate I didn't like it. I was just surprised you painted yourself that way."

Evelyn's lips curled into a wicked smile. "Welcome to my dark side." She touched my arm and pointed to a slab of reclaimed wood hanging above the painting that announced the gallery's name.

The Death of Me
An Evelyn Sinclair Gallery

Her complexion beamed a confident glow as I pondered the name. "Does that mean you died? In the metaphorical sense, or a near-death experience?"

"The interpretation belongs in the eyes of the beholder. Art is meant to bring out the feelings and experiences of the individual. It may be metaphorical to some, and literal to others. I hope that everyone sees something unique that speaks to their soul."

In my line of work, when I ask a question, I expect an answer. Precisely, the truth. If someone had played that "interpretation is in the eye of the beholder" crap on me in my world, they would've had the pleasure of meeting the not-so-charming side of my personality.

"Could you just answer the question?" I asked politely, but I'd been told my social skills could use a tune-up.

Work was my life, and I ended up spending more time with corpses and killers than I did with good and decent living people. I'd spent time with a lot of beautiful women who didn't understand my commitment to the badge. There were a lot of things in life that I was good at. Making women happy to be with me was not one of them.

I waved my hand to erase my jackass response. "What I meant was, I'd like to hear more about your work." I hoped she read my sincerity and cut me a break. This was my warm-up to the third reason I had walked Evelyn back to work—I wanted to ask her out.

Evelyn held her gaze on mine for a moment to gauge my sincerity, then reached into her purse and pulled out an invitation. "I'm having a small private event here on Friday for my friends and patrons. My fellow artists and I are doing an informal Q&A and discussing our fall collections. I'll be sharing the life-changing experience that inspired my paranormal style."

The invitation was embossed with the name of her gallery in bloodred letters.

"The Death of Me." Her *death*, in whatever form, had apparently influenced her artistic style.

I tapped the card as I read the details on the invitation. "I've never been to an art show before. What do I wear to something like this, a tux?"

"Yep. It's a super-formal event," she said melodramatically. "A tux is the required dress code, along with shiny black shoes, a tall top hat, a dapper walking cane..."

"Perfect. That's how I usually dress on Friday nights."

Evelyn had an infectious laugh and a genuine smile. I pictured her as the funny girl in her friend circle and imagined how she would replay the story of our impromptu meeting. "I was sitting in the coffee shop, minding my own business, drawing strangers like I always do..."

A horn honked to get my attention. My partner had arrived to pick me up for work.

"Thanks for the invite, Evelyn. Duty calls." As I opened the door of Parker's truck, Evelyn called my name.

"Hey! You never told me what you do for a living."

I slid my jacket aside and flashed the Chicago PD star clipped to my belt. "Detective Leo Ricci, Violent Crimes Task Force."

Evelyn put her hand on her hip and nodded as if my statement answered a million questions. "Glad you're one of the good guys."

As much as I would've loved to spend more time with Evelyn, Parker and I had a crime scene to process. As my partner drove to the scene of our latest homicide investigation, I watched Evelyn in the rearview mirror waving goodbye.

I focused on her until her image disappeared in the early morning fall haze. One moment she was there. The next, she was gone.

Damn.

OUT OF MY MIND—LEO

I CRANKED UP THE HEAT IN THE SHOWER AND INHALED THE steam as I de-stressed after a long couple of days. Murder was a nasty business, and I was looking forward to some time off.

It was Friday, the day of Evelyn's art show, and I hadn't decided which way to go on the invitation. Evelyn was the most interesting and confident woman I had ever met. Her paintings were courageous, disturbing, and, however you say, *really fucking cool* in art terms.

But what was stopping me was what I'd learned about her from her website—Evelyn claimed she had the ability to communicate with the dead. I'd dug into her past and cross-referenced the information on her website. Her artist statement about her near-death experience lined up with the details in her accident report.

I believed the part of her story about being clinically dead then coming back to life. However, the part I was having trouble accepting was her alleged *gift*—the ability to connect with ghosts through her dreams. I didn't believe in paranormal phenomena. When you died, your spirit either went to heaven or hell.

There was no in-between stage. No lingering souls haunting the living. Scary stories about the undead were made up for horror movies and Stephen King novels.

If Evelyn put on this schtick to promote her art show, so be it. No crime was committed. We were heading into October, and with Halloween coming up, the spooky stuff was great advertising for the Final Friday Gallery Walk at the end of the month.

But if Evelyn wasn't pretending and believed she could see ghosts, I could never date her. In my line of work, I had the unfortunate task of examining the corpses of murder victims and bringing justice to their killers.

It would be disrespectful to the living and the dead to engage in that mindset. My association with a medium could undermine my credibility as a detective. There was no way I could have a relationship with someone like Evelyn purely because of the optics.

As I lathered up and cleansed my body, I fantasized about seeing Evelyn again. She was beautiful and funny and different from the women I usually found attractive. I admired her bravery in painting herself the way she had, putting it on display for the world to see. She was fearless and talented. Bold and sexy. Drop-dead gorgeous and off-limits.

I wanted to attend her party and hear all about her life-altering experience and see her thriving in her artistic element. Still, something inside of me warned me to keep my distance. We were too different. Her art was toxic to my reputation.

I'd convinced myself a million times over to stay away from the beautiful and witty artist. Still, there was a problem with that logic—I couldn't get her out of my mind.

HAUNTED—EVELYN

Opening night. My stomach fluttered with nervous excitement as I mingled with our guests and sipped a dirty martini.

The clink of appetizer plates and cocktail glasses, along with the murmur of our friends, filled the gallery and breathed life into the once-abandoned building. While the collective hum of activity energized my soul and validated my decision to open my gallery, part of my anxiety stemmed from anticipating seeing Leo again.

He never RSVP'd to the event and never said if he was coming when I'd invited him. "Thanks for the invitation," was all he'd said. I couldn't tell if that meant that he had accepted the invitation—which would explain why he hadn't formally RSVP'd. Or if Leo had meant *thanks for inviting me* but never intended to come.

I'd met him under the most awkward circumstances imaginable. It was never like we were on a date, so he had no obligation to respond to the invitation. Either way, tonight was about celebrating the opening of my new gallery with art lovers and friends. I was grateful to my fellow artist, Luis, and our fearless and energetic gallery manager and social media goddess, Gibson, for all their hard work.

I steered my thoughts away from Leo and focused on the guests in attendance.

As I rocked my shoulders to the beat of our acoustic guitar duo, I noticed a man watching me from across the room. He was stylish and handsome and seemed enthralled by my ghostly art. He admired one of my paintings from the fall collection, *Above and Below*.

The subject was an 1800s-era female, dead in body but alive in spirit. Her corpse stretched out along the shoreline at the bed of a creek. She wore a lilac dress dotted with tiny blue flowers and white polka dots. Her wet hair was tangled and covered her face like writhing snakes while her arms stretched wide.

The pose suggested the woman had clawed her way out of the murky water and dragged herself to shore, only to succumb to the elements.

The woman's ghost kneeled beside her remains. Her ghostly hand touched her body, and her eyes shot a damning glare at the viewer. I painted the woman just as she had appeared to me in a dream. Angry. Resentful. Oozing with a toxic mix of betrayal and revenge.

Whether the woman was murdered or died by someone's negligence, the apparition was determined to remain earth-bound to seek justice for her untimely death. Her clothing suggested she had died decades ago. I didn't know her name or any other details about her. All I could do to keep her memory alive was use my gift to share her story.

The well-dressed man crossed his arms as he studied the painting, seemingly deep in thought. He looked familiar, but I couldn't place where I'd met him. Maybe we'd crossed paths at another gallery. I didn't want to stare, so I turned away.

Inside, I was silently cheering that my art profoundly affected at least one of our guests.

I scanned the crowd in search of Detective Ricci, but apparently, he wasn't coming. Part of me was disappointed that he would miss my chat about my near-death experience, but my practical side was relieved.

While I'd sensed the mutual attraction, I couldn't imagine Leo and I being compatible as a couple. He was a serious, all-business detective. I was an artistic medium who communicated with the dead through my art. I couldn't turn my gift on and off at will, and I had no control over what information I received through my dreams.

Given the fact that Leo was a homicide detective, my gift and his job could lead our relationship down a tumultuous path. Leo was a tough guy. He could handle the scrutiny of his cop friends once they found out about my gift. That is, if he genuinely wanted to get to know me.

But was I willing to be grilled and possibly ridiculed by his inner circle?

The reason why relationships never worked out for me was for that reason. I hadn't dated anyone seriously since the accident because I never felt I could trust anyone with my feelings. I had signed up for the matchmaking service. I'd gone on several dates, but none of the men I met gave me the spark I'd expected.

In fairness to Leo, he did seem impressed and hadn't made me feel weird about my artistic expression. I didn't blame him for being skeptical. That's why I hoped he would hear my story. Once he found out what had happened, maybe he wouldn't think my gift was unfounded.

Leo was a detective. If he had any interest in seeing me on a personal level, he would've run a thorough background check into my past. The months I spent in a mental health facility were thanks to my closed-minded family. My frequent moves. My name change. Knowing that put me at ease.

If Leo had decided not to come based on what he'd found out, then it was for the best. No need for awkward explanations or the insecurity that came when strangers formed opinions about my credibility—or sanity—depending on who was doing the judging.

If Leo miraculously showed up, it was because he wanted to get to know me despite my past.

TOXIC—LEO

I drove to Halsted and parked my Charger across the street from Evelyn's gallery.

I lowered my window and used a pair of high-powered binoculars to check the scene before deciding whether to attend the event.

The brown paper that had covered the windows had been torn down, revealing the interior of the newly remodeled gallery. I had expected bright-white lights, neatly framed artwork lined up on the walls, and stuffy patrons noshing on canapés and sipping champagne.

Not even close. Once again, Evelyn had blown my mind.

Instead of going with the expected, Evelyn obliterated the concept of a safe bet. From my vantage point on the street, I spotted a heavily tattooed server in a short black dress, sporting glittery devil horns as she circled the crowd delivering well-dressed Bloody Mary cocktails.

I zeroed in on her tray and noted the drinks were garnished with a skewer of black olives and a mini grilled cheese sandwich wedge. The gallery was crowded with a laid-back group of guests mingling and enjoying the show.

I had made the right choice when I dressed in my usual off-duty wardrobe of dark jeans, cowboy boots, and a black leather jacket. I glanced around in search of Evelyn, but she hadn't made her appearance yet.

Wait a minute...

Evelyn Sinclair cruised into the gallery, drawing the attention of everyone in the room. Her long sandy-brown hair spilled over her shoulders and her lips twisted in a way that seemed she was holding back a delicious secret she was dying to tell.

She was dressed in a pair of worn-out jeans accentuating her curves and a white tank top with one of those gauzy scarves she loved with muted fall colors. *Nice ink.* She had a full sleeve of tattoos running up and down both arms. I wondered if she had tats over her firm and toned yoga body.

Evelyn's hair was styled in loose waves, and her makeup was lightly applied as it was the first time I'd set eyes on her in the coffee shop. No fake eyelashes. No bright lipstick. Evelyn's relaxed and casual style complemented her natural beauty.

I lowered my binoculars and ran a gut check before deciding my next move.

Do I engage or retreat before moving in the wrong direction toward a beautiful woman who may or may not be dead wrong for my reputation?

My job was full of risks. Every time I clipped on my star, I knew I might not make it home. While I considered myself brave on the job, why was I indecisive about Evelyn when the answer was obvious?

THE DEATH OF ME—EVELYN

Gibson flashed the lights and invited our guests to the small seating area by the stage at the back of the house. Our statuesque gallery manager, wearing a red satin suit, mile-high stilettos, and black-rimmed glasses, upstaged everyone with her flashy clothes, platinum-blonde Marilyn Monroe hairstyle, and commanding presence.

She lifted the mic to her painted red lips. "In keeping with the spooky vibe of the season, *The Death of Me* is proud to introduce our inaugural collection, Haunted History."

The massive chandelier illuminated the room on cue, followed by a chorus of *oohs* and *ahhs*. It cost a fortune to restore the fixture to its original glory. Still, that Gothic-era matriarch was the lifeblood of the gallery.

Sydney had negotiated a reduction in the studio's sale price after the dismal inspection, and I invested the savings into the restoration budget. She had even introduced me to a reliable contractor—her brother-in-law, Braydon, who had done a fabulous job remodeling her new townhome.

Thinking of Sydney, I wondered where she was. When I invited her, she was so excited to see the new gallery.

"Please welcome our artists, Luis Franco and Evelyn Sinclair."

Luis grasped my hand on the way to our makeshift stage and gave me a gentle squeeze of encouragement. Luis, a successful custom tattoo designer, raised his glass to the crowd. He wore a short-sleeved silk shirt to show off his personally designed tattoos. The classy silver fox wore his shoulder-length hair slicked back behind his ears. He emitted a glow of grace and appreciation.

Luis was not only a talented artist, but he had a flair for theatrics. Since his tattoo designs were intended for the skin, not a canvas, he displayed samples of his work on live models using temporary ink that would wash away.

Gibson handed Luis the mic as he introduced his living works of art. His friends served as models who shared his enthusiasm for the limelight. As Luis's crew danced to an upbeat club mix, our guests marveled at the artwork inked on their skin.

Luis had taken the Haunted History theme back to the Prohibition era. He ran with an outlaw collection featuring Al Capone and his cohorts and the working-class clientele dancing and drinking behind the green doors of the heavily guarded speakeasies.

As the music faded and Luis turned the mic back over to Gibson, I mentally prepared for my moment in the spotlight. Just as I flushed the memory of Leo from my mind, a tall, muscular man with intense eyes entered the gallery.

Detective Leo Ricci is in the house.

My cheeks warmed when I met his gaze. Leo lifted his drink and gave me a nod. His subtle and sexy greeting sent a rush of excitement to my core. He was dressed in all black and wore his shirt unbuttoned at the top, revealing a stylish silver rope chain—more understated than the jumbo-sized religious cross I had penciled into his sketch.

I returned the greeting to the handsome detective with a soft smile before taking a deep breath to calm my nerves. Gibson slid down the dimmer switch and brought the candelabra lights and sconces to a whisper.

The room was silent except for the raindrops hitting the windows and the faint rumble of thunder that served as the soundtrack for my spooky story. Once the mood was set, a single spotlight shined down on me.

"Before we get started, I have a serious question." I held up a flashlight and scanned the crowd, making eye contact with each person in the room. "Is anyone afraid of the dark?"

A mix of laughter and words of encouragement emerged from the crowd. I nodded to Gibson, who then prompted her assistants to hand out small, vigil-like candles to our guests. As the flames were lit, a warm glow spread throughout the room.

"Have you ever been alone and sensed someone watching you? Have you heard someone whisper your name only to turn around and find no one there?"

The crowd murmured in the affirmative.

"What if I told you we're never alone? Want to know the truth about ghosts? They're everywhere. Roaming the city streets, haunting houses, zapping the energy from electronics, wandering the woods in the dead of night, creeping around barns, spooking the animals, lurking in basements, hiding in attics, possessing their worldly trinkets and treasures, hovering over crime scenes…"

No one uttered a sound, giving me a moment to breathe and absorb the energy in the room. "What do these restless spirits want? Why are they here?"

I took a dramatic pause. "All ghosts have the same problem—they don't want to be dead. Not every soul is ready to transition when their time is up. Death is confusing.

Frightening. And many don't know what to do when the tunnel appears, beckoning them to step into the light."

"Spirits remain earthbound when something in this life is holding them back from moving on to the next. From my experience, there are only three reasons a soul stays behind: Fear, love, or revenge. In a few rare cases, it's a combination of all three."

I aimed the beam of a flashlight at my painting, *The Death Coach*. "In this case, the subject fears judgment." The artwork featured a 1900s-era horse-drawn carriage that carried a ghostly figure with wide, horrified eyes. His expression was riddled with guilt, terror, and remorse—exactly how the middle-aged ghost had come to me in my dream.

"For others, the lust for revenge keeps their spirits earth-bound." I shined a flashlight at my painting, *Above and Below*. This piece held the attention of the well-dressed man that I was certain I recognized but wasn't sure from where.

"Still others experience a love so strong, they refuse to move on without their beloved." I shined a light on my favorite oil painting, *Ghost Bride*. The subject was a sickly sweet apparition floating around the afterlife in her wedding dress. With a bend to her neck, the bride kept the pious smile of a virgin bride.

"Before the bride could recite her vows, she tripped over her dress, tumbled down the wooden stairs, and broke her neck in front of her family and bridegroom." I held up a finger as if a thought had just occurred to me. "But the ill-fated bride's sister later married the groom-to-be, which leads me to wonder if she really fell or was she *pushed* down the stairs?"

The guests murmured excitedly at the idea of an old-fashioned wedding day homicide.

"Being a ghost sucks. I should know. I used to be one."

I aimed the light at my self-portrait, *The Death of Me*. This was the one Leo had seen when he'd walked me back to the gallery from the coffee shop. Since he was brave enough to come to the show, I hoped he'd keep an open mind as I shared details of my near-death experience.

"Who wants to hear a ghost story?"

GHOST STORY—EVELYN

"MY GHOST STORY BEGINS WITH MY DEATH. FIVE YEARS AGO, I was swimming in Lake Cumberland and decided to dive under a waterfall. All my friends had done it and bobbed back to the surface. But when I went under, I kept my life jacket on, which proved to be a deadly mistake."

I glanced around the room, taking in the spooky vibe of the flickering candles.

"While the pressure of the waterfall pushed me down, the life jacket's buoyancy tried to lift me to the surface. The two opposing forces kept me trapped underwater. I was under for more than five minutes before my friends could rescue me."

I paused to let the weight of my story settle in. "When my friends heaved my body onto the pontoon boat, I wasn't breathing. I had no pulse. My lips were blue. One of my friends made a frantic call to 9-1-1 and said I had died. She was right."

I lowered the mic and inhaled a deep breath. "By the time I reached the hospital, the paramedics had resuscitated me. I had a pulse, but I hadn't regained consciousness. While in a coma, I was aware of my surroundings. My spirit floated over the bed, and I could see and hear everything going on around me while my body was in a deep sleep. A nurse with long black braids and gentle eyes held my hand and whispered words of encouragement as I fought for my life," I said.

"Nurse Gwen told me the doctors didn't think I would wake up, but not to let that discourage me. She smiled and squeezed my hand. 'What happens next is not up to doctors. It's not your decision to make either.' I couldn't speak in my dreamlike state, but I understood Gwen's message. A higher power was deciding my fate," I explained to the audience.

"Gwen was kind and patient while she waited at my bedside. Then, after I'd been in the hospital unresponsive for three days, she grasped my hand, gave me a maternal smile, and informed me the decision had been made. Then, she lifted a precious little beagle onto the bed." I smiled at the memory.

"The little guy was soft and warm and had the most adorable, angelic little face. Gwen said his name was Georgie, and he would stay with me while she checked on her other patients. When Gwen left the room, Georgie snuggled up and rested his chin on my chest. As he stared into my eyes, I felt a wave of positive energy flowing through me. It was the moment my body and soul had been reunited for the first time since the accident," I said.

"A series of electronic beeps and the murmur of voices around my bedside stirred me from my coma. Gwen scooped up Georgie and headed for the door just before I opened my eyes. Before leaving the room, she aimed her finger at me and said a single word. That one word is why I am standing on this stage today."

I shifted my gaze around the room, sensing the anticipation. "The word was *Halsted*." I met Leo's gaze. He seemed as enthralled with my story as the rest of the audience.

"When I opened my eyes, my mom and dad were at my bedside with a nurse who was *not* Gwen. As my family asked me a million questions about how I was feeling and what I remembered, I asked the new nurse if she could bring Gwen back to my room so I could thank her for staying with me."

"The nurse, an older woman with silver hair, stared at me in shock and explained that no nurse named Gwen had been in my room. I shook my head in confusion. Gwen had been with me the whole time. She brought her dog Georgie to visit me. How could this kind and wonderful woman have left the hospital before finding out my fate?"

I picked up my sketch pad off a side table and held it to the audience for reference. "Before the accident, I never considered myself an artist. I was dead set on a career in finance and didn't have an artistic bone in my body. But I had been so certain Gwen was real, I asked for a pad of paper and a pencil so I could draw a picture of her and Georgie."

I aimed my flashlight at a framed sketch of a sweet beagle and an angelic woman, wearing scrubs, in her early sixties.

"What I had drawn was surreal. The portrait was so realistic with meticulously added details. It could've passed for a photograph of Gwen snuggling her precious little dog. When the nurse saw my sketch, she nearly passed out." I laughed with the audience.

"She recognized the woman in the portrait and told me a nurse named Gwen had worked at the hospital for thirty years, but she had suffered an aneurysm and passed away the previous year. She also confirmed the dog's identity and said Georgie had passed away years earlier. Still, Gwen drank from a photo mug with his picture on it," I explained.

"Since my near-death experience, I still dream of ghosts. When I sleep, I walk with the dead—some from the distant past, others from our time. But unlike Gwen, ghosts don't talk—at least not to me. The way I communicate with the dead is through my art."

I gave Gibson a nod, and she motioned to the gallery as the lights lifted. "Allow me to introduce my latest collection, *Haunted History.*"

Gibson took over the mic. "I know you are all *dying* to add an original Evelyn Sinclair to your private collections, but please be aware her ghost paintings are not for sale. They will remain on display in the gallery as part of our permanent collection. Her other works featuring Chicago's historical landmarks painted with Evelyn's stylistic spooky vibe are all available for purchase. Enjoy the show!"

As I stepped off the stage to applause, Luis offered me a hug and a glass of champagne. We clinked glasses, congratulating each other on a perfect evening. Then Luis's husband, Hector, and their friends swallowed him up in a sea of hugs and well-wishes before sweeping him back into the crowd, freeing me to say hello to Leo.

"I'm glad you came." I took a sip of my drink to settle my nerves. I wasn't accustomed to the spotlight. Although I found the experience exhilarating, I was still coming down from the adrenaline rush.

"Me too, but I don't think I'll sleep with the lights off tonight," Leo teased. "What parts of your ghost story are true, and what parts are made up for your Haunted History theme?"

"All true. Every word of it." Leo was standing close enough that I caught a whiff of his cologne and a sneak peek of a tattoo peeking out from under his shirt. Leo was insanely hot, and my mind drifted in a sensual direction.

"So, these ghosts. You say you dream of them? That means they're not real, right?"

I laughed at his linear thought process. Leo was a detective, and I understood Leo's need for definitive answers. "Yes, the ghosts come to me in my dreams—but that doesn't mean they're not real."

The handsome blond man I had seen earlier approached, stealing my attention from Leo. "Hello, Evelyn. Excuse me for interrupting. I'm Dr. Vaughn Reynolds, Sydney's husband."

Ah, that's right. I recognized him now from Sydney's pictures. I'd never met him in person, which was probably why I hadn't immediately placed him. "So nice to meet you, Vaughn. Where's Sydney?"

"I don't know. She was supposed to be here. I had to check on a surgical patient, so we planned to drive separately and meet here. I assumed she'd be here already." Vaughn glanced around the room as if Sydney might've come in while he was talking.

"Maybe she's running late," I said.

"When did you last speak to her?" Detective Ricci asked.

"Not since I left for work at five o'clock." Dr. Vaughn seemed annoyed Leo was butting in but was too classy to make anything of it. He shifted his gaze between us. "Did you two meet through the—"

"No," I cut him off before he said Armstrong Agency. I was sure Sydney had mentioned I had signed up with the matchmaking service, but I didn't want him to mention it in front of Leo. "This is Detective Ricci. We met a few days ago at the coffee shop. It turns out he's a huge art fan." I tossed Leo a grin.

Vaughn initiated a handshake. "Thank you for your service to our community, Detective. Isn't Evelyn's work breathtaking?"

"She had me at Ghost Bride." Leo delivered his witty response with his characteristic dry tone.

Vaughn rechecked his phone. "I think I'll go home and see

what's keeping Sydney. Congratulations on your new gallery, Evelyn. Your art is beyond fascinating."

As Dr. Vaughn walked away, I recalled Sydney questioning me about the day I died. *Did you know you were going to die?* She was frightened. Of whom I had no clue. At the time, she was gushing over her new husband. Fear and love. That was an unsettling combo.

Dr. Vaughn passed through the doorway, into the night, as the sinking feeling crept over me that Sydney's insecurity was somehow attached to her new life with the good doctor.

WANTED—LEO

When Vaughn left, Evelyn invited me upstairs to tour her studio.

We climbed the staircase to the third floor. Evelyn unlocked her door and led the way to a vast open space filled with art supplies, multiple workstations for all her mediums, and a cozy seating area with a couch and chairs on the far side.

Evelyn's studio was an organized mess of paintbrushes tucked into pottery vases with tubes of oil paint and turpentine littered around the room, and an abundance of reference photos and drawings attached to the wall with blue tape.

About six hundred repurposed coffee mugs were scattered, along with piles of magazines and sketchbooks stacked on every surface. Evelyn waved at her works in progress and explained she earned most of her income from commissioned work.

"The ghost paintings are part of my personal collection and will remain on display indefinitely. Gibson uses them as examples of my style to potential clients. My sales come from private collectors who want paintings of famous landmarks and family portraits—*of the living.*"

"You are crazy talented, Evelyn."

She glanced up at me and smiled, motioning for me to join her on the couch. "I'm glad you came." She kicked off her boots and plopped down on the couch. For the first time that evening, I had all her attention. Her gorgeous blue eyes were fixed on mine.

"Like you said, I'm a huge art fan."

Evelyn laughed and tapped my chest playfully, admonishing me for teasing her. "Well, if you can handle *Ghost Bride*, I guess I'm not so scary."

"Speaking of ghosts, I want to understand how it all works. How you see them." I was relieved Evelyn only dreamed of the subjects of her paintings. Still, I wanted to be sure I understood how she perceived her alleged paranormal gift.

"Can you walk me through one of these ghost dreams of yours? What do they show you? Do they reveal their cause of death? Guide you to crime scenes? Point out their killers?"

"When ghosts appear to me, each one is unique. I never know what to expect," Evelyn explained. "Sometimes they lead me to places like their home or even a graveyard. Sometimes they show me their dead bodies—like the painting of the corpse with her vengeful ghost beside her. Sometimes they want to show me something else, like a memory."

"So, the only time you see ghosts or have any contact with them is in your dreams? You sleep, and you see ghosts. You wake up, and that's it?"

"Pretty much," Evelyn said.

Pretty much was not the truth. I was trained to detect lies. Uncovering bullshit was my specialty. "There's more to your story. What are you hiding from me?"

"Some things are better left unsaid."

"Are you afraid of what I'll think if you tell me the truth?"

Her blue eyes held a touch of sadness. "The truth is, I don't divulge everything publicly. Coming out and saying I dream of ghosts is safe and believable. Giving too many details gets me into trouble. Some people don't like the idea of ghosts spilling their secrets to the living."

"You've pissed people off before?"

"Big time."

She's afraid. Finally, an admission I could understand. "You can lie to everyone on this planet, Evelyn, but I'm asking you not to lie to me." She had every right to shoot down my request, but it was a relationship deal breaker for me. If she couldn't be honest with me, I was out.

"Telling the truth hasn't worked in my favor. If you want me to make that promise, I need to know I can trust you." She held her gaze on mine.

"You have my word."

Evelyn paused as she considered my request. "Sometimes, a ghost stays with me after the dream. I feel their presence around me while I'm awake. There's more they want to show me."

"Why? Do they want something from you?"

Evelyn nodded. "The ones who stay need my help. I draw for them. It's a paranormal phenomenon called *automatic drawing*. I communicate with the dead through my art. I get into a relaxed state and let my gift take over. I never know what I'll draw then, but it's important."

"How do you know what they want?" I asked.

"Occasionally, a random word pops into my head, and I have no idea what it means. Sometimes the word is for someone I know, or it could be for a complete stranger. I never understand it, but I know the message will make sense to the person I'm meant to deliver it to."

"Like when your ghost nurse said, *Halsted.*"

"Exactly. I had just woken up from a coma. I had never been to Chicago, had no artistic skills, and no idea what it meant or why it was significant. Of course, the word couldn't have been more spot on."

"Did a word pop into your mind when you met me?"

"This line of questioning feels more like an interrogation than a conversation." An ornery smile crept up on Evelyn's face. "Do you want to crank up the lights so you can watch me sweat under pressure? Offer me a cigarette to gain my trust? Slide a pad of paper and a pencil across the table to get my confession in writing?"

As a detective, I'd dealt with plenty of wisecracking suspects during my investigations. None of them had ever rendered me speechless. Evelyn sensed my hesitation and moved in for the kill. "If you want me to confess, you'll have to work for it, Detective Ricci."

Challenge accepted. I stood from the couch and towered over her as I reached for her hand. I pulled her to her feet and backed her against the wall, leaving only an inch between us. I placed my hands on the wall, blocking her from trying to move past me.

"You better watch your tone, Miss Sinclair. If you get on the wrong side of me, I'll put you in handcuffs and lock you up in my interrogation room."

Evelyn's cheeks warmed. She covered her face with her scarf to hide her embarrassment as she blushed at our sexually charged interrogation game. "Fine. You win." She took a deep breath to recover. "I haven't heard a special word about you. Maybe it will come, maybe it never will. I have no control over what I receive."

"Anything else I need to know about you?"

"No. Is the interrogation over now?"

"Not yet. I have one more question."

Evelyn sighed dramatically as if exhausted by my line of

questioning. *God, she's gorgeous.* My eyes drifted to her chest. Her long hair covered her breasts, and a whisper of a smile crept upon her lips.

"This is the last one, Detective. Then it's my turn to interrogate *you*." She pointed a stern finger at me and playfully poked me in the chest with her pointy fingernail.

Her touch gave me a sexually charged rush of adrenaline that prompted me to change up my line of questioning. "Can I kiss you?"

Evelyn's sultry gaze landed on mine as she gave me a nod of acceptance.

I brushed her long hair aside with my fingertips and lifted her chin as I pressed my lips against hers. I moved slowly at first, savoring her taste, the warmth of her mouth, and the faint scent of vanilla on her skin.

I slid my hands to her hips and guided her away from the wall. A quiet moan escaped her lips as she snaked her hands up my back and felt the ripple of muscles under my shirt. The sensation of her touch aroused me, and I kissed her harder and deeper as I ran my fingers through her hair and slid my tongue down her neck.

Evelyn explored my body, kneading my muscular shoulders, running her fingers along my six-pack, playing within the safe zone above the belt while avoiding the area that would take our passionate kiss to the next level.

I followed her lead and kept my own hands within the same boundary. Evelyn was petite compared to my six-two frame. As we kissed, her body melted into mine. Her breasts rubbed against my chest as we made out. The erotic sensation of her body against mine drove me wild.

From the moment I locked eyes with her, she had been at the forefront of my mind. All my thoughts kept circling back to the sexy artist who had a talent for commanding my attention. But there was a problem with my attraction to her —I didn't *date* the women I was attracted to.

My career was too demanding for committed relationships. Falling in love was not an option. Evelyn was energetic and alluring, and if anyone could change my mind, I had no doubt it would be her. But my commitment was to my badge. Dating Evelyn would be a distraction.

Evelyn slid her fingers under my shirt collar and lightly scratched her nails at the nape of my neck, then moved to my chest, where she traced the outline of my tattoo. Only a hint of ink was visible under my shirt, but she had noticed it.

Every little touch aroused me. I moved my hands down her back and massaged her tight ass. I'd been covertly admiring her body since the day I walked her back to her studio. The way her hips swayed in her worn-out jeans. The gentle bounce of perky breasts as she fast-walked to keep up with me on the sidewalk. The curve of her shapely silhouette...

A knock on the studio door interrupted our heated make-out session.

Evelyn pulled back and gave me an apologetic grin. "I have a party to get back to." She moved to the door as she straightened her clothes and wiped her mouth with the back of her hand.

She conversed with Gibson and assured her she was on her way back downstairs. I slid on my coat and took the hint that my private tour of her studio had ended. As we walked down the stairs to rejoin the party, I picked up Evelyn's hand and interlaced her fingers with mine.

She glanced over her shoulder and smiled at my gesture.

Right then and there, I knew I was in trouble. What I *wanted* from Evelyn was limited to a physical relationship. Still, my attraction to her was burning on all cylinders. When we hit the landing, I wished her a good night and escaped before Evelyn changed my mind.

My phone vibrated with an incoming call as I headed to the Charger. It was late, which meant it was work related and urgent. I lifted my cell from my jacket pocket and checked the screen. It was my partner, Parker. "What have we got?"

"A missing person. The husband came home and called 9-1-1 when he discovered signs of a break-in and his wife missing. We need to act now. Evidence in the bedroom suggests an abduction."

"Right. Shoot me the address. I'll meet you at the scene," I said. "Who's our victim?"

"A real estate agent from uptown—Sydney Reynolds."

TAPS—EVELYN

WHEN I GOT HOME, I FLOATED UP THE STAIRS THAT LED TO MY apartment with a euphoric pep in my step.

The soft opening at the gallery with our friends and patrons was a huge success. The goal was to give The Death of Me, or *The DOM*, as we affectionately referred to it, a warm welcome and generate buzz for the highly anticipated Final Friday Gallery Walk at the end of the month.

According to Gibson, our mission was accomplished. I was thrilled the evening had turned out so well—especially my unexpected *moment* with the hottest cop in Chicago.

When I crawled into bed that evening, I let my mind wander with erotic thoughts about Leo. His hands sliding to my hips, the sensation of his warm and wet mouth trailing kisses down my neck, the strength of his rippling muscles… I'd never imagined I'd find someone so different from me so attractive.

Aside from the fact that he was the sexiest man I had ever met, he had an alluring aura that pulled me to him. The way he commanded my attention and kissed me passionately without going too far, considering it was our first kiss.

Dating a detective was surprisingly sexy. Leo was a take-charge guy, and the sensual side of me wanted him to dominate me with his strength and give me orders he expected me to obey. I rolled over in bed and closed my eyes, hoping my erotic fantasy would spill over into my dreams.

Tap...tap...tap...

Someone knocked on my bedroom window.

I sat up in bed and darted my gaze around the room, searching for signs of life. I moved to the window, pulled open my curtains, and looked down the alley.

Not a living soul in sight.

My apartment was on the third floor of an old brownstone that faced the alley. I kept the rickety fire escape pulled up to the window, so there was no quiet or easy way a creeper could sneak up the metal stairs and into my personal space.

That's when I realized the tapper was no longer among the living.

This is a dream.

A ghostly figure materialized as I stood at the window and stared at the glass. Her image was blurry, obstructed by a haze of fog. I couldn't see her features clearly, but I was sure the ghost was a young woman.

Slim. Long hair. Freshly dead. No—freshly *murdered*.

Her eyes bulged out of their sockets as she tapped on the window, desperate for my attention. The woman's expression, visible to me as a reflection in the glass, showed the sheer panic, horror, and helplessness she had experienced in her final moments of life.

As the ghost tapped on my window, her lips twisted. Her mouth opened and closed like a fish desperate to breathe out of the water. She was trying to communicate by vocalizing her plea, but the words were trapped inside, unable to escape.

When her attempt to speak failed, she pressed her palm against my window. There was something in her hand. It was a note or maybe a photo, but it was scratched up, and I couldn't make out a word or a picture.

It wasn't easy to see through the fog that shielded her features. I couldn't decipher what was on the paper either. In my dreams, information was never delivered on the nose. My gift never appeared in clear, tangible images—only snippets of clues.

Frustrated by my lack of understanding, the ghost pounded on the window with enough force to break the glass. With the heat of her rage bubbling to the surface, the woman's face came into focus, and I recognized the ghost's identity—Sydney.

Oh god.

Overcome with a rush of horror, I forced myself to concentrate and focus my energy out the window. There was a reason Sydney had come to me. There was something she wanted to show me. Judging by the condition of her body, she might be trying to identify her killer.

Sydney reached out her hand and beckoned me to follow her. I concentrated on her shadowy form and watched the ghost float down the alley behind my apartment. When I lost sight of her, the dream version of me ran into the kitchen, pulled open the curtains, and craned my neck to see where she had gone.

Sydney was pointing to a dumpster behind my building. I feared her ghost was trying to tell me she was inside. Her corpse had been dumped there, and she wanted me to discover her body. My heart was racing so fast. I felt as if it might explode.

"Wake up," I told myself. "Wake up! Wake up!"

A loud rumble of thunder shook the windows, waking me from a deep sleep. As I recovered from my nightmare, a single word popped into my head.

"Captiva."

I bolted upright in bed and pressed a hand to my pounding chest. I sucked in deep breaths to fill my lungs with air as the reality of what I had witnessed brought on a new round of terror. While I panted and wiped my sweaty hair off my face, I felt the presence of Sydney's ghost, still lingering after my dream.

She tapped her finger on my drawing hand, signaling she wanted to communicate. I rushed to my living room and lit a trio of white candles to energize the room. I gathered my sketchbook and pencils and prepared to draw.

I spread a throw blanket on the floor, got into a comfortable position, and closed my eyes. I tuned in to the elemental energy of the thunderstorm that had lulled me to sleep during the midnight hour. The gentle pitter-patter of raindrops on the glass created the rhythmic white noise I needed to meditate.

When I relaxed, I let my gift of automatic drawing take over. My hand began to move as I served as a guide for the spirit world. While I was trancelike, I had no clue what I was drawing and didn't know what I would discover once my work was complete.

When my hand stopped moving and my energy was zapped, I opened my eyes and studied my work. I'd drawn a beautiful young woman with a crooked smile, long hair, a heart-shaped face, and thick eyelashes.

While her beauty and Mona Lisa smile characterized her personality in life, the portrait I'd drawn of Sydney was postmortem. Dark shadows pooled under her eyes, and gory black lines sprouted from her luscious full lips. Her long, slender neck held the imprint of choke marks and finger bruises that revealed Sydney's tragic cause of death.

Strangulation.

As I stared at her portrait, my pencil rolled off my lap and onto the floor. The reality of what I had witnessed brought on a new round of terror.

Sydney had been murdered.

DAMNING—LEO

THE BEST-CASE SCENARIO FOR SYDNEY REYNOLDS WOULD'VE been a ransom demand. A money-for-her-life act of greed.

The worst-case scenario was that Sydney was the object of her abductor's desire. When people fell prey to sexual predators, the victims were in grave danger.

Sydney had been missing for up to eight hours. I would've welcomed a ransom call. While my team processed the crime scene at the home of Dr. And Mrs. Reynolds, I got a call from Evelyn. I dreaded telling her that her friend had been abducted, but she'd have to learn somehow.

I stepped away from my team to take the call in private. "Evelyn? I'm afraid I have bad news."

"Have you found her?" Evelyn's voice sounded distressed as if she had been crying.

So, she knew already. She must've watched the early news. We'd gotten word out to the media quickly, in case viewers had tips. "No. We're doing everything we can to track her down. I'm sorry, but I need to get back to my team. I'll call you if—"

"I have information about the case," Evelyn said.

"What do you know? Has Sydney contacted you?"

"Yes." I heard a lighter flicking in the background. Evelyn wasn't a smoker, which made me consider she wasn't alone.

"Is she with you now? Is Mrs. Reynolds okay?"

"No," Evelyn said.

"Do you mean *no*, she isn't with you, or *no*, she isn't okay?" Adrenaline pumped through my veins as I waited impatiently for Evelyn to explain what she knew about our missing person. If Mrs. Reynolds was with Evelyn, we needed to get her to the hospital. There were signs of a struggle at her townhouse and bloodstains on her bed.

I quickly considered the possibility that Mrs. Reynolds had escaped from her attacker and made it to Evelyn's. Surely one of them would've called 911, but news of a call hadn't reached me yet. I needed to know Sydney's location to get her the urgent medical attention she needed. "Evelyn?"

She didn't answer.

Evelyn's silence spoke volumes. She was either traumatized by what she had witnessed, or someone didn't want her to talk. "Are you at the gallery or at home? I'll come over and—"

"Sydney is dead. The killer placed her body in a dumpster."

"Where?"

"I'm not sure."

"Then how do you know she's dead? Did you witness the crime? Overhear someone bragging about the murder? Did someone reach out to you and confess?"

Evelyn was silent, probably spooked by my rapid-fire questioning. I didn't want her to feel overwhelmed and hang up, so I softened my tone to keep her talking. "You are the first person to come forward with information. Please, tell me everything you know so I can help your friend."

The lighter flicked again. Thunder rumbled in the background.

"Sydney came to me this morning at four a.m. I was asleep in my apartment. She tapped on my window and woke me up, asking for help."

It was almost eight a.m. now. I wanted to fire off a million questions, starting with, *Why the fuck didn't you call 9-1-1 when Sydney Reynolds entered your apartment?*

Sydney's story had hit the early morning news. The city had become instantly engrossed with the newlywed who was abducted from her multimillion-dollar townhouse. Violent crimes happened in the streets. Usually gun or gang related. It was rare for a break-in and abduction to have been carried out in the upscale neighborhood on the east side.

Everyone in violent crimes knew we had to find Sydney fast. Evidence at the scene suggested the kidnapping was personal. Sydney had been targeted.

"I'm assuming she was still *alive* at four a.m. That was three hours ago, Evelyn. If she was alive when she asked you for help, then why the hell are you telling me she's—"

"Remember our conversation last night?" Evelyn paused, giving me time to let her question settle into my bones. "Sydney was not alive when she visited me. I'm a medium, Leo. Sydney's ghost contacted me after she was murdered."

Fucking hell. When I laid eyes on her morbid self-portrait, I should've run from Evelyn.

"I'm not crazy, and I'm not making this up. I have proof. I don't know exactly where her body is, but I have pictures that will help you locate the crime scene. She's in a dumpster. I would narrow your search to the art district. I sense she's near the gallery."

I was one-hundred-percent sure Evelyn was selling me a bullshit story. Still, if she had a photo or any physical evidence to help my team track her down, I would do everything humanly possible to help our victim. "How did you get the pictures? Did you take them?"

"I drew them."

"Do you know who murdered Sydney?"

"Not yet."

"How did she die?"

"She was strangled to death."

"When?"

"Just before she tapped on my window."

The call went dead, then my phone pinged when a series of texts came in. *Holy hell.* I swiped through a string of professional sketches of a beautiful young woman. I recognized her immediately as my missing person, Sydney Reynolds.

The woman, described by her friends and loved ones as bubbly and outgoing, was portrayed in the drawing as a brutally murdered corpse disposed of on a bed of dumpster trash. There were a total of six pictures. Four of them were from different vantage points at her crime scene.

As for the other two, Evelyn had drawn Sydney as a translucent ghost with strangulation marks on her neck, wearing kinky lingerie. Like the other ghost paintings in Evelyn's gallery, Sydney appeared as a tortured soul. Her mouth was agape as if trying to scream, eyes bulging, gaze locked on me—the viewer.

The last sketch was the most damning. Sydney was outside Evelyn's window, staring through the glass with what appeared to be a photograph in her hand with the faces scratched out. The idea that Evelyn could draw her friend that way—her critically missing friend—made me realize how dark and shallow the artist's mind truly twisted.

As I stared at the horrific depiction of the woman my

team and me were working around the clock to save, Parker banged on the door. He let himself into the room where I had taken the call. I could tell by my partner's urgency to get my attention there had been a development in the case.

"Give me good news, Parker."

"Sorry, Leo. We have a body."

UNEARTHED—LEO

By the time Parker and I arrived at the crime scene, the block had already been cordoned off, and a crowd had formed behind the yellow police tape.

Sydney's remains had been discovered by the sanitation department in a dumpster. Near the art district—just as Evelyn had described.

Hordes of curious onlookers peered down the alley, hoping to sneak a glimpse of the body while swarms of reporters and news crews were setting up for their breaking news reports.

I wore dark sunglasses and a baseball cap pulled down low to keep a low profile in front of the media. I preferred to keep my identity under wraps and let my commanding officer handle the reporters and press conferences.

I was a big guy and couldn't exactly hide, but as a homicide detective, my job was to solve murders and hunt down killers. I let the brass handle the ugly stuff. "Is it her?" I asked a uniform at the scene.

"Yeah, it appears to be Sydney Reynolds." The officer

shook his head as if to erase the gruesome scene he had already witnessed. "It's bad."

Once we were behind a tarp that shielded the crime scene from public view, I slid off my shades and met Parker's gaze. "Are you ready for this?"

"Never."

The CSI photographer had just finished up and stepped aside to allow us to examine the scene. *Christ.* The victim wore a thick coat of lipstick and her hair had been brushed and styled as if the killer had groomed her after her death for the crime scene photos.

Mrs. Reynolds was dressed in a negligee, her body was covered in red and white rose petals, and there was a teddy bear tucked at the crook of her broken neck.

Anger bubbled inside me that someone had the gall to mock her murder. What hit me harder was the thought that some sicko enjoyed what he'd done to this innocent woman.

From what we knew, the crime had been elaborately planned and carried out. The kidnapper had known Sydney's habits and committed the crime while her husband was at work. A knocked-over glass picture frame and a small amount of blood were the only signs of a struggle. No screaming or banging had alerted the neighbors.

Sydney's abductor had meticulously planned and carried out the crime. There were clues left at the victim's home, Location *A*, that suggested the assailant knew intimate details about her life. While we hadn't ruled out Vaughn as a suspect, we were tracking down all leads.

"What the fuck brand of psycho are we dealing with here?"

Parker exhaled a mournful sigh as he studied Sydney's remains. He was the youngest and newest member of our team. On the job, he dressed in dark suits with crisp white shirts and plain ties.

Off duty, he dressed like a gamer who lived in his parents' basement. The guys were constantly giving him hell about it. Still, he was an expert FBI profiler who had an uncanny ability to penetrate the minds of the criminally insane.

"The killer has formed an emotional attachment to the victim. Sydney knew him or at least was aware of him. Knowingly or not, she rejected him. *This* is her punishment." Parker lifted a pen from his jacket and carefully swept Sydney's hair away from her neck.

Deep purple and red finger bruises dotted her slender neck—just like Evelyn's drawing.

"Stalker?"

"Likely. Her killer wanted his face to be the last she'd see in this lifetime. He wanted to watch the light leave her eyes. He loved her, and, in his mind, her rejection ruined everything."

If I lived a thousand years, I would never be able to shake that image from my brain. I had four sisters. Knowing that could happen to one of them was all the motivation I needed to find this sick fuck before he struck again.

"Nothing in her social media or reported by her husband about a stalker. Yet. We'll dig into that," Parker said.

Using a small brush, I dusted aside a pile of rose petals and unearthed a piece of paper tucked in Mrs. Reynold's hand. "The victim has been given a message to deliver."

Parker waved over the photographer before we removed the evidence.

After documenting the finding, I used a pair of tweezers to lift the paper from her stiff hand. We leaned closer to examine the image.

"It appears to be a photograph with the face scratched out." I turned the paper over to examine the back. It was blank. No time stamp or markings to identify where it had been printed. "He's angry."

"Agreed. Could be an ex-lover, boyfriend, or a man she barely knew—"

"Or her husband," I finished the sentence.

Parker nodded as he regarded the corpse with pity, then turned his attention back to the scratched-out face in the photograph. "We need to find out this person's identity. It could be the victim, a perceived romantic rival, or the killer himself."

I bagged the photo and marked it as evidence, hoping the lab could work its magic and turn the image into a lead.

While Parker recorded notes from the scene, I slid out my phone and reexamined Evelyn's sketches. Her drawings were dead on, right down to the placement of the rose petals scattered over Sydney's corpse. While I didn't know how or why Evelyn had come upon this information, I was sure it hadn't come from the ghost of our victim.

There were only two scenarios that would lead to this level of knowledge. One, she had been at the scene before she called me and had drawn the corpse as she stood over her friend's dead body. Two, the killer had taken a picture and sent it to the artist, who then rendered her sketches from the photos.

Either way, Evelyn had guilty knowledge of the crime scene, and at this point, I had to treat Evelyn as a witness—or a suspect. Either way, I was done with her ghost stories.

I had already divulged to my team that I had been at the same art show Dr. Vaughn had attended just before he discovered his wife missing.

Naturally, I had to explain why I had been at Evelyn's gallery. Now everyone with a star knew about my relationship—what little there was of one—with the hauntingly beautiful artist and alleged medium, Evelyn Sinclair.

While Dr. Vaughn Reynold didn't fit the profile Parker had described, I'd been a detective long enough to know no one had a perfect marriage. Life was never without complications, and even seemingly perfect people had enemies whether they realized it or not.

I wasn't ruling anyone out as a suspect until I conducted my interviews and discovered more about the happy couple. There was always trouble in paradise, and I needed to investigate every angle of Sydney's life.

I felt sick as I walked away from the dumpster that held the remains of a woman who didn't deserve the horrors inflicted on her. The killer's message was clear: *"This woman is trash."*

It was my job to send a message back. *No one gets away with murder on my watch.*

HEARTBREAKER—LEO

THERE WAS NO EASY WAY TO TELL DR. VAUGHN REYNOLDS that his beloved wife had been murdered. Instead of dragging him down to the station and putting him on display for the media circus to devour, we met the victim's family at Sydney's real estate office, now being used as a war room.

Volunteers were printing *"Missing Person"* flyers, assembling to canvass the neighborhood, and praying for a miracle. They didn't know that right now, Sydney's body was being lifted out of a dumpster.

I hated that we hadn't arrived with good news instead of a tragedy. The victim's family had stayed out of the activity and gathered in a private meeting room on the top floor of Sydney's agency.

Her parents were huddled on a love seat, holding hands and comforting each other. At the same time, Vaughn stood by the window with his brother Braydon beside him. While the entire family was fearful and grief-stricken, Vaughn appeared the worst of them.

His face was paler than a sheet of paper, and his eyes were bloodshot and glossed over from stress and lack of sleep. His skin was blotchy, and he kept shaking his head and running his fingers through his hair as if he could chase away the agonizing images of his beloved wife begging for mercy from the violent man who had stolen her from the safety of their home.

"Did you find our daughter?" Sydney's mother whimpered, breaking the silence. A hopeful twinge of optimism shone in her watery eyes.

Her husband held his frail wife as she clutched a photo of our victim as a young girl hugging a smiling golden retriever. A stack of photo albums was on her lap, and a box of tissues was tucked at her side.

"We did," I answered.

There was a collective gasp in the room. Dr. Vaughn, his brother beside him, practically holding him up, stared into my eyes as if he could extract the information from my soul.

When it came to delivering bad news, I never sugarcoated the information. No matter what language I used, I couldn't soften the blow or change the outcome. Now that Sydney's case had gone from missing person to homicide victim, my role in the investigation had changed.

My job was to catch her killer.

From that moment on, I was searching for suspects. Family members and friends were always on our short list of suspects in any murder investigation. Judging by how we found her corpse, her mother and father were not involved. No siblings. The most likely suspect—statistically speaking— was the victim's husband, Dr. Vaughn Reynolds.

Parker and I approached delivering bad news to victims' families as an opportunity to assess the reactions of those closest to the deceased. Some might've deemed that cruel or insensitive, but our job was to seek justice for the victim. My partner and I learned a lot from each individual's reaction.

While Parker resembled a technology nerd who camped

out on the sidewalk to be first in line to get the latest iPhone, he was sharp, well educated, and skilled at reading people and their reactions. Plus, his baby face and likable-guy persona helped soften my all-business style.

"Is she in the hospital? Can we go see her now?" Sydney's father asked. His bottom lip trembled as he clutched his wife. His blue eyes widened as he held on to a sliver of hope that his daughter still had a fighting chance against the man who'd abducted her.

"No, sir. I'm sorry to tell you I have bad news. Your daughter is no longer alive."

Since the parents were not suspects, I shifted my gaze to Dr. Reynolds.

From experience, there were only three ways victims' families responded to this tragic news. One, they were in complete denial. They would shake their heads, wave their arms, and call us out for being idiots for not knowing a dead body when we saw one.

This denial was followed by a wave of questions meant to invalidate our information. *How do you know it's her? Did you run DNA tests? Maybe the woman you found just looks like her....*

The second reaction was more common, the complete and total meltdown. When the family member believed the information I delivered, they reacted with immense grief—like Sydney's parents. Wailing, crying, fainting dead away. The victim's mother and father embraced as they digested the news that their daughter had been murdered.

The third reaction was less common, but since Dr. Vaughn wasn't crying or disputing his wife's fate, I braced for what he was about to do next.

The doctor's eyes were sharp and vexing. Instead of being distraught, his face reddened with rage. Dr. Vaughn set his sights on me and aimed his finger between my eyes. "Where were you? Why didn't you find her in time?" Vaughn came at me with the vengeance and veracity of a street dog in survival mode.

He evoked the "kill the messenger" coping mechanism. I was the scapegoat for his snowballing grief.

"Vaughn, man. Hold on. It's not his fault." Brayden subdued his brother and held him back, but Dr. Reynolds was delirious with rage. I had just informed him that his wife had been murdered. I had given no details, no context as to where her body was discovered and had not suggested a sexual assault.

As detectives, this was a crucial moment for us. I kept Parker in my peripheral vision as we kept silent and let Vaughn continue his rage. While he was either in shock about the news of his wife's murder or was putting on a show for his in-laws, we wanted him to keep talking.

Suppose Dr. Reynolds knew anything about his wife's disappearance. In that case, he might let something slip about the crime that only her killer would know. As it stood, we had a few leads but no prime suspect who had abducted Mrs. Reynolds. It could've been a stranger or the man she loved and trusted most.

"You're a fuckup, Detective. You don't even care that she's dead. Just one crime you have to solve. She's my wife! You fucking loser. You too, you little shit." He shifted his gaze to Parker. "You're so fucking smart. Why couldn't you figure out who took her?" Vaughn struggled to free himself from his brother's bear hug, but Braydon was stronger than his inconsolable sibling.

"Vaughn, please," Sydney's mother whimpered.

A loud knock came on the door. "You alright in there, Ricci?" It was Officer Santoni, the uniform stationed outside the door. A buddy of mine from the neighborhood who used to help me swipe beers out of my dad's garage fridge when we were in fifth grade.

Santoni knew I was alright. Christ, I had a gun. It was just his protective nature to look out for one of his own. Parker opened the door and asked Santoni to escort Sydney's parents and Braydon to a quiet room where they could grieve. The compassionate soul that he was, Parker had the decency to warn them not to watch the news.

While my loyal friend ushered the family away, Dr. Reynolds composed himself. As tears streamed down his cheeks, he closed his eyes and lifted his head. My partner and I stood silent, giving the doctor time to process the soul-crushing news.

After a few moments, Dr. Vaughn opened his eyes and blinked to regain his focus. "Forgive me, gentlemen. I don't know where that came from."

"Grief," Parker said. "I can't imagine what you're going through." My partner lifted an eyebrow, reminding me to show compassion to the guy.

"I'm sorry for your loss. Can I get you anything?" I gestured to a conference table and suggested we all take a seat. I poured Vaughn a glass of water and slid a box of tissues in his direction.

"Where did you find my wife?" Vaughn asked as he sank into a chair.

"In an alley. An area south of here, near the art district," I said.

"How did she die?"

"We're waiting for the medical examiner's report. The autopsy will take place in a few days."

Vaughn swallowed hard, heartbroken at the thought that his wife's body was in the morgue. "Any suspects? Have you caught her killer?"

"Our investigation has just begun," I said.

Vaughn's gaze landed on a shelf on the opposite side of

the room. He smiled mournfully at a framed wedding photo Sydney had proudly displayed in her conference room.

"We've only been married four months. We had a small ceremony on Captiva Island." Vaughn pointed to the photo for reference.

Parker offered a bittersweet smile and commented on how happy they looked.

"Do you know anyone who would want to hurt your wife?" I asked. "Did she have any enemies? Jealous ex-boyfriends harassing her?"

"We've been over this a hundred times. Why are you asking again about exes?" Vaughn shifted his gaze between the two of us. It seemed something occurred to him that he hadn't considered before. "Was my wife sexually assaulted?"

"We can't reveal details about an open investigation."

"Oh god." Vaughn's face blanched, and he covered his mouth as if about to be sick. He bolted out of his chair and paced the room like a caged animal, trying desperately to escape the nightmare unfolding in his mind.

"Some fucking psycho broke into our home and captured my dear Sydney and… and… fuck!" He picked up the photo frame that held their wedding photo and slammed it against the wall, shattering it to pieces.

He went into a self-destructive rampage, flinging books and glass awards from the shelves, destroying everything in his path. Dr. Vaughn Reynolds was either a fantastic actor or a grief-stricken widower. I intervened and wrapped him in a bear hug to prevent him from hurting himself.

While subdued, he wailed in agony as the reality settled in that his beloved bride had been brutally murdered. I would hold my judgment about his guilt or innocence until I had hard evidence.

I lived by the creed "Innocent until proven guilty," but I

couldn't bring myself to feel sorry for the guy until I knew for sure that he didn't do it.

My next official business was to track down and question Evelyn Sinclair. Once I got her down to the station, she would tell us what we wanted to know. My interrogation style wasn't pleasant, but a woman had been violently murdered.

I wouldn't let my personal feelings for Evelyn hinder my investigation.

LOSING BATTLE—EVELYN

My call to Leo had been a complete disaster, as expected.

At best, my hot new *almost* boyfriend thought I was a whacko. At worst, Detective Ricci believed I was involved with Sydney's murder. The news was reporting that a body had been recovered. While there was no official confirmation of the victim's identity, I knew it was Sydney.

I'd communed with plenty of dead people, under terrible circumstances, but never a friend.

Oh god, Sydney.

And now I knew the detective on the case. That had never happened before. In the past, I'd given information to the cops anonymously when I had clues that could help them solve a crime. I never wanted to get actively involved in a case—until now.

Once Leo and his team recovered her body from the dumpster, and my friend's corpse was staged exactly as I had sketched her, Chicago PD would come banging on my door and drag me down to the station to interrogate me. I knew what was coming and needed to prepare.

The problem was that I had little faith Leo or anyone else in law enforcement would believe my story. Knowing that I needed to find out as much as possible from Sydney before I had to face Leo again. Solid, indisputable evidence was the key to getting him to believe my gift was real. Who better to get the truth from than the victim herself?

While it pained me to see my friend's ghost, I needed to connect with Sydney so that I could gather clues that would help solve her murder. Her restless spirit was no longer around me, so I needed to track her down.

The most logical place to start was at the scene of the crime, but I sensed there was a more direct path to finding my friend. If Sydney was out for justice, she might be following the detective charged with tracking down her killer.

My meeting with Leo was unavoidable, so I shoved my sketchbook into my purse, grabbed my travel mug, and headed out to avoid Leo and his team storming the gallery. I bottled up my outrage and sadness over the murder and set out to offer my paranormal services to the all-business detective who didn't believe in ghosts.

I realized I was heading into a losing battle. Still, with or without Detective Ricci's help, I would unravel the clues and solve the mystery of who killed Sydney Reynolds. My confrontation with Leo was unavoidable, so I decided to meet on my terms.

I sent Leo a text: **Meet me at the coffee shop.**

THE MESSENGER—LEO

I HATED SURPRISES. BUT WHEN I ARRIVED AT THE COFFEE SHOP and found Evelyn seated in her usual spot, drinking her coffee, with my favorite green smoothie waiting for me, I admit—it was the good kind of surprise.

Sunlight shined in from the window and brought a warm glow to Evelyn's complexion. When her bright-blue eyes met my gaze, I had to remind myself that I was there on official business—not because I wanted to see her again.

Whatever we had going at her studio was over. She wasn't the fun and nice person I had believed her to be. *Nice* people didn't sketch horrid pictures of their murdered friends and try to sell some ghost schtick to law enforcement.

Still, since she appeared to be cooperating with my investigation, there was no need to treat her like a hostile witness —unless she wanted to keep going down the damnable ghost path.

Maybe she was delusional, or someone was coercing her into feeding me false information. If she had more information about the crime or the killer, I would uncover the truth.

Evelyn greeted me with a sad smile and slid a chair out with her foot, inviting me to join her.

"Any news?" Evelyn asked.

"We're doing everything we can to find her killer. My team is interviewing her friends and coworkers, checking security footage, and tracking down all the leads we have. Which is why I'm here to see you."

Evelyn nodded. "Good. I'm ready to get to work." She patted her sketchbook, indicating her contribution to the case. "Where do we begin?"

While I was pleased Evelyn was trying, she was delusional if she believed we would be working as a team. I was the detective. She was the witness. I wanted nothing more to do with her ghost stories. "Let's start with the truth."

"I couldn't agree more, Detective. Have you run a background check on me?"

"Yes."

"You know my real name?"

"Lauren Murphy."

"Did you look up the details of my accident report?"

"I did."

"Before or after you came to the art show?"

"Before."

"Why?"

"I was curious. I wanted to know more about you." It was imperative to establish a good rapport with my star witness. By being honest with Evelyn, I hoped to earn her trust.

"Do you believe what I told you about Sydney, or do you think I'm crazy?"

"I don't think you're crazy." That was the truth, but I knew her information about the crime came from a source that still had a pulse. "I'm running a murder investigation. My job is to follow leads. My partner wants to ask you some specific questions about the drawings. He's into—*that kind of stuff.*" I gestured to her sketchbook.

Evelyn seemed satisfied with my answer and agreed to come to the station and meet Parker. As we walked down the sidewalk to my car, our shadows stretched before us on the sidewalk. Evelyn studied our elongated silhouettes as she twisted a long strand of her hair around her finger. "If you don't think I'm crazy, does that mean you believe me?"

With Evelyn, I had to be careful about how I approached her version of reality. I considered the idea that someone was coercing her. She had guilty knowledge about the crime, that much I knew, but she had divulged things she couldn't have known unless she had witnessed the crime or the killer had shared pictures with her.

"Talk to me, Leo." She touched my arm, boomeranging my attraction back to center. I had to chuck the idea that Evelyn and I would ever have a shot at a romantic relationship. I had to remain professional. I was the one who asked for the truth. I owed her the same courtesy.

"If you want to change your story, now is the time." I guided her away from foot traffic, giving her a moment to make the right choice. "Look, if someone threatened you and coerced you into showing me those drawings, I can help you. Tell me, Evelyn. Who gave you information about the murder?"

"I've already told you the truth. I can't help it if you don't like the answer."

Fair enough. I gave her a chance. Since Evelyn was sticking with her ghost story, I would have to use an interrogation approach she wouldn't like. I had a job to do—track down a killer. If I had to hurt her feelings, call her a fraud, or make her curse the day she met me to get to the truth, I wouldn't let my personal life get in the way of doing my job.

When we reached the Charger, I clicked the remote and

unlocked my vehicle. I opened the door and placed my hand on her back as I helped her into the car. I caught a whiff of her vanilla-scented skin, another reminder of our passionate kiss last night.

Before the call in the early morning hour, I was looking forward to seeing her again. I had even planned to invite her to dinner the next time I had a night off. Something I rarely did with the women I spent time with. I paused before shutting the car door, giving her one last chance to come clean.

We locked eyes as we each waited for the other to speak. I needed to come up with the right thing to say to get to the truth. I could help her. She just needed to let me in. "I will never let anyone hurt you, Evelyn."

"I know."

"All I need is a name."

"I have no control over my gift. I'm just the messenger."

I gave her a nod and closed the door. I wasn't up to speed on the paranormal playbook. Still, Parker was giddy over the idea that we had an alleged clairvoyant witness interfering with our case.

As for me, I wanted nothing to do with this nonsense. Evelyn knew more about our investigation than she was telling me. I believed she knew the killer's identity but was afraid to turn him in. The truth about her guilty knowledge had nothing to do with a ghost.

I wondered if Sydney had mentioned any of the men she dated before marrying Vaughn. She had been a client of the Armstrong Agency, a high-end matchmaking service.

My team was in the process of checking into the men she dated. Vaughn had already told us that he and Sydney had met through the service, and she had gone on dates with several other clients before they met and fell instantly in love.

Since Evelyn and the victim were friends, Sydney

might've said something about a jealous ex-boyfriend, a man who had been harassing her after she had broken off the relationship, or even an affair that continued after the marriage.

The other scenario I considered was Evelyn may be staying silent to protect her friend's dignity. An affair would've been scandalous and devastating to Dr. Vaughn. Maybe Evelyn's motive for lying was loyalty.

Either way, I would uncover the truth and discover what Evelyn was hiding.

CAPTIVA—EVELYN

Leo and I rolled up to the back entrance of the station. He parked the Charger inside a compound surrounded by barbed wire and security cameras, with armed guards controlling who came and went.

Inside, Detective Leo Ricci checked in with a uniformed officer stationed behind a desk. He gave the officer my name, and she buzzed us inside the underbelly of the historic precinct.

The *click, click, click* of my heels echoed off the brightly lit hallway as I kept up with Leo's fast pace. I dropped my gaze to the dirty tile floor and avoided eye contact with Leo's fellow officers. Maybe I was paranoid, but I felt like the entire precinct knew who I was—and why I was with Detective Ricci. I was confident he had to divulge that he was in the presence of Dr. Vaughn last night—because he was at the gallery to see me.

As I did my *walk of shame that I never had the pleasure of enjoying*, Leo led me down a hallway, up two flights of stairs, and then through a huge room filled with detectives behind desks, clicking away on laptops, talking on cell phones, and interviewing people who would certainly rather be anywhere but there.

Leo steered me into a smaller, more private office and shut the door. Behind a wall of paperwork and a stack of books sat the man I presumed was his partner. The tall, thin man with a bushy ponytail, soft-brown eyes, and a genuine smile rushed to greet me.

"Evelyn, I'm so glad to meet you. I'm Agent Parker Williams." Parker, sporting a standard-issue crisp white shirt tucked into dark pants, initiated a handshake.

"*Agent?* You're not a detective?"

"I'm with the FBI Chicago Field Office. Detective Ricci and I work together on the Violent Crimes Task Force. I'm a criminal profiler. Our agency collaborates with law enforcement on cases that require more resources than a single jurisdiction can handle," Parker explained. "Kidnappings, murder for hire, battery with sexual assault, serial killers—"

"Let's get started," Leo interrupted as he pulled out a chair and invited me to take a seat.

I exhaled a rush of nerves as I weighed the gravity of my situation. *I'm a witness in a highly publicized murder case.* My phone call to Leo meant my secret was out. If the media discovered my involvement and how Sydney's ghost had led me to her crime scene, my face would be plastered all over national news stations.

This is not what I want or have ever intended.

Yes, I wanted to share my art and gift with the world—but only the details I felt comfortable sharing. Dreaming of ghosts was safe. Admitting that the restless spirits wanted my help solving their murders was a fact that could get me killed.

While sharing my near-death experience and painting the ghosts who visited my dreams was something I was passionate about, getting myself tangled up in a present-day murder investigation was dangerous.

The subjects of my paintings at the gallery were old ghosts whose deaths occurred decades ago. But now that my friend had become the victim of a homicide, I would do everything in my power to help Leo and his team solve the crime.

Leo spread out photocopies of the drawings I'd texted him of Sydney's crime scene. I glanced at my work and then turned away. It pained me to see my Sydney's face immortalized in terror as her remains were laid to rest on top of a pile of garbage.

Leo and Parker stalked me like a pair of hunters as they gauged my reaction. Parker smiled politely as he absorbed the essence of my being. Leo leaned on the edge of his desk, waiting to go for my throat if I showed any signs of deception or guilt. One wrong move, and my head would end up on their trophy wall.

"I'm sorry about what happened to your friend," Parker said. "What can you tell me about these drawings?" Parker's nonconfrontational style was the opposite of Leo's tough and intimidating aura. Parker was the brains of the Violent Crimes Task Force, and Leo was the beefed-up intimidator in the *good cop, bad cop* scenario.

"I think they speak for themselves. Is there something specific you want to know?"

"You admit you are the artist of these pictures?" Leo tapped his finger on Sydney's portrait.

"Of course. I never denied it. I called *you*, remember?"

"Just establishing facts for my partner." Leo nodded as if mentally marking a check in the box. "When was the last time you spoke to Sydney Reynolds?"

"That's a loaded question, Detective."

Leo exhaled an exacerbated breath as he re-formed his

question. "When was the last time you spoke to Sydney —*while she was still alive?*" His eyes sharpened, angry I had forced him down a paranormal path of questioning in front of his colleague.

"A few weeks ago, after my gallery manager, Gibson, sent out invitations to the private event. Sydney sent me a text to congratulate me. She placed the invitation next to a bouquet of roses on her desk and sent me a pic. She was thrilled and said she and Vaughn wouldn't miss it."

Parker lifted a finger and said, "That's the event last night, correct? The one Detective Ricci attended as your guest?"

Here we go. I was certain Leo had already confessed he had been there as my guest. I imagined his buddies were curious as to why he was at an art show, and Leo had to present me, the artist he'd hit on at the coffee shop, as Exhibit *A*.

The idea of Leo's buddies razzing him about getting involved with the "crazy" lady who sees ghosts made me cringe as a round of self-deprecating thoughts swirled around my head. That was why I hadn't let myself get too close to the men I dated through the agency.

When one of my dates raised an eyebrow about my paranormal art, I mentally slammed the door. If a guy didn't like my paintings, I didn't care. I was out if he thought I was lying about my near-death experience. If I never let anyone in, no one could hurt me.

"That was the last time you communicated with her? The text about the art show?"

I didn't like Detective Leo Ricci's harsh tone. If he didn't believe in ghosts, fine. If he wanted the truth, he would have to deal with my reality.

"I've already told you. I'm a medium—*I see dead people.* The last time I was in contact with Sydney was last night. The time was around four a.m. She had already passed when she visited me."

Parker lifted his eyebrows in a curious rather than judgmental way. "Do you have the original drawings with you?"

I nodded as I lifted my sketch pad out of my bag. I flipped the pages to the first drawing and turned it around so the guys could study my work. Parker flipped through the sketches while Leo leaned against the desk with his arms crossed.

"Fascinating," Parker said. "How long did it take you to draw these?"

"A couple hours, I think. I'm in a deep state of relaxation when I draw. It zaps my energy. Sometimes I fall asleep by the time I finish."

Parker flipped the pages, scrutinizing each one. "When you called Detective Ricci, you stated that the killer had disposed of her remains in a dumpster. How did you know that? I don't see evidence of that detail in your work."

Good question, Agent. You are paying attention. "Sydney first came to me in a dream. She beckoned me to follow her, and when I did, she pointed to a dumpster."

"Did she talk to you? Tell you anything about the crime? Every detail could be important."

"*Captiva*," I said. "I keep hearing the word. I don't know why she wants me to pay attention to this, but I know it's important."

"You're clairaudient?" Parker asked. "You hear voices from the spirit world?"

Leo folded his arms as if annoyed by his partner. His muscles rippled, and his black T-shirt rode up his arm, exposing another piece of his *tattoo puzzle*. Had I gotten this peek outside the interrogation room and under different circumstances, I would've been hungry to see more.

But the ghost ship had set sail, and I was no longer interested in pursuing a relationship with a man who believed I was either a liar or a lunatic.

"Yes. Just a word or a short phrase. When Sydney came to me, she wanted to communicate more, but the only word I heard was *Captiva*."

Parker twisted his lips and nodded excitedly as he flipped to the last sketch. "And this?" He pointed to the note Sydney held in her hand. The message she was so desperate for me to pay attention to. I liked Parker. Not only was he intelligent, but he was also a probing investigator.

"Thank you for bringing that up." I shot a sideways glare at Leo, who suddenly seemed interested in what I had to say. "Sydney was trying to show me something important on that paper, but it was blurry, and I couldn't figure out what it was. I think it's a photograph—but the face was scratched out."

The guys exchanged glances. Something I'd said made a connection.

BEST SHOT—EVELYN

DETECTIVE RICCI PACED AS HE WORKED OUT HIS NEXT LINE OF questioning. "If I've just been murdered, and my ghost is wandering around in search of help, why do I come find you? Why not seek out me or my partner or someone in law enforcement who could actually help me?"

I stared at Leo incredulously. "I am helping Sydney."

"You're right, Evelyn. That didn't come out the way I'd intended. Unlike my partner, I'm new to this ghost stuff. Help me out here." Leo gestured for me to continue.

Knowing that Leo didn't believe a word of my ghost story made it difficult to explain how things worked in the in-between stage of the afterlife. I shot my gaze to Parker, hoping he would step in and defend me, but he seemed curious to hear my side of the story.

"Let me explain something to you, Detective Ricci." I scooted my chair back, moved to the whiteboard by the back wall, and picked up a marker. "Sydney was murdered. A man kidnapped her from her home, dragged her away, did unthinkable things to her, and strangled her to death."

I illustrated her graphic murder using a blue dry-erase

marker. "And dying was just the beginning of the hell she is currently experiencing. Death is terrifying for souls that choose to remain earthbound. You don't always go through the warm, golden tunnel into paradise when you die. When you stay, it's by choice."

"Fear, love, or revenge?" Detective Ricci asked.

"You were paying attention last night." I was impressed Leo had remembered the details of my presentation. I felt a twinge of regret that our perfect evening had evolved into *this*.

I drew a circle representing the path to *the other side*, then drew an *X* over it. "You are correct, Detective. Sydney would love to speak to you, your partner, Vaughn, and all her loved ones—but she can't. The only person she has left in this world is me." My voice trembled, causing me to pause and compose myself.

"She's terrified, confused, devastated, and pissed off that some loser stole her life. The problem is, *you* can't hear her because *you* are not a medium. That's why she came to me!" I tossed the marker back onto the ledge. I hated that I had to justify my intentions to Leo. What other reason would I have to make this stuff up?

"I can't imagine how difficult this must be for you, Evelyn." Parker stepped in to defuse the situation while Leo clenched his jaw to prevent something probably extremely nasty and hurtful from escaping his lips. "I understand you —and *Sydney*—are trying to help us track down the killer. I'm listening." Parker gave me an apologetic smile and glanced at his partner.

Whether or not Parker believed me, he was at least a good sport. However, Leo was still not on board. Not only was he skeptical of my paranormal gift, but his expression was also tinged with animosity, like I was wasting his precious time.

Instead of sitting there and letting Leo grill me, I took

control of the interrogation. "Detective Ricci, you are a skeptic. I hear you loud and clear. Honestly, I don't give a damn what you think. My only motive is to help solve Sydney's case. If you think I'm crazy, I don't care. All I want you to do is listen to what I have to say and believe me when I tell you it's true."

I opened my arms, inviting him to take his best shot. "What can I do to convince you I'm telling the truth? I have nothing to hide. Ask me anything. No topic is off-limits. Hit me with your best shot."

"Why did you change your name?"

I inhaled a sharp breath, unprepared for a painfully personal question. "That has nothing to do with this case."

"Who are you running from, *Lauren*?"

"No one." Feeling exposed, I sank down in the chair and crossed my arms. "I meant you could ask me anything about Sydney or the case or my gift. This line of questioning is out of bounds."

"You said you had nothing to hide. No topic is off-limits. Why won't you answer my questions? Who are you afraid of?" From the moment I'd first set eyes on Leo, I knew he was the strong and serious type. His job demanded it, and if his motive was to intimidate me with his body language and cold, hard stare, it was working.

My skin dampened with perspiration, but I was determined not to crumble under pressure. "My family doesn't understand my gift. My parents checked me into a mental hospital after I started drawing dead people. Once I was released, I cut them out of my life and changed my name to get a fresh start. *Lauren* wasn't brave enough to stand up to them. *Evelyn* doesn't give a fuck what they think of her."

Leo held my gaze as he absorbed the answer. I sensed he would've taken my parents' side if the opportunity had presented itself.

I was over being shamed for something I had no control over. If Leo wanted to look down on me because of my connection to the spirit world, I would find a way to help Sydney without his help. "Anything else, Detective?"

"Do you know who killed Sydney?"

"No."

"Had you ever met Dr. Vaughn Reynolds before last night?"

"No. But I know his brother, Braydon. He was the project manager for my gallery remodel. Sydney recommended him."

Parker jotted down the note on his iPad.

"Do you know anyone who would want to harm your friend?"

"No."

"Did Sydney ever talk about ex-boyfriends or unwanted attention?"

"No."

"Is Sydney here with us now?"

I couldn't believe what I was hearing. Had I convinced Leo I was telling the truth? Was he cracking open the nonbeliever vault just enough to give me the benefit of the doubt? "No. She's not here."

Leo sighed dramatically. "That's a shame. It seems now would be the perfect time for the victim of a homicide to show up. You know, when you—*the medium*—are standing in front of the two guys who can help solve her murder. Did Sydney's ghost have something more important to do this afternoon? I mean, she stayed behind to bring her killer to justice, right?"

And to think, I had given Detective Ricci the benefit of the doubt. Not only was he an ass, but he wasn't a very good detective. If he believed Sydney's motive for remaining earthbound was revenge, his detective skills needed a refresher class on motives.

While I stood there, reeling from Detective Ricci's mockery, he opened the door to his office. "Thank you for your time, Miss Sinclair. You are free to go now."

WALLEYE—LEO

Evelyn shifted her gaze between Parker and me, stunned by her dismissal. "I'm not making this up. This isn't some sort of act. The drawings mean something. I know you recognize—"

"If we need anything, we know where to reach you." I gestured again for Evelyn to leave my office.

She huffed in frustration, gathered her art supplies, and stuffed them back into her purse. She pushed her chair back and headed for the door—but paused before leaving. "Look, I get it. I'm sure you deal with delusional people all the time."

I opened my mouth to argue, but Evelyn cut me off. "But please understand, I'm not doing this for myself. I have an obligation to deliver the messages. What you decide to do with it is out of my hands. But if you take me to her crime scene, I might be able to—"

"Get a lot of publicity for your upcoming art show?" I snapped, losing patience with her ghost bullshit. I had already done my digging into Evelyn's personal life. She had invested a small fortune into her new business. Sure, her ghost paintings were not for sale, but she had already divulged that most of her income came from commissioned work.

Conjuring up the ghost of her murdered friend would be a fantastic way to promote her work and bring in new clients. Her first art show in her new gallery had to be putting a lot of pressure on her. Perhaps her ghost stories, paired with the murder of her friend, gave her the idea of jumping into a high-profile case as a "psychic investigator." It would make an excellent story for the evening news.

From my experience, people rarely do something for nothing. And this story she conjured up about wanting to help ghosts solve their murders would have the media salivating to break the story. A beautiful and talented young woman helping Chicago PD solve murders they were too dense to figure out on their own.

I was out of patience and needed to get back to work and stop wasting my time on an opportunist. While I had been attracted to her, any hope of moving forward with a romantic relationship was DOA—dead on arrival.

Evelyn's jaw dropped, and her eyes were wild with indignation. The shock of the accusation floored her. Instead of pleading her case or bothering to defend herself, she slung her bag over her shoulder and marched out the door.

As Evelyn retreated, she stopped dead in her tracks and turned to face me. "*Walleye.*" She spat the word as if it were laced with venom. As she waited for a reaction from me that never came, she turned her back and clicked down the hallway, making no further effort to plead her case, defend her honor, or meddle in my investigation.

"Hold on. Let me drive you back." Evelyn was stubborn enough to walk home from the precinct alone, even though it was in a dangerous neighborhood.

Evelyn's response came in the form of a one-finger salute.

Fine. I deserved that.

I watched her storm through the corridor and waited until she was out of sight before I went back to my office to confer with Parker on the interview. I knew we wouldn't agree on everything, but Evelyn had hit the mark when she described the photograph in Sydney's hand.

Parker may believe the information came from the great beyond. Still, her description validated my theory that Evelyn knew more about the murder—or murderer—than she was willing to admit.

Her attempt to convince me she had a paranormal gift had failed. However, the one-word *clairaudient* thing defied logic. When Evelyn had said "Captiva," it was a safe bet. It was no secret that Mr. and Mrs. Reynolds had a destination wedding and tied the knot on a remote island in Florida.

No big mystery. No *aha!* moment.

What had me reeling, though, was what she'd said to me. If there was a single word in the universe that could deliver a sucker punch to my gut, she'd found it.

Walleye.

THE VISION—EVELYN

IF DETECTIVE RICCI HAD CALLED ME CRAZY, DELUSIONAL, psychotic, or a witch, I wouldn't have flinched. I've heard it all before, which was why I had to change my name and relocate to seven cities in five years. But accusing me of being an opportunistic media whore was an all-time low.

What brand of crap detectives do we have in this city?

There was a murderer on the loose, and Chicago had the town's worst, most self-absorbed asshole running the investigation. While I mentally revved up ideas of how I could help Sydney without Leo's help, I buried Detective Ricci's condescending assessment of my character and concentrated on the greater good.

I had a direct line to the victim. All I had to do was follow the clues from Sydney and track down her killer. Once I had a name, I could hand deliver the information to Chicago PD without ever having to speak to Detective Ricci again.

The news had reported a candlelight vigil that evening at the location of Sydney's crime scene to honor her memory. While I paid my respects, I would seize the opportunity to connect with Sydney.

I stormed back to the gallery with an empowering sense of renewed energy. I went straight to my studio to examine my drawings to see if there was anything important I may have missed. As I studied my sketches, my cell buzzed with an incoming text.

GIBSON: Are you at the gallery? Mega good news!
EVELYN: Here. Can't wait!

Moments later, Gibson's stilettos clicked on the hardwood. She was talking to someone, and I could hear a pair of tennis shoes padding beside her.

Maybe a person is the surprise?

I pushed the rolling chair back from my drafting table and left my office to meet her. From the landing, I spotted Gibson schmoozing with Jeremy, the photographer from the Windy City Beat.

The magazine had arranged an artsy photo shoot with Jeremy at the gallery back when it was still in the remodeling phase. The photographer had loved the work-in-progress setting with billowy drop cloths over the windows, scattered paintbrushes on worktables, and my beloved chandelier out of commission on the floor.

Jeremy was carrying a cardboard box, and Gibson was grinning so hard I feared she might spontaneously combust. The Beat had interviewed me ahead of the October Final Friday Gallery Walk, and I reasoned the issue that featured the gallery was ready for distribution.

"Hey, Jeremy. Nice to see you again," I said as I trotted downstairs.

"Hi, Evelyn." He was the broody artist type who wore black and never had time for chitchat. He took his work seriously and was a stickler for details with respect to camera angles, lighting, shadows, and backgrounds.

We had worked for hours to get the perfect shot, but Jeremy assured me the extra effort would pay off. *"I'll know it when I see it."*

I couldn't wait to see which photo the magazine chose to feature in the arts section distributed all over town in bars, restaurants, and newsstands. The gallery promo would probably be a small mention buried inside. Still, I was thrilled to even make it into the magazine.

"Have you seen it yet?" I asked Gibson.

"No, but I approved several of Jeremy's amazing photos. I don't know which one they decided on."

Jeremy set the box next to Gibson's desk and pulled a box cutter out of his jeans. When he lifted the box flap, I nearly choked on my tongue when I saw the cover design. My jaw dropped, and my eyes widened in surprise.

It was me. *On the cover.*

Specifically, a closeup of my face with my eyes standing out as the focal point. Jeremy had worked some Photoshop magic on my picture. He added a blue-tinted filter and reduced the saturation level of my face from the nose down, giving my portrait a ghostly, translucent glow.

Jeremy had nailed the vibe of the gallery and my own personal brand. Although the photo shoot had been long and tedious, every moment and uncomfortable pose was worth the effort a million times over.

I stifled a scream when I read the headline:

THE DEATH OF ME: INTRODUCING EVELYN SINCLAIR

"Oh my god." Gibson's bangle bracelets jangled as she grabbed my arm and squeezed.

I shook my head, stunned and overwhelmed with gratitude.

"Oh, my freaking god, Evelyn!" Gibson snatched a magazine off the top for closer inspection. We flipped through the pages and were pleased to see a considerable spread featuring my fellow artists from all the fantastic galleries on the block.

As Gibson and I basked in our Chicago art scene glory, Jeremy stood still and quiet, enjoying our reaction to his incredible art.

"Thank you, Jeremy. This is beyond what I could've imagined. This had to have taken you hours and hours. Your vision is amazing."

Jeremy beamed with pride as he absorbed my flattery. "Your work speaks to me. I wanted to capture the essence of your artistic soul."

Gibson fluttered around her office like a vegan leather-clad butterfly and packed up a swag bag for Jeremy. She stuffed it with a gallery-branded Yeti, T-shirt, postcards, and all the promo goodies that would fit in the canvas tote, along with an invitation to a press event coming up at the gallery.

As Gibson and I walked Jeremy to the door, I realized it was getting dark. While I was happy for a short reprieve from the sadness and drama, I had a memorial service to attend, a detective to prove wrong, and a ghost to track down.

PRYING EYES—EVELYN

LUMINARIES LINED THE SIDEWALK THAT LED TO SYDNEY'S VIGIL. The soft glow of candlelight created a somber mood along the sidewalk that led to the crime scene where her body had been discovered.

Mourners gathered and delivered flowers, pictures, stuffed animals, and shiny balloons on sticks to a makeshift memorial blocked by police barricades and a chain-length fence. Sydney was a huge supporter of local businesses and donated her time and money to many nonprofits that supported our community. Her death had been a shock and tragic loss to many who loved and respected her.

While I wanted to pay homage to my friend's memory, I attended the vigil to try to connect with Sydney's ghost. Since Detective Ricci had no more use for my opportunistic, media whore, paranormal services, I made it my mission to track Sydney's killer on my own.

What I wanted more than anything—even more so than bringing her killer to justice—was to help Sydney find closure so that she could move on and find peace on *the other side*. Knowing she came to me in our hour of need, there was no way I would turn my back when I might be her only hope.

Even if Leo didn't want my paranormal guidance, I could anonymously send the information to his team or call in a tip to the hotline and lead detectives toward the killer. When I figured out who the murderer was, I would find a way to bring him to justice.

I lit a candle and joined the swarm of well-wishers that gathered to pray and offer affirmations of hope and healing for those left behind. An a cappella chorus gathered, holding hands and singing a harmonized rendition of "Amazing Grace."

The ensemble swayed in time with the music and formed a semicircle around a framed portrait of Sydney that had been propped against the chain-length fence. Seeing Sydney's face among the flowers and tributes paired with the somber music and the warm glow of the candles whirled past me in a surreal haze.

I hadn't known Sydney well, but she was someone I admired and adored. Ambitious and confident. An intelligent and decisive businesswoman. A fun-loving, confident person who didn't deserve to be murdered and dumped on a pile of trash.

Pangs of guilt swirled in my gut as I remembered how worried she was when we toured my gallery. Something had been bothering her. I should've asked her why she was concerned about dying.

Her fear seemed out of place, considering she'd claimed to be so happy with her new husband, Vaughn. I couldn't figure out why or who had provoked her anxiety. Had she been truthful when claiming she was overwhelmed with her new, perfect life?

Or was something sinister brewing under the surface that had her regretting her whirlwind marriage? I knew from experience that everyone had secrets. Some were tiny white lies, while others were doozies that would wreak havoc on a person's social life or end a career.

Had Sydney uncovered one of Vaughn's secrets? Was it too big to bury? Had the discovery led to her death? Or was there a random psychopath roaming the streets of the Windy City? The what-ifs bounced around my mind and gave me a head rush.

I took a deep breath and focused on the growing memorial along the fence. Hundreds of gifts, cards, and pictures were placed around her crime scene. As I studied the tributes, I had an uneasy feeling someone was watching me.

I glanced around the crowd, searching for the culprit, but no one stood out. Still, my instincts were never wrong. The creepy feeling made my stomach turn. The intense feeling was overwhelming, and I decided to leave, but as I turned to go, I felt an urge to draw.

Sydney is here.

There were too many people around, and the closeness of bodies made me nauseous. The flickering wave of candlelight blurred my vision. The sea of mourners had swept me into the current, and I needed to break away.

I broke away from the swarm and found a less crowded area across the street. I slumped down on the sidewalk against a brick wall to shield my drawing from curious passersby. I closed my eyes, concentrated on Sydney's energy, and held the tip of my pencil to a clean sheet of paper in my sketchbook.

As my mind quieted, my hand began to move.

While my gift of automatic drawing took over, the unsettling feeling that someone was watching me broke my concentration. I opened my eyes when I sensed someone was taking my picture. I scanned the crowd to see who it was, but no one around had a camera aimed at me.

Still, the sensation made me paranoid. I stuffed my sketchbook into my purse and hustled down the sidewalk to escape whoever had noticed my paranormal practice.

When I reached my apartment, I studied my work. It was a series of drawings of a young woman with long hair, hauntingly beautiful eyes, and a long slender neck. The sketches were loose and grainy. I had interpreted that design element meant that time had passed since the event had occurred.

In one of the drawings, the young woman was walking alone down a path in the woods. A shadow trailed behind her. In the next, I had sketched a stack of photographs that showed her innocently standing naked in a bedroom, unaware someone was violating her privacy.

Someone had tucked a teddy bear beside her corpse in the last one. The young woman was not Sydney, and I reasoned a different restless spirit had made contact with me at the vigil.

I slid my sketchbook back into my bag, trying to figure out why this particular ghost had made contact with me at the vigil and how it related to Sydney's murder. As I processed the information, I sensed a connection between the victim and the color red.

LOVE LETTERS—LEO

TWO DAYS HAD PASSED SINCE WE RECOVERED THE REMAINS OF Sydney Reynolds from the dumpster. In that time, my task force had interviewed family, friends, and coworkers, canvassed the neighborhood around the crime scene, and was looking into the men she dated from the Armstrong Agency, a high-end dating service where she'd met her husband.

The autopsy had confirmed the cause of death—strangulation. Murders of this type are personal and almost always carried out by someone the victim knew.

No fingerprints or body fluids were at the scene other than Dr. Vaughn and his brother, who had been doing renovations at their townhome. At the time of Sydney's murder, Braydon Reynolds had a weak alibi. He said he was at home, and his wife corroborated his story.

Since Braydon had access to the Reynolds' home, he was on my short list of suspects. Even if he hadn't physically abducted Sydney, he could've made a copy of the key and given it to an accomplice or aided Vaughn in committing the crime.

Braydon had a record of misdemeanor drug charges and got into trouble selling stolen goods. Still, he hadn't done jail time and had no record of sexual assault or domestic violence.

We had eyes on him, but since he had volunteered to come to the station to answer questions and submit his DNA without lawyering up, he didn't appear to be the killer—but that didn't mean he wasn't involved.

Then there was the interesting fact we uncovered about Dr. Vaughn—his ex-girlfriend had filed a temporary restraining order against him. The two had broken up a year ago, and Vaughn had contacted her repeatedly to reconcile. The woman claimed he had shown up at her work and apartment and had angrily confronted her about having an affair.

Vaughn has a temper.

After interviewing Sydney's coworkers at her real estate office, one of her colleagues gave a statement that she had witnessed Mrs. Reynolds crying in the bathroom days before she went missing. When the woman asked her what was wrong, she brushed it off as nothing, just stress.

Another coworker stated that Sydney had received a package at work. He had no idea what it contained but said that Sydney didn't seem pleased about the contents. He believed she was hiding something.

The owner of the real estate firm gave us permission to search Sydney's office without needing a warrant. What we found became our first real lead in the investigation. A series of handwritten love letters—*signed with a heart.*

Sydney had torn them up and stashed them in the back of her desk drawer. The notes were familiar, as if the sender knew her well, but also disturbingly sexual in nature. Based on this evidence and how her corpse was staged at the crime scene, it appeared that Sydney Reynolds was the object of a dangerous obsession.

The working theory was that Sydney had been abducted and murdered by a stalker.

As Parker and I stepped into another interview, I thought of Evelyn. I had not spoken to her since the interrogation. She knew more than she was leading me to believe. I suspected she knew the identity of the killer.

If that was the case, why wouldn't she tell me? Why would she cover for a violent killer? The only logical reason was fear. If Evelyn knew who killed her friend, she would be in grave danger.

Even though I was sure she never wanted to speak to me again, I needed to talk to her and make sure she was alright because my gut told me her involvement would get her into serious trouble.

CALLER UNKNOWN—EVELYN

My cell vibrated on my desk.

Caller Unknown.

I ignored it. I'd been getting weird calls from numbers I didn't recognize for the past few days. I'd answered the phone a few times, thinking maybe it was a client, but the caller hadn't said anything each time I'd picked up.

The only sound was of a male, breathing heavily. I chalked it up as some random weirdo who got off on the sound of my voice. He probably habitually dialed random numbers until someone gullible like me picked up.

"Do you need to answer that, Evelyn?" Gibson pushed her glasses up her nose and pointed at my phone.

"It's not important." I didn't want to worry her, so I slid my phone into my bag. The thing that bothered me about the calls was that the harassment had begun after I had attended Sydney's vigil, and I felt someone had been watching me.

My cell stopped buzzing, paused, and then went off again. Whoever was calling wasn't giving up. Finally, after I'd ignored it for the umpteenth time, a text pinged. I slid my phone out of my purse and checked the screen.

CALLER UNKNOWN: Go to the window. I want to see you.

Disgusting. The strange thing was, I was usually in my studio at this time of day, working in front of a window to take advantage of the natural light. Today, however, I was meeting with Gibson in her office nestled inside the gallery on the first floor.

Does the caller know that? I shook off my paranoia. My studio was on the third floor of the building and faced the alley. No one could see me from that angle.

At least, I don't think so.

The office landline rang.

"Thank you for calling The DOM, Gibson speaking." She flicked her gaze to mine as she listened to the caller. "May I tell her who's calling?" She covered the receiver with her hand. "He wouldn't give his name but said it's urgent. You should probably take it." She handed me the phone before I had a chance to refuse.

I shifted uncomfortably as I lifted the phone to my ear. "Hello? This is Evelyn."

"How did it feel when your soul left your body?"

The man harassing me on my phone had found out my name and where I worked. He could've just dialed random numbers until he found a woman who picked up. It was one thing when a stranger called and acted like a perv, but now that he had found out my name and where I work—and that I had died—it was personal.

He knows who I am.

"Don't call again." I slammed the phone into the cradle. I didn't want to dump a load of drama on Gibson, so I told her it was a telemarketer.

While I was ninety-nine percent sure the unknown caller was just some random weirdo, my mind kept circling back to the fact that Sydney's killer had not been caught. I was surprised Leo hadn't contacted me since the interrogation from hell. Still, I hoped they were closing in on the killer and no longer needed my help.

My phone buzzed when a text came in. I turned it over and checked the screen, mentally preparing to unleash on the sicko.

TESS: Happy hour at Marlin's tonight?
ME: Perfect! See you there.

I turned off my phone and stuffed it into my purse. I apologized to Gibson for the distractions and gave her all my attention. As we discussed the menu and goody bags for the preopening media event, I couldn't shake the feeling that the calls were not random.

Someone is trying to scare me.

BOYS AND BEER—LEO

I HAD ALL THE WORKING PARTS SET INTO MOTION, AND MY next order of business was to grab a beer with my buddies. As much as I wanted to catch the killer, I trusted my team and needed to keep my sanity.

Everyone had instructions to inform me if we had any breaks, but unless something changed, I was going off duty for a few hours.

Officer Santoni and I met at a dive bar in the neighborhood we'd been going to since we got our first set of fake IDs in high school.

The bar was packed for a weeknight. There was a hockey game that night, and the place was shoulder to shoulder with Hawks fans. A couple of our buddies, fellow cops, waved us over to a high-top table in the corner of the bar by a serveyourself popcorn machine and a barrel of free peanuts.

It was bucket-o-beer night, and our brothers had a round of cold brews waiting for us when we arrived. I felt a weight lifted as I took a long swig off a Pabst Blue Ribbon and let the stress of the job melt away.

As I downed my first beer, my thoughts circled back to

Evelyn. I wanted to check on her and make sure she was alright—and apologize for accusing her of using her friend's brutal murder to promote her art show.

As much as I didn't want to admit it, I missed seeing Evelyn. *Her smile, beautiful eyes, wry sense of humor, warm mouth, the scent of her skin, sensual curves...*

"Leo, pass me another one." I shook off the memory of our intimate moment in Evelyn's studio and handed out another round of beers.

Santoni had the guys rolling as he recalled a story about the two of us getting busted at a Clark Station for trying to buy a pack of smokes at the ripe old age of ten.

Fucking Santoni. He was a great storyteller, but he had a way of twisting the details and exaggerating the stupid shit we did as kids to make us out to be heroes.

True, we did forge a note from his mom saying it was okay for us to buy a pack of Camels for her. And yeah, we were idiots because the lady at the cash register knew his mom from their book club. But in the end, our stupid plan worked. We got the cigarettes and smoked a couple on the way home, only to have both our moms waiting on the front porch of his house with fire in their eyes.

"The last thing you want to do is piss off an Italian woman. Am I right, Ricci?"

I lifted my beer in salute. I'd heard this story a billion times, and my attention drifted to a raven-haired, voluptuous beauty summoning me from the bar.

I'd seen Rochelle casually for a few months and tossed her a nod. We weren't dating, but we'd hooked up enough that I needed to say hello. I hadn't even sent her a text since Sydney Reynolds went missing.

I stepped away from the guys to grab another round and check in with the Sicilian bombshell. Her low-cut red dress accentuated her curves, and with her legs crossed, the fabric rode up her bare thighs, revealing her long, shapely legs. A swarm of guys buzzed around her, but she shooed them away when she'd captured my attention.

She was from the neighborhood and a regular at the bar. Still, she looked more like a beauty queen with her perfectly applied makeup and hair styled in an updo and sprayed to withstand a Category 4 hurricane.

Based on appearances, Rochelle didn't belong in this shitty bar with a bunch of off-duty cops guzzling beers with their buddies instead of going home on their off nights. But she was born in this town and would die here like so many other loyal Chicagoans—including me.

"Hey, Rochelle. How's it going?"

Instead of a friendly hello, I got a pouty smile. "I saw on the news you found that missing rich lady. Such a bummer you didn't find her while she was still alive."

A bummer. "Yeah, I've been busy with her murder investigation. Sorry I haven't called."

Rochelle stirred her amaretto sour as she processed my apology. She set down her drink and leaned closer, giving me a fantastic view of her cleavage.

"Did you miss me?" She uncrossed her legs and tossed me a sultry grin.

"I did." We never talked much, but I'd gone back to her place a couple times and we'd enjoyed each other's company.

"I'll be honest with you, Leo. You're a good-looking guy. The sex is mind blowing, but I don't want to be some girl you hook up with from the bar when you feel lonely. I mean, just take me out to dinner once in a while. Let me show you off to my friends, alright?"

It seemed every woman I hung out with wanted the same thing from me, besides "mind-blowing sex," that I couldn't give them—*time*. I had an obligation to the badge and the good people of Chicago to track down killers.

I couldn't commit to Saturday afternoon barbecues, dinner and a movie, or even church on Sunday morning, because I had victims who took precedence over birthday parties and family get-togethers.

"You're right, babe. I understand how you feel, but you know my job keeps me busy. I'm not always available."

She leaned in close and whispered, "Are you *available* tonight, Leo?" She nibbled on my ear and trailed kisses down my neck.

I placed my hand on her bare leg and caressed her silky-smooth skin, tempted by her offer. I leaned in and planted a kiss on her lips. Memories of our wild nights gave me a rush of excitement.

A night under the sheets with Rochelle was the remedy I needed to get my murder investigation—and Evelyn—out of my head for a couple hours. But I had a gnawing sensation in my gut that Evelyn was in danger.

We had a surveillance team at Sydney's memorial. Evelyn had been there drawing. It seemed Miss Sinclair was playing junior detective and had visited the crime scene to connect with the "ghost."

Evelyn didn't realize how dangerous it was to stick her neck out. Everybody in town knew who she was now—her face had been on the cover of a popular magazine. My team was there because we believed the killer might be there, too, admiring the damage he had caused.

I needed to talk to her and tell her to stay out of my investigation—and to be careful.

I put the brakes on my make-out session with Rochelle and stepped away to make a call. Even though I was certain Evelyn didn't want to hear from me, I wouldn't be able to sleep until I knew she was safe.

BUZZED—EVELYN

Tess smiled and waved from the bar. She looked stunning and stylish in a maxi dress with bold chandelier earrings. Her natural hair was swept back with an emerald-green headband that matched the rims of her trendy glasses.

My fashion designer friend had already ordered a pitcher of margaritas and a basket of chips and salsa, our favorite happy hour combo.

I shrugged off my heavy plaid coat and slung my purse over the barstool as I slid into my seat. My anxiety level had reached the tipping point. My sixth sense kept alerting me that I was being watched. The unsettling feeling that someone had taken photos of me at the vigil weighed heavily on my mind.

Thanks to Gibson relentlessly promoting the gallery opening, my picture had been circulating in the papers, art magazines, and all over social media. While it was possible someone had recognized me and was watching out of curiosity, the sensation felt more sinister.

Tess lifted her margarita glass and offered a toast. "Happy Monday. You survived." She gave me a once-over. "Rough day? Did one of your paintings come to life and try to drag you to hell?"

I cracked up, self-conscious that I looked as shitty as I felt. While Tess and I downed our first round and devoured a couple cheap tacos, I dished about my flash romance with the hot detective. I omitted the parts about his involvement in Sydney's case. Still, I gave her the lowdown on how we'd scandalously made out in my studio during the party at the gallery.

The alcohol and my dating therapy session with Tess helped settle my nerves. After all the drama and heartache over the last few days, I needed to let loose, laugh, and revive my ailing soul—and mingle with some of the hotties hanging out at the bar.

A band had set up on the stage and started their first set, bringing a fresh round of energy to the bar. When the guys played one of our favorite covers, Tess grabbed my arm and led me to the makeshift dance floor.

As Tess and I danced our stress away, I couldn't stop thinking about Leo. I'd made light of my flash romance with "the hot cop from the coffee shop," but the truth was, I couldn't get him—*or his rocking body*—out of my mind.

The chemistry between us bordered on lethal. Our first kiss had enough atomic energy to blow the moon out of orbit. I was still angry with him for dismissing my drawings —and making a mockery of my gift—but my aggravation and hurt feelings never cooled my attraction.

My sexual fantasies starring the annoying detective played on an endless loop, and my wild imagination didn't end on the canvas. I craved his muscular body and longed for him to wrap me in his strong embrace as our bodies synced in a sensual rhythm.

Detective Ricci's alpha male energy torched my core. He had playfully threatened to handcuff me. Had he meant that literally? Was Leo the kind of high-octane Dom who would please his inexperienced little kitten with sex toys, lotions, safe words, and physical demands that would require my signature on a contract to proceed to his interrogation room?

"So, if I sign this, I'm yours? You can do whatever you want to me?"

I snapped out of my daydream when I felt again that someone was watching me. I shot my gaze around the room as I sang along with the cover band and moved to the beat of the crowd-pleasing pop music.

A couple lookers. No one creepy stood out, but my sixth sense was tingling. Maybe I was dancing a little too sexy as my fantasies about Leo dominated my thoughts. I had a healthy buzz and needed to chug a gallon of water and head home before I got too wasted.

When the band took a break, Tess and I headed back to our seats at the bar. I reached for my purse that I'd hung off the barstool to pay my tab, but it was gone. I scooted my chair back and searched the floor, hoping it had fallen off the chair, but it wasn't there.

"What's wrong?" Tess asked.

"Someone stole my purse."

A rush of panic washed over me when I realized someone had my driver's license that showed my home address and the freaking key to my apartment. That, along with the paranoia I couldn't shake, left me with the horrible feeling that the theft wasn't random.

As I stood at the bar, dumbfounded, my cell buzzed. I lifted it out of my pocket and checked the screen. Damn. I wasn't in the mood for this conversation, but I answered anyway in case it was urgent. "Hello?"

"Hey, Evelyn. How's it going?" Leo asked, sounding suspiciously casual for the snappy detective.

"Fabulous. You?" I covered my ear so I could hear him over the noise.

"Sounds like you're in a bar."

"Busted. Nice work, Detective. What can I do for you?" It wasn't my intention to be rude, but I wanted him to cut to the chase about the nature of his call.

Tess tapped my shoulder to get my attention. "I think we should call the cops, Evelyn. This is fucked up."

"What's fucked up? Where are you?" Leo must've overheard Tess and was ready to pounce into action. A guy who hunts down killers for a living would probably be disappointed by my boring case of a missing purse.

"Someone stole my purse from the bar at Marlin's. I don't need you—"

"I'm on my way." Leo ended the call before I had a chance to talk him out of it.

MISSING—LEO

With Santoni riding shotgun, we rolled up to Marlin's five minutes after I'd found out Evelyn needed my help. Rochelle was fifty shades of pissed when I told her I had to run and wouldn't blow her mind that night.

That is the exact reason I can never be in a committed relationship.

Inside the bar, I pointed out the victim, a gorgeous young woman with long honey-blonde hair, sulking at the bar with her worried friend.

"Holy smokes." Santoni elbowed me in the ribs, chastising me for holding back relevant information to the case. "That's Evelyn? Now I know why you were in such a rush to deliver your detective services. Did you dump Rochelle because of her?"

"She's a witness in the Reynolds investigation. That's it."

"If you say so, buddy. What have we got to go on?"

The victim was young, beautiful, and, judging by the empty margarita glass in front of her barstool, a little buzzed. An easy target for a predator searching for his next victim.

Sure, someone down on their luck or a drug addict in

need of a fix may have slipped in and done a quick sweep for valuables in a crowded bar. But I ran a quick assessment of the situation. If the perp wasn't after money, another likely scenario was that whoever had taken Evelyn's purse was after her personal information. Name, address, cell phone…

But two days ago, I pulled an innocent woman's corpse out of a dumpster and had no credible leads on her killer. And Evelyn was somehow involved.

When I approached her, Evelyn's reaction to seeing me was comical. There she stood, hand on her hip, head tilted, and instead of graciously accepting my offer to help, she rolled her eyes and turned her back on me.

Lucky for her, I didn't take offense. After I'd had some time to think about how I'd treated her, I realized what a jerk I'd been.

Evelyn didn't need to run a con to bring attention to her work. Her paintings were terrific. She was on the cover of an art magazine. Plus, Evelyn's manager had been promoting the gallery opening as the most significant event to hit the city since the Chicago World's Fair.

I'd been working day and night on my murder investigation and failed to reach out to her to apologize. "Evelyn," I spoke her name and waited for her to face me.

When she met my gaze, her gorgeous blue eyes held no joy in seeing my face. I hated that I had such a negative effect on her, but I hoped I could make amends.

"I already told you. I don't need your help."

I slid my jacket aside and flashed my star. "Serve and protect. It's what I do. Where was the last place you saw your purse?"

"Oh, shit!" Her drunk friend yelled. "*This* is the guy? This is the hot cop you made out with in your studio?" Tess shoved Evelyn on the shoulder. "Why'd you guys break up?"

Evelyn's distaste for me dissolved into utter embarrassment. I didn't mind being objectified by her friend, and I enjoyed watching Evelyn squirm with humiliation. Her cheeks warmed, but she got back to business and pointed to the barstool.

"It was there before we hit the dance floor. I didn't notice it was gone until I needed to pay the bill. Tess also left hers at the bar, but the thief didn't steal anything."

Tess held up her Chanel clutch to illustrate the point.

That's not a good sign. Her friend's purse was worth a couple grand, not including whatever she had inside. Whether she realized it or not, Evelyn had become a celebrity. I didn't want to scare her, but my detective brain worried that Evelyn's newfound fame had made her a target.

"Can I talk to you in private?" I asked.

Marlin, the nervous bar owner who didn't like cops swarming around his customers, had been within earshot. He tossed me the keys to his office and told me we could meet in there, away from the noise.

Once we had privacy, I took the opportunity to right my wrongs. "Evelyn, I owe you an apology. I had no right to question your motive. It took courage to call in the information you had, and I was wrong to accuse you of having an ulterior motive."

She seemed surprised by my admission of guilt. "It's okay. I'm over it." She waved her hand as if she could erase the hurt feelings I'd caused her. "You're not the first person I've ticked off with my drawings."

I was relieved Evelyn didn't hate my guts, but I doubted she had forgiven me. "I was way out of line. I treated you like a suspect instead of a witness, and I'm truly sorry. Your art is amazing. I've kicked myself a hundred times for even suggesting you had bad intentions when you—"

A heavy fist banged on the door. "Hey, Ricci! Are you still looking for a purse? I'll give you a hint, it isn't in Marlin's office." I could tell by Santoni's triumphant tone that there had been a development in the case.

Santoni stepped inside the office, dangling Evelyn's purse straps by his finger.

"Oh my god! Where was it?" Evelyn placed her hand over her heart, relieved to have her stolen property returned.

"In the bathroom. An old guy saw it in the trash can and turned it into Marlin. I already checked it for tracking devices. Nothing there. Don't get too excited, though. The thief probably cleaned you out."

Evelyn opened her bag and checked the contents. She pulled out her wallet and was relieved to find her license and credit cards all accounted for. She said sixty bucks in cash was missing and a pair of sunglasses, but other than that, everything else checked out.

Santoni and I exchanged glances, both coming to the same conclusion. The motive wasn't money. Evelyn had been targeted. The purpose of snatching her purse was to find out personal information about her. Now the thief knows where she lives from her license.

Evelyn gave my buddy a grateful smile. "Thank you for helping. Are you a cop?"

"Officer Christopher Santoni. Just doing my job."

"Well, you're off duty, but thank you for your service."

Santoni bowed his head appreciatively. Being a cop and serving our hometown was more than a job to him. He loved our city and helping our community. He beamed with pride whenever a civilian recognized his service.

"I need you to do one thing for me, though. Let Detective Ricci take you home. I don't want to scare you, but the guy had your purse in his possession for some time. We'd all feel better if Ricci checks your house and stays with you until a locksmith arrives."

HOVERING—LEO

I ordered Evelyn to stay in the living room while I cleared her apartment. With my gun drawn, I searched each room to ensure no one had made a copy of her key and used it to enter her apartment.

Once I finished my sweep, Evelyn invited me into the kitchen and asked if I wanted a drink while we waited for the locksmith. I'd had a couple beers already and declined her offer. Evelyn looked comfortably buzzed yet poured herself a nightcap, pulled a bowl of strawberries out of the fridge, and slid it between us.

Then she lit a trio of candles on the bar in her kitchen. As the flames danced, she slid onto a barstool and rested her chin on her fist, mesmerized by the fire. Evelyn was quiet by nature, but her bright, thoughtful eyes revealed her wild imagination was working something out. She moved her hand over the flames as if absorbing the energy.

"Whenever I think of Sydney, I'm compelled to light three candles." She lifted her gaze from the flickering flames and shot me a quizzical look. "Does that mean anything to you, Detective?"

I studied her body language as she sipped her vodka and soda. "No. What are you thinking?"

She bit her lip and tapped her fingernails on the bar before sharing her insight. "Three candles. Three spirits. I'm sensing Sydney isn't the killer's only victim."

I should've been used to it by now. The way Evelyn blew my mind every time we had a conversation. Her creative mind was always coming up with new ideas. How could anyone look at a couple of candles and devise a serial killer scenario?

"Have the murders already taken place... *in your mind?*"

Evelyn stared at the candles. "I think so, but I'm sensing the murders were spread out. There was a lapse between victims." She moved her hand over the flames as if absorbing the energy.

"The *candles* tell you that?"

"Fire is a powerful element. It heightens my sixth sense. I don't have details, but I trust my instincts." Evelyn lifted her gaze and met my eyes. "Does the color red mean anything to you?"

My first thought was *blood*, but I was fascinated by Evelyn's train of thought. "Red in what context?"

"As it relates to the case."

There were red rose petals at the scene of Sydney's home, a teddy bear holding a red satin heart and a small amount of blood splatter in the bedroom. "I can't discuss an active murder investigation."

"Right," Evelyn said, shaking off her obsession with the candles. "How long do you think it will be before the locksmith arrives?"

I'd called a buddy who owed me a favor to do the job. He said he would be at Evelyn's in fifteen minutes, but I told him to take his time because I wasn't in a rush to get out of there. I feared for Evelyn's safety and didn't want her to be alone.

"He's running behind. It might be a couple hours. I'll stay up and wait for him to get the job done if it gets too late."

Evelyn carried her drink into the living room and turned on some acoustic guitar music. She plopped down on the couch and invited me to join her. I followed her lead but reminded myself the last time we sat on a couch together, we made out like savages.

The attraction was still burning, but I had to stay professional for the sake of the investigation.

"Why did you call me tonight?" Evelyn curled her legs on the couch and snuggled into a more comfortable position.

"No reason. I was off duty, having a couple beers with my buddies, and I just wanted to check in and make sure you were doing okay."

Evelyn played with the fringe on a throw pillow. "Sorry I ruined your night off with my purse-snatching drama."

What I found attractive about Evelyn was her calm demeanor. She was bold and fearless on the canvas while understated and thoughtful in the flesh. "I'm still off duty, and while I have the chance, I want to talk to you about something unrelated to the case."

Evelyn eyed me curiously. "About what?"

"Us." I fixed my gaze on hers. "I'm sorry things ended so abruptly. How I cut you down. It was never my intention to hurt you or for things to end between us."

Evelyn gave me a soft smile. "We would've never made it anyway. Maybe it was best to end it sooner rather than later."

"Why do you say that?"

"I could never date a man who doesn't believe in my gift."

That stung. I hated that the one thing keeping us apart was out of our control. "Then you're right. We never stood a chance."

Evelyn downed the rest of her drink and set her glass on

the coffee table. "What will you do when you find out you're wrong?"

"About what?"

"My gift." She pulled a pillow onto her lap and eagerly waited for my response. She had stripped off her sweater and scarf while I searched her place and wore only a tank top tucked into her jeans. Evelyn never wore anything revealing, and I took a quick peek at her trim waistline and perky breasts.

"That will be a hard sell because I don't believe in ghosts. Therefore, I won't accept you can talk to them. We can't knock down that wall."

"Allow me to rephrase my question." She tapped her fingers on the pillow. "What are you going to do when one of my sketches is so undeniably real and true, and you know in your heart there is no way I could have knowledge from any source other than a being from beyond the grave?"

Evelyn's chest heaved when she took a big breath. "To rephrase, what will you do when you can no longer deny the truth that I was right and you were wrong?"

I loved the way she never backed down. Her confidence was admirable—and sexy—and dammit, I wanted her to be right.

I wished the goddam ghost of Ebenezer Scrooge would float through the wall and shake his fists at me, cursing my name for doubting the gorgeous and talented medium staring right at him and drawing his fucking picture.

"This may surprise you, Evelyn, but I wish I was wrong." I tugged on her elbow and drew her close. "Because if I could solve the one problem keeping us apart, I could kiss you right now."

Her lips curled into a bittersweet smile as she placed her hand over my heart. "Maybe we'll get our second chance in another lifetime, Detective." Evelyn moved to the bar and blew out the candles.

As the flames died, she watched the billows of smoke rise from the wicks as if reading a hidden message only she understood. "Good night, Leo."

I finally met the woman of my dreams. The only woman I could see a future with. But there was one thing hovering in our way—*ghosts*.

SILENT—EVELYN

I woke before the sun came up to the sound of a chainsaw slicing my refrigerator in half. I rolled over in bed and checked the time: *Too damn early.*

I slid on my robe and stepped out of my bedroom to see what was going on in my kitchen. Of all the scenarios running around my mind, Leo making cappuccinos and cooking a full breakfast was not one of them.

"Good morning, Miss Sinclair. Hope you're hungry." Leo had a dish towel slung over his shoulder and was sprinkling cheese over a freshly cooked omelet. The kitchenette was set with sugar cubes for my coffee and a green smoothie for my uninvited houseguest.

"What are you doing?"

He folded the omelet onto the plate and added a couple slices of toast.

"The locksmith left an hour ago. I had time to kill before work. Thought you could use a good breakfast."

As I stood by the bar with a slack jaw and a severe case of bed head, Leo carried our plates to the table and motioned for me to have a seat. Then he made a second trip and delivered my cappuccino.

"Where did you find food?"

"I'll tell you a secret. There's something called a *market*. It's about a block away from your apartment. That's where people find food and coffee beans for their expensive machines that sit unused on their counters."

I tapped my temple in response to his smart-ass answer. "Good to know."

A normal person would've been delighted to wake up to find a handsome Italian man in her kitchen, preparing a delicious meal and catering to her every whim. However, I was *not* normal and questioned his motive.

Leo dug into his omelet and aimed his fork at a bakery bag in the kitchen. "I got some of those cinnamon things you like if you're not in the mood for eggs."

"That was very thoughtful. Thanks." I slid into the chair across from him and plunked a couple sugar cubes into my coffee. Leo and I had made peace last night, and I hoped this meant he would be open to hearing about my drawings from the vigil.

The creepy sketches of the beautiful woman I didn't recognize had been at the forefront of my mind. "Um, after breakfast, do you think we could—"

His cell vibrated, stealing his attention. As he read whatever information had been delivered, his eyes narrowed, and his lips tightened while he processed what he was reading. He remained focused on the content and then shifted his gaze to mine.

I sensed that what he was reading involved me—and it was not painting me in a good light.

"What's wrong?"

Leo set down his fork and patted his mouth with a napkin. The fire in his eyes could've melted titanium. "Have

126

you ever heard somebody say something that didn't make sense, and afterward, your brain kept circling around the conversation, trying to figure it out?"

I didn't like where this was going.

"Remember the night of the art show when Vaughn introduced himself?" Leo drummed his fingers on the table.

"Yes."

"Vaughn looked at me, then looked back at you and said, *'Did you two meet at—'*" He lifted his hand and gestured to me. "Finish the sentence, Evelyn. What was Dr. Vaughn going to say before you cut him off?"

I slunk down in my seat, willing the universe to suck me into a black hole.

Leo stole glances at me as he waited for me to confess using a high-end dating service, the Armstrong Agency, to find a suitable match. Early in his investigation, he had to have known that Sydney and Vaughn had met through the service.

His team undoubtedly had dug into her profile and checked out the men she dated. I wasn't a detective, but I deduced that Leo had probably only very recently—*like right this second*—found out that Sydney had given me a referral to join the elite matchmaking agency, and I had accepted the invitation.

And had gone on dates with a dozen different alpha male billionaires.

I wasn't ashamed of my decision to use a dating service. Still, the thought of Leo searching for information in my profile made me question his motive.

I couldn't control what Leo or anyone else thought, but this line of questioning was personal and had nothing to do with the case. I had the right to remain silent. Detective Ricci could glare at me until his freshly made omelet decomposed on my plate before I would apologize for not telling him about my personal life or offer up information that was absolutely none of his business.

"You do understand your friend was murdered by a man who was very angry with her. Did it occur to you that one of the men she dated from the agency could be the killer?"

Leo jumped back into interrogation mode and was not letting up. "What if *you* dated one of the same men Sydney went out with? Don't you think you should've told me so I could check them out?"

I scooted back my chair and moved to the window to put some space between us. I didn't like being interrogated in my home. I felt trapped and needed to get away from him.

"I asked you if there was anything else I needed to know. You told me no. I don't like being lied to."

He's accusing me of lying now?

Enough. I would not let him assassinate my character again. "Leo, you asked me that question on the night of my party. Sydney was still alive. There was no murder investigation at that point. I had no obligation to tell you I was seeing other people."

Leo leaned back in his chair and nodded as if I had just confessed to a murder. "Honesty is the cornerstone of every relationship. You should've told me."

Now he had crossed the line. "Really? I asked you what you were up to last night before you came to my rescue at the bar. And unless your buddy Santoni smears red lipstick on your shirt collar when he drinks beer, you lied straight to my face about who *you* were with."

"That's different, Evelyn. We're not seeing each other. I didn't want to hurt your feelings."

"Exactly. What kind of bitch would I have been telling you about all the guys I dated before I made out with you?"

Our conversation had blown over into an argument. We both needed to cool down, and trading accusations wasn't going to solve anything. "You need to leave." I pointed to the door.

"I have questions. Official business. Do you want to do that or go to the station?"

I huffed, shocked by his callous attitude. "I'm not answering your questions, and I'm not going to the station."

Leo shook his head as if my stubbornness was the root cause of the argument. "Evelyn—"

"I know my rights. You're not getting a word out of me. If I need a lawyer, I'll get one."

"I'm sure you will. You've got what, a million-dollar stock portfolio to pull from? Another detail about your life I had to read about in a report."

"My net worth is none of your business," I snapped. Before the accident, I was dead set on a career in finance. Even though I'd changed careers, I still had a savvy business mind. Instead of wasting my money on a degree I never intended to use, I invested my college savings in the stock market. It was a calculated risk that paid off big time, but that was none of Leo's business.

He grabbed his coat and moved to the door. "I'll find out what I need to know with or without your cooperation. If you want to do this the hard way, you have the right to waste my time." Once he was in the hallway and headed for the stairs, a word popped into my head.

"Leo, wait."

He stopped in the stairwell and turned to face me.

I wished to God I didn't have to say it, but it was my obligation, and I had to do it—damn the consequences. I aimed my finger at him and said, "*Blackwater.*"

When Leo realized I was having a *clairaudient* moment, he closed his eyes and raked his fingers through his hair. "Are you fucking kidding me?"

I was on the verge of an emotional meltdown between

the accusations and what he probably perceived as a pitiful attempt to get his attention. "No. I'm not fucking kidding you. Believe me, I wish I was fucking kidding you, but sadly, I'm dead fucking serious."

"Let me make this easy for you, Evelyn. Stay out of my investigation. Stop visiting my crime scenes. Stop coming up with fantasies about magic candles, and stop pretending you can talk to the dead."

A dog on the first floor started barking. My elderly neighbor Maxine opened the door and stepped into the hall-way. I could see her holding her little guard dog in her arms from the landing. She shifted her gaze between Leo and me. "Are you alright, Evelyn?"

As if the situation could get any worse, now the entire building could hear our fight. "Hi, Stella," I said to the agitated little princess pug. "Sorry to bother you, Maxine. My friend was just leaving."

Leo apologized to my neighbor for the disturbance and made a quick exit. When he left, my heart raced with anxiety.

Why is Leo so angry with me?

SIXTH SENSE—EVELYN

AFTER I KICKED LEO OUT OF MY APARTMENT, I WENT BACK TO the living room, plopped down on my couch, and decompressed for a few moments.

I'd had so much turbulence in my life over the last few days that I hadn't had a moment to process everything happening. My stomach was growling, but I was too nauseous to eat. I wanted coffee, but my hands were trembling, so I settled on a cup of calming herbal tea.

I cracked open my window to get some fresh air and spread a blanket on the floor to serve as a yoga mat. I did sun salutations to get my blood flowing and circulate air into my lungs. As I tried to tune out the negativity, my thoughts circled back to the purse-snatching incident.

Why had someone bothered to steal my purse if they only wanted cash? They could've easily just swiped my wallet. Curious, I retrieved my bag and dumped the contents onto the coffee table to double-check if anything else was missing.

The fact that my money was gone came as a relief. That's what robbers do. Take things of value. Wasn't it a purse snatcher's job to know a thing or two about his resell market? I picked through the rest of my stuff on the table and separated the junk from the valuables. My pencil pouch that held my art supplies was all there, as was my sketchbook.

I'd had a moment of paranoia back at the bar when I thought maybe the person watching me at the vigil was also the same person who had stolen my purse. What if someone was curious to see what I had drawn at Sydney's memorial?

My sixth sense alerted me that something was off about my sketchbook. I flipped through the pages and gasped when I got to the middle of the book. The pictures I'd drawn at the vigil were missing, hastily torn from the book.

My thoughts boomeranged back to the bar. The moment my purse had gone missing, Leo called to check on me. Then he arrived on the scene five minutes later, and his buddy miraculously found my stolen property. What if it was a setup? What if Leo wanted to see my drawings and orchestrated the purse-snatching scenario?

It seemed far-fetched that two respected law enforcement officers would stoop to that level. My imagination was hard at work, but I preferred the bad cop scenario over the idea that a stranger had followed me to the bar and stolen my work.

At least I solved one mystery. The thief wasn't after my ID or the keys to my apartment. I was targeted because of my automatic drawings.

Have I attracted the attention of the killer?

BLACKWATER—LEO

I'd solved many mysteries in my line of work, but the case of Evelyn Sinclair's clairaudient messages defied logical thinking.

Blackwater.

That word wasn't a lucky guess. She couldn't have found it through research and had never heard it from me. I hadn't a clue how she came up with it, but what had me reeling was that Evelyn was on to something.

My Italian blood ran hot, and when I'd found out Evelyn hadn't been honest with me about being a client of the Armstrong Agency and that she was a millionaire, I'd blurred the lines between doing my job and acting like a ticked-off boyfriend.

Which was even more messed up because we weren't even dating. I needed clarity, and my partner was the only person I could talk to about this delicate situation. I needed his sharp brain to help me work things out.

Even though Parker and I were off duty, guys like us were workaholics, so I reached out to him to ask for his advice. When I told him I needed to confer with him on a "paranormal matter," he was on my doorstep fifteen minutes later wearing a graphic T-shirt, torn jeans, and a pair of expensive sneakers.

"Her clairaudient clue was *Blackwater*?" Parker exhaled and slumped down on my couch. "What are the odds she would come up with a word from one of our unsolved murder cases?"

"Impossible," I said.

When our homicide victim was a teenager, her mother had taken her to a festival in Blackwater Falls, Virginia. The mother had said she had bought her a mood ring from a crafter that Erin always wore. When we recovered the victim's remains, the cheap silver keepsake was missing from her finger.

"The detail of Erin Messer's missing ring was never released to the press. Evelyn couldn't have come up with that information from any other source—"

"Other than from the ghost of the victim," Parker said.

"Or the *living* killer," I added.

Parker scoffed. "Why can't you give Evelyn the benefit of the doubt? There are many credible stories about people who have survived a near-death experience and come back with paranormal abilities. Law enforcement agencies have used mediums and psychics to help solve cases."

"I'm a detective. I need proof." I brought my laptop to the living room and opened Erin's case file. I brought up the pictures of the crime scene where her body had been discovered in a back alley behind a run-down strip mall.

"Maybe this is the evidence you're looking for." Parker aimed his pen at a piece of paper that looked like trash marked at the scene. It was about four feet from the body and appeared to be a photograph with the subject scratched out. The photo had appeared to be random street trash at the scene. We had no reason at the time to believe it was anything else, and no reason to think of it when collecting clues at Sydney's crime scene. *Shit.*

Now it seemed we had a link between two murder investigations.

Is there a pattern between the victims? Both had personal items stolen. Erin's sentimental ring had been taken from her body, and Sydney's earrings had been stolen from her home. Both women were in the spotlight. Sydney was a successful real estate agent with her face and contact information on ads, postcards, and online advertising. Erin owned a bakery and posted daily about her small business, with pictures of herself posing with her treats at the bakery.

"Are you thinking the same thing?" Parker asked.

"Erin and Sydney were killed by the same person. Chicago has a serial killer in the making."

It took three murders, with a time lapse in between, for an individual to earn the rank of a serial killer. After witnessing what the monster had done to the first two victims, my question wasn't if he would kill again—it was who would be his next victim.

SABOTAGED—EVELYN

For the first time since Sydney's murder, I gave myself permission to relax. After a photo shoot with my neighboring gallery owners, I was alone in the studio and took advantage of some needed downtime.

I cranked up my favorite country music playlist, kicked off my boots, and cozied up on the sofa in my studio—the same couch where I'd made out with Leo a week ago.

I lifted a throw pillow and sniffed. The scent of Leo's heavenly cologne lingered on the fabric. I hated to admit it, but that night and that kiss had been the best thing that had happened to me in a long time.

I wasn't ashamed to admit that domineering, protective men turned me on. When Leo and I met, our sexual energy was hot enough to melt the skin off my bones.

Even though he had cut me to the core with his accusation about trying to capitalize on the murder of my friend and yelled at me for not telling him I dated a dozen different guys in as many weeks, I still fantasized about spending an evening with Leo in my bedroom.

What does that say about my sexual desires?

I knew we weren't compatible as a couple—me, the ghost girl, and Leo, the homicide detective—and I needed to extinguish my hot and wild attraction to him.

My cell rang as I tried to delete the memory of our intimate moment. I checked the screen and was surprised when I recognized the caller's name.

"Hello?"

"Evelyn, good to hear your voice. How are you?" Tomas asked. I met the billionaire businessman through the Armstrong Agency. We had dinner and had a lovely time, but after our date, he said he was going out of town on business and would call when he returned.

But that never happened. At the time, I thought that was his polite way of saying he wasn't interested in seeing me again. Maybe I was wrong.

"I'm good," I said, not wanting to bring up all the drama in my life.

"Wonderful to hear," Tomas said. "You've been on my mind. I'd love to see you. Are you free this evening?"

I sat up and shook my head in disbelief. "Tonight? Well, I'm at the gallery working late. I don't think—"

"Have you eaten dinner?" Tomas asked.

"No."

"Then we'll dine together. Nothing fancy, I promise. Let's enjoy a nice meal, so you can tell me about your upcoming exhibit. I saw your beautiful face on the magazine cover and the article about your paintings. Your talent amazes me."

My cheeks warmed, embarrassed by his flattery. While my sensible side came up with a thousand excuses why I should say no to the sexy Brazilian businessman offering to bring me dinner, my thrill-seeking side agreed before I sabotaged an impromptu and exciting evening.

"Okay. What time do you want to meet?"

"Let me in. I'm already here."

No way. I moved to the window and spotted a black Bentley parked in front of the gallery. Tomas stood beside his car, holding a couple restaurant take-out bags. When I had moved back the curtains, his gaze landed on mine. He tossed me a confident smile, moved to the door, and studied my self-portrait on display in the window.

While I was a tad unnerved Tomas had shown up unexpectedly, I was attracted to take-charge alpha men and found the gesture sexy.

Tomas was the distraction I needed to vanquish Detective Leo Ricci from my fantasies.

WHIPPED—EVELYN

As I trotted downstairs to open the door for Tomas, I checked my phone for the billionth time. I kept thinking Leo would call to apologize, yell at me again, or order me to show up to the station with my lawyer... my phone buzzed.

CALLER UNKNOWN: Is death painful, or did it feel good when you crossed over?

Disgusting. I deleted the text and turned off my phone.

Tomas greeted me with kisses on my cheeks, a warm smile, and a bounty of carryout food from a celebrity chef restaurant where it was impossible to get a reservation unless you had a connection.

He oozed boss-man class in a dark tailored suit and flashy jewelry glistening with diamonds. His slicked-back brown, shoulder-length hair was perfectly tousled, and his beard was trimmed to perfection. I felt seriously underdressed compared to the billionaire businessman, but this was me in my natural habitat.

"Look at you, Evelyn. The famous artist of Halsted." He focused all his energy on me and seemed pleasantly surprised to see me in jeans, boots, a casual blouse, and my one-of-a-kind, handmade scarf. When we'd gone on our date, I had worn a little black dress and mile-high heels for a fancy evening out. An upgrade from my weekday artsy style.

I invited Tomas into the conversation area in the gallery, away from the window, where we could dine without the whole neighborhood seeing us. If Tomas was interested in seeing my art, I would gladly show him, but I didn't want to give him a tour unless he wanted one.

If he was genuinely interested in me, he would want to see my work. It wasn't a test, per se, but my style wasn't for everyone. If he hated my ghosts or was turned off by my macabre subjects, we weren't a good match.

Better to axe the paranormal elephant in the room before falling for the wrong guy again—I'd learned that the hard way.

Damn. Stop thinking about Leo, Evelyn.

"It's spooky in here," Tomas teased as he eyed my paintings on the way to a table and chairs I'd set up. "I hope I'm going to get a private tour."

I laughed and promised to show him around after dinner. I had been so stressed lately that it felt good to take a break from the fear, sadness, and Leo's investigation for at least a few hours. I would never let Sydney down, but my soul needed a respite from the drama.

Tomas grinned as he unpacked our impromptu meal while I turned on some music and lit a few pillar candles to energize the room. He spread a plaid tablecloth over an old wooden door we had repurposed into a table. He set out a vase of flowers, wineglasses, bottled water, and a charcuterie course complete with a bottle of vino.

Not only had the restaurant whipped up a carryout meal, but they had also provided the dishes, table setting, and decor to complement the restaurant's trendy vibe. *He must be a special patron.*

Before he uncorked the wine, Tomas showed me the label. "I remember how much you love Chateauneuf du Pape. Tonight, we will celebrate you and your accomplishments." His gaze drifted to my chest as he reached for the corkscrew.

When I busted him checking me out, Tomas tossed me a flirty grin. A not-so-subtle reminder that I had gotten a tad frisky after we knocked out our second bottle on our first date. We were having a lively conversation about Cezanne's Postimpressionist paintings, and we talked for hours about art, my gallery, and the Chicago art scene.

I ended up drinking more than I'd intended. After dinner, we made out in the back seat of his limo on the way home. He had invited me to his place, but I declined the offer. The next day after I sobered up, I was so embarrassed I had lost my inhibitions and led him on. I was not surprised when he hadn't called for a second date—until tonight.

Tomas poured the wine, and I noticed another bottle peeking out of the bag. I made a mental note to keep my drinking to a minimum so I wouldn't lose my inhibitions around him again.

"I can't wait to see your Haunted History collection. Perhaps we could enjoy our wine when we return from our tour?"

He must really be interested in art. As I led him into the gallery, Tomas picked up my hand. He kissed the inside of my wrist as we stood in front of *Above and Below*, the painting of the ghost alongside her corpse along the riverbed.

Most people recoiled at the sight of the vengeful ghost. Maybe Tomas was really into the dark side of my personality.

"You are a beautiful woman, Evelyn." He pulled me in for a hug, moved his hands down my back, and slipped his finger inside the back pocket of my jeans.

"I hope we can pick up where we left off on our last date."

He grinned and rubbed his hand down to my hip as he moved in for a kiss. His suggestive gesture was out of place and a total turnoff. As he leered at me, I noticed his eyes were red. He appeared to have had a couple of drinks before arriving.

Did he call me because he's drunk and wants to get laid?

I tried to pull back, sickened at the idea that he assumed I was easy, but Tomas held me firmly, not wanting to let me go. I felt a rush of panic. I didn't like how possessively he was treating me.

Is Tomas the guy following me and sending me harassing texts?

I needed to stay calm and make my intentions clear. Our date was over, and I was about to tell him to leave when someone banged on the gallery's glass door, causing a yelp to escape my lips.

I peeked around the corner to see who was at the door—Detective Ricci.

TWISTED—LEO

Evelyn opened the door a crack but didn't invite me inside. She was surprised to see me at her gallery after hours and immediately assumed something was wrong.

"What happened?" Evelyn asked.

I glanced over her shoulder and noticed a light on around the corner. Otherwise, the gallery was dark. Acoustic guitar music played in the background, and the warm glow of candlelight spilled into the darkened room.

"Are you alone?"

"No."

"Is this a bad time?"

Evelyn checked behind her and then shook her head. "You're scaring me. Has there been a development in the case? Did you catch the killer?" she whispered, not wanting whoever was in the other room to hear our conversation.

"Is everything alright, Evelyn?" A man in a shiny suit with slicked-back hair strolled out of the candlelit back room into my line of sight. The guy had a drink in hand, and his shirt unbuttoned a couple notches.

I considered Evelyn was entertaining a client, but when I

smelled something warm and savory wafting in from the back room, paired with the romantic music and mood lighting—not to mention a half-million-dollar Bentley parked outside—I realized this prick was seducing her.

Christ. Is this a fucking date? Is this rich guy her latest match from the Armstrong Agency?

"Yeah. All good. My friend just needs to talk to me for a moment," she said to her date, then turned her attention back to me. "What can I do for you, Detective?"

"Official business. You didn't answer your phone, and I need to ask you a few questions."

Evelyn excused herself, but instead of letting me in, she grabbed her coat and met me outside. Under the streetlights, Evelyn crossed her arms to shield herself from the frigid night air. I wanted to pull her into my arms and keep her warm, but that privilege had been lost.

She watched me cautiously, bracing herself for another interrogation. Her wounded expression gave me a fresh round of remorse for losing my temper with her about the dating thing. I was wrong for expecting her to hand over her dating history before our first kiss—but I sure as hell had the right to be upset that she had withheld information relevant to the case.

"I'm here because I could use your help."

"About what?" Her body remained rigid as if protecting herself from another one of my verbal blows. She seemed upset, but I couldn't tell if it was because of me or if there was another reason why she was acting uneasy.

"Have you seen this woman?" I lifted my cell and showed her a picture of Erin Messer—the Blackwater connection.

Evelyn studied the photo and then shook her head. "She doesn't look familiar. Is she dead? Do you want to know if I've seen her *recently* like the way I see Sydney?"

I walked straight into that one. I kept a placid expression

but wasn't in the mood for another batch of ghost stories. "No. I'm asking if you have ever met her as a *living* person."

She narrowed her eyes and studied the picture again. "No. Did you need anything else? I'm cold."

"Who's the guy?"

Evelyn gave me a sharp stare. "That sounds like a personal question, Detective."

"Just tell me his name so I can check him out."

"Why do you care who I spend time with?"

Damn. I hated that I couldn't tell her about the connection between Erin and Sydney. The information had not yet been released to the public. Parker was looking into a possible connection to the Armstrong Agency, but I hadn't gotten the verdict yet.

In case there was a link, I needed to warn Evelyn without giving her privileged information about the newly connected cases. "There are a lot of bad guys out there. I want to make sure he isn't one of them." I gestured to the expensive car in front of her gallery.

Evelyn turned back and looked through the glass door of the gallery. Her date was watching us. Her lips tightened as if considering what I had said. Had she sensed something off about that prick? Was she unnerved he was watching her? If she hadn't picked up on his smarmy vibe, I sure as hell had.

"The date isn't going so well. I could use a ride home." Evelyn tightened the belt on her coat and glanced behind her again.

I hated that her date made her uncomfortable, but I was grateful Evelyn asked for my help. I had a standing order with my sisters and friends from the neighborhood that if they were ever out with a guy that wasn't treating them right, all they had to do was call me, and I would pick them up, day or night.

"I'll take you anywhere you need to go. Do you want to wait in the car while I ask him to leave?"

Evelyn twisted her lips as she thought it over. "No, I can do it. Just come inside with me while I tell him." I wanted to honor her wishes and hang back and let Evelyn handle the situation, but I didn't have a passive bone in my body. The idea that some asshole made her uneasy in her sacred space revved my protective nature into the red zone.

Her date sized me up as I escorted Evelyn back inside. His gaze bounced between us as he sipped his wine.

"How do you know Evelyn?" He was a big guy, tall and muscular like me, but I could drop him and have him in cuffs in a nanosecond if the situation required force.

"That's none of your business, buddy." I widened my stance and let that motherfucker know I was not a guy he wanted to piss off.

"Is there a problem?" He glared at me and then set his sights on Evelyn.

"Everything is fine, Tomas. I just need you to leave." She aimed her finger at me to serve as her excuse. "Detective Ricci needs to ask me some questions in private about a crime I witnessed. It's urgent. I need to leave with him immediately."

Once Evelyn announced I was a cop, the guy got the hint, packed up, and was in the back seat of his Bentley before his driver had a chance to pour him a glass of champagne for the ride home.

CURIOUS—EVELYN

After Leo dropped me off, I was exhausted and humiliated from my impromptu date with Tomas and wanted nothing more than to get a decent night's sleep.

I grabbed my purse and reached for my phone to charge it for the night. I had turned it off and hadn't checked my messages. As I scanned my texts, I was peeved to find I had another message from *him*.

CALLER UNKNOWN: Were you happier when you were dead?

How many burner phones does the creep have?

As I stared at the message, I considered texting him back. It was a bad idea. The guy sending me messages wanted me to interact with him. The best way to handle it was to either delete the message and not respond or report the harassment to the cops.

I tapped my nails on the kitchen counter as I deliberated my next move. *Screw it. I need to exterminate this pest.* I picked up my phone and decided to text the caller—just once— hoping I could scare him off with a nasty response.

EVELYN: Back off, loser! Stop texting me. Stop calling. Get a fucking life!!!

The message dots bounced. A chill ran through my blood. The moment I'd hit send, I knew I'd made a terrible mistake. My heart raced with anticipation as I waited for his response. The dots bounced, then disappeared…bounced, then disappeared… then it rang.

CALLER UNKNOWN.

I gasped, startled by his boldness. I stared at my ringing cell, too shocked to pick up but too curious to send the call to voice mail. I tapped the screen and lifted the phone to my ear.

Heavy breathing. *Of course. Asshole.*

I waited for him to speak, not wanting to give him the satisfaction of hearing my voice, but as I remained on the line, the breathing got heavier, and the man began to pant.

Disgusting. I had gone this far, and I needed to find out the man's identity so I could report him to the cops. A dozen burner phone numbers wouldn't help track him down, but a name would. "Who are you?" I held my breath as I waited for his answer.

Is he someone I know? A casual acquaintance from the art scene? An obsessed fan morbidly curious about my past?

"I don't want to ruin the surprise."

The line went dead.

HE DOESN'T DESERVE YOU— EVELYN

I LEFT EARLIER THAN USUAL IN THE MORNING AND TOOK A different route to my studio—in case he was watching me.

My tall suede boots clicked on the sidewalk as I navigated the pedestrian traffic on Michigan Avenue. I held my keys firmly in my pocket. First, so I would be ready to open the door to the gallery and get inside. Second, to use as a weapon in case the weirdo who'd been texting me approached me on my way to work.

I hustled through a blinking walk signal and stopped cold when I reached the sidewalk and sensed I had a tail. Michigan Avenue during rush hour. There were tons of people and cars buzzing past on the busy street, but what I felt was different.

I pulled off to the side to stay out of the flow of foot traffic, grabbed my phone, and pretended to tap out a text as I covertly checked my surroundings. I scanned the crowd, and no one suspicious jumped out.

Stop living in fear. Call Leo.

No. I wasn't going to pull him away from his homicide investigation to report a couple of unsavory phone calls and texts. Even though it was unnerving, it seemed reasonable that some weirdo had read the article about my near-death experience, found my cell number, and got off on harassing me.

Not exactly a crime worthy of a detective.

I'd noticed more foot traffic around the gallery and people dropping by to see the paintings on display ahead of the opening. I considered that maybe I had a fan who was overly curious about me or about my paintings that hadn't yet been revealed to the general public.

Which would also explain the nature of the disturbing phone calls.

"How did it feel when your soul left your body? Is death painful, or did it feel good when you crossed over? Were you happier when you were dead?"

I made it to the gallery and upstairs to my studio without incident. I'd skipped my daily trip to Taboo in case he was watching me. Instead, I choked down a stale granola bar I'd unearthed from the back of my pantry. It was so hard and chewy, I worried I might rip out a filling.

This is my punishment for being a paranoid disaster.

I considered calling the cops instead of bothering Leo. Even though there were tiny instances of my privacy being violated along with the sensation that someone was watching me, nothing happened. Cops had actual crimes to investigate and real victims to assist.

Other women had to deal with violent predators and domestic abuse from boyfriends, husbands, and people they once trusted. Their complaints were valid. The cops would probably be pissed off at me for wasting their time over nothing.

"Let me get this right, Ms. Sinclair. Some asshole sent you a couple of unwanted texts. He called you and breathed heavily? Stole

a couple of pages out of your sketchbook? Did he hurt you? Threaten you in any way?"

I slid my dizzying thoughts to the back burner of my brain and concentrated on my work. It was a painting day, and I wouldn't let some random loser steal my attention away from my art. Today I would focus my energy on the mystery ghost I had sketched at Sydney's memorial.

The ghost that has me seeing red.

Normally, I would tape my sketches to the wall for reference, but the vigil drawings were the ones that had been stolen from my sketchbook. Luckily, I had taken pictures and scanned through the photos on my phone to refresh my memory.

I locked myself inside my studio, silenced my phone, and cranked opera music to awaken my artistic muse. As I faced the coldness of a blank white canvas, I dove in and marked the area with random brushstrokes and splatters.

My hand moved quickly as I hastily slapped the first layer of paint on the canvas. Then I dipped my brush into a pool of black paint and loosely outlined the trees and a nature trail that cut through the woods. Then I painted the form of a teenager peeking over her shoulder. Behind her, I added a long shadowy figure of a man.

Creepy.

I didn't know why ghosts wanted me to use my gift to share their stories—that was my assumption, anyway. I was given my gift for a reason, so when ghosts made contact with me, I had a sense of duty to immortalize them on the canvas. In this case, my vigil ghost felt different. She was bold and seized an opportunity to connect with me outside of a dream.

This ghost must really want my attention.

I knew I couldn't choose my gift, but I wished I had the ability to see into the future rather than focusing on the past.

If I could stop this poor girl from being murdered, I would do it without hesitation. Saving a life was a risk worth taking. Instead, I was painting the final moments of her life with no way to change the outcome.

Sorry, sweet girl.

Once I had the background mapped out, I added Prussian green to the landscape and lightened the trail to highlight the ominous figure lurking behind her. I had never seen the ghost in my dreams, so I took some artistic liberties with her expression.

I selected a thin brush and painted her facial features. I gave my subject bright-blue eyes with a sharp, vexing glare. Her focus was set on the shadow and her lips drawn tight, warning her would-be killer to back off.

As I painted in the details, I sensed the ghost's energy, and the world around me appeared tinted in red. What a color had to do with the ghost was beyond my grasp, but I followed her lead artistically and let her spirit guide me.

I like your attitude, Red Ghost.

I grabbed a medium brush and squeezed cadmium red onto my pallet and dabbed in ivory black to darken the color. I thinned it down with turpentine and rolled my brush into the mixture until the paint was the right consistency for her bloodred dress.

After working for hours, I stepped away to take a break. I glanced at the clock. It was nine o'clock at night. Even though I was exhausted, I was thrilled to have gotten so far along without a distraction. After the eerie texts from Caller Unknown last night, I feared I would have to face a new batch of harassment.

I made a deal with myself that if I got one more text or call from him, I would report the harassment to Leo. No more chances.

I checked my phone.

No new messages from *him*.

I breathed a sigh of relief and was thankful I hadn't bothered Leo with the stupid calls. I put my phone back in the drawer, grateful the harassment had only been temporary. The guy was probably bored with me and moved on to his next unsuspecting victim.

My head was throbbing, and I was ravenous with hunger. I desperately needed an energy boost so I could continue working. I grabbed my purse and coat and headed out of my studio, into the gallery.

When I opened the door, there was a flower arrangement on the ground, right in front of the door. It had a note with my name scrolled across the center. Gibson knew not to disturb me while I was painting and must've left it for me so I would see it when I resurfaced.

I picked up the notecard to see who had sent the exotic arrangement of wildflowers.

He doesn't deserve you. The card was signed with a hand-drawn heart. No signature.

Who would send something so personal? I had a sickening feeling as I considered the list of suspects. Since I had ended my date abruptly last night with Tomas, I wondered if he had sent the flowers as a mean-spirited gesture because I had left with Leo.

I barely knew the man and doubted he had given me a second thought after I asked him to leave the gallery. A rich and powerful man like Tomas probably had a harem of women on standby. I wasn't special to him—*he just thought I was easy.*

Then if it wasn't Tomas, I wondered if Leo had sent the flowers. His way of trying to woo his way back into my good graces? Leo was a stand-up guy who had bent over backward to make sure I was safe. He probably hated seeing me with an entitled ass like Tomas, especially after I asked for his help to get me out of a sticky situation.

But if Leo had sent me flowers, he would've written something nice or romantic. He wouldn't have ruined the gesture by insinuating another man wasn't good enough for me.

There was no denying Leo and I were still attracted to one another, but it seemed out of character for Leo to try to patch things up with a generic gesture. If he wanted to see me or had something to say, he would show up on my doorstep or pick up the phone and call me.

As I considered the motive, an unsettling thought came to mind. Had Caller Unknown been watching me? Had he seen me at the gallery having dinner with Tomas and leaving with Leo?

He doesn't deserve you.

I didn't scare him off last night. *Crap.* And now he was getting bolder since I gave him the attention he craved. *Stupid, Evelyn, Really stupid.*

I gripped my keys, making sure one poked out between my fingers so I could use it as a weapon to take out an eye. Caller Unknown might be a real threat after all. The phone harassment seemed to be building into something more sinister.

Is he out there now? Waiting for me to leave?

MELTDOWN—EVELYN

I WOULD NOT LET A DERANGED STRANGER DICTATE HOW I LIVED my life. The coffee shop was three stinking blocks away. The street was well lit, and there were plenty of people and cars cruising around the arts district.

If I walked straight there and back, there was no way the guy would try to grab me—if that was his intention—because there were too many witnesses around.

I trotted downstairs, locked the door behind me, and pulled my hat down low to cover my face. I stayed alert and quickened my pace to make it to the coffee shop without drawing attention to myself.

My long sandy-brown hair blew in the frigid, late fall wind while I held an umbrella to shield me from the splattering of icy rain. I tried to look confident and strong in case he was watching. Still, I felt vulnerable knowing some disgusting pervert might be lurking around the corner.

Watching. Learning my daily routine. Waiting for the perfect moment to pounce...

I peeked over my shoulder and saw a man in a thick wool coat trailing behind me. I crossed the street before he got too close and blended into a lively pack of twentysomethings as they left a bar. I used them as my personal fleet of body-guards and flowed with the crowd.

At the coffee shop, I breathed a sigh of relief when I stepped inside. I headed to the counter to place my order and glanced around for a familiar face. No one unusual stood out.

I ordered a cappuccino and a slice of cheesecake, then settled into my usual spot by the window to see who was coming and going. *Stop.* I was acting like a paranoid disaster. I made up my mind to call Leo in the morning and report the harassment. No one had the right to frighten me to the point of not wanting to be alone in public.

I pulled out my sketch pad and flipped to a clean page. I jotted down a time line of the harassment, starting with the first calls and texts I received after I visited Sydney's memor-ial. The more I thought about the boldness of the calls, the more frightened I became.

My hand trembled. *Someone is watching me.*

As my heart raced, I tried to act natural so as not to alert him that I was aware of his presence. Perspiration dampened my skin, and my mouth went bone dry. I slid my hand into my purse to retrieve my cell but remembered I'd left it in my studio.

The coffee shop was populated with a scattering of patrons, with one employee behind the counter. Caller Unknown had never shown his face or revealed his identity, at least as far as I knew. I reasoned he wouldn't risk blowing his cover by confronting me in public.

Maybe he is outside, watching me through the window.

With my pencil in hand, I flipped to a new page. I was tired of being afraid and feeling like I was being hunted. I needed to switch to offense and lure him to me. If I could see

Caller Unknown's face, I could sketch him and turn him in to the cops.

On the paper, in big, bold letters, I wrote:

THANKS FOR THE FLOWERS.

I scooted my sketch pad into the center of the table and displayed it face up, inviting him to read my message. I stared out the window, terrified and exhilarated, waiting for him to come into sight. In my peripheral vision, a shadowy figure approached my table—inside the coffee shop.

Slowly, I shifted my gaze from the window and turned to see who had come up behind me.

Dr. Vaughn Reynolds.

I gasped at the sight of him. Vaughn's face was paler than death. His cheekbones were gaunt, skin sallow, and dark circles pooled under his bloodshot eyes. The grief-stricken widower appeared more like a strung-out drug abuser than a respected heart surgeon.

"You see her, don't you?" Vaughn lunged at me and clasped my arms, squeezing tightly so I couldn't escape. The mental torture he was enduring was evident in his wild eyes. Dr. Vaughn had been reduced from a suave and confident doctor to a disheveled man, filled with rage and desperation, on the verge of a meltdown.

"What does she want? What did she say to you? Did Sydney tell you who killed her?"

His grip was so firm, I couldn't shake free. I feared he would hurt me, but in one swift motion, a man came up behind him and yanked him off me—Braydon, Vaughn's brother.

Braydon was bigger and stronger than Vaughn and held him in a vise grip as he spoke gently to calm him down. Once Vaughn stopped fighting, Braydon turned his attention to me. "I'm so sorry, Evelyn. Vaughn's losing his mind. He left the house talking smack about you seeing Sydney's ghost, and I've been running around the city trying to track him down. Are you alright?"

I had known Braydon for a few months. He was the project manager in charge of the gallery remodel. He was friendly, on the quiet side, and did a fantastic job hitting our completion milestones.

The pain of Sydney's death and its toll on the family were evident in Braydon's weary eyes. With my hand over my chest, I nodded as I caught my breath. "I'm okay. You need to get him to a hospital. He is not well."

Without waiting for a response, I grabbed my sketch-book, shoved it into my purse, and bolted from the coffee shop. No more stalling. I had to report this to Leo—*tonight*.

DISTURBING THOUGHTS—LEO

I HAD TWO CONNECTED MURDERS AND NO MAIN SUSPECT.

I wanted more than anything to bring Evelyn in on the case. I knew it was reckless to trust a civilian who claimed to have the ability to communicate with the dead, but the killer had taken two lives. I feared time was ticking away before he struck again.

This paranormal thing went against my belief system. Still, at this point, I was convinced Evelyn's clairaudient clues were the real deal. Parker and I went to the station to share the latest information about the connected murders with the team. As we pored over the evidence, lightning struck twice.

Talia, my fellow detective on the task force, burst into our office with a triumphant grin and an evidence folder in hand. "We just got the photo analysis we've been waiting for from the crime lab." She slammed the file on my desk as if she had delivered the secrets of the universe.

"Take a look at this." Talia tucked her dark curtain of bangs behind her ear, slid on her reading glasses, and revealed the first piece of evidence. A layer of the photograph had been separated from the scratched-out original found in Sydney's hand.

"She's next," I read. Our brilliant crime lab had unearthed a secret message that had not been visible to the naked eye. The original photo had scratch marks over the face and most of the body, leaving only traces of the image. I reasoned the photo's subject was a woman who had already been on the killer's radar before Sydney's murder.

"The killer is taunting us by revealing his next victim," Parker said. "He's a narcissist."

"Tell me we have an ID on the woman in the photograph," I said.

"Not quite." Talia flipped to the next photo. "We got a face, but it's not human."

Parker and I exchanged glances.

"What does this look like to you guys?" She pointed to a snippet of clothing the woman was wearing. I reached into my desk drawer and pulled out a magnifying glass. I moved it across the paper and identified a furry face with sharp fangs and a pair of dark eyes staring back at me.

"Is that a primate?" Parker asked.

"Sure looks like one," Talia said. "It reminds me of—"

"Bigfoot," I said. *Fuck.* I recognized the artistic style of a one-of-a-kind scarf designed by the woman I ordered to stay out of my investigation. "The woman in the picture is Evelyn Sinclair."

As I barked orders to my team, I tried to reach Evelyn. When she didn't answer her cell, I grabbed my coat and ran out the door. With Parker behind me, I cursed myself for not doing more to keep her safe.

Disturbing thoughts of processing Evelyn's crime scene raced through my mind. Would the killer dump her body in an alley as he had with the previous victims? Would Evelyn's last moments of life be spent blaming me for not catching her killer?

I tapped her number again. No answer. If anything happened to Evelyn, her blood would be on my hands.

MURDER VAN—EVELYN

I SHOULD'VE ASKED ONE OF THE BARISTAS TO CALL THE COPS, but I was so busy trying to escape Vaughn that I'd lost my sense of reason. Once outside, I upped my pace and jogged as swiftly as possible on the rain-slicked sidewalk.

When I was a block away, I checked over my shoulder to ensure no one was following me. No sign of Braydon or Vaughn—or the man in the thick wool coat I'd seen earlier.

While Vaughn had frightened me, I didn't believe he had killed his wife. Nor did he fit the profile of a man who would spend his days tracking my movements and harassing me.

Still, Vaughn believed I was communicating with Sydney and the phone calls were centered around death. He was desperate for answers, and his own brother said grief was causing him to act irrationally.

I was done guessing. Someone was following me. It might very well be Sydney's killer. My next order of business was to call Leo and tell him everything.

I returned to the gallery, hurried inside, and locked the door behind me. When I marched upstairs and reached the landing, my gaze landed on the wildflower arrangement still outside my door.

"He doesn't deserve you."

Once inside my studio, I plunked down in my office chair to calm myself before calling Leo. My hands were trembling as I rubbed my arms to soothe the pain from Vaughn's polarizing death grip.

I took a series of calming deep breaths and pulled out the list I'd created at the coffee shop, detailing the harassment I'd been experiencing—

My cell vibrated inside my desk. I yanked open the drawer and grabbed my phone. I was shocked to see I had a dozen missed calls and as many messages from Leo. As I held the phone, he called again. Whatever he wanted, it had to be urgent.

"What's wrong?"

"Where are you?"

"At my studio."

"Are you alone?"

I paused, trying to process why he wanted to know.

"Answer me!"

Leo's harsh tone startled me. "Yes."

"Make sure the doors are locked. I'm on my way."

"You're scaring me. Has the killer struck again?"

"I'll explain when I get there. There's been a development in the case that involves you. I don't want to frighten you, but Sydney's killer may be after you. Stay on the phone with me until I get there."

My body stiffened as a rush of panic washed over me. I wasn't being paranoid. The harassing calls and flowers were related to the case. I stepped out of my office and headed for the stairs to check the security of the doors on the main floor.

"Strange things have been happening," I said. "Phone calls, flowers, and someone has been following—"

All the lights went out.

The gallery fell pitch black.

The streetlights shone in from the window, and it didn't appear the electricity was out on the whole block, just my building.

"Evelyn? What happened?"

"The lights went out." I held my breath and listened for signs of an intruder. I covered my mouth and choked back a scream.

Glass broke. The back door creaked open.

No, no, no... this is really happening.

"Talk to me, Evelyn. What's going on?"

I crouched down on the stairs, too frightened to move. "He's here," I whispered. "Someone just broke in from the alley. He cut the electricity."

"Lock yourself in your studio and hide. I'm two minutes away. Find a weapon to defend yourself in case he reaches you."

My legs were rubber as I crept back up the stairs. As I moved stealthily along the wall by the landing, a fluorescent beam from a flashlight shot across the gallery below.

"He's searching for me."

"Find a place to hide! If he finds you, bash him in the head with whatever you can get your hands on. Claw out his eyes if you have to!"

Footsteps pounded up the stairs.

"Run, Evelyn! Lock yourself inside a room."

He's on the landing. I'll never make it in time.

There were three studios under construction on the second floor. If I could lock myself in any of the rooms, I could hide until Leo arrived. I kept one hand on the wall and ran until I found the door to Luis's studio. I twisted the handle. *It's locked.*

The footsteps charged toward me and the beam from the flashlight cut across my face. My fight-or-flight instincts kicked in, and I ran upstairs back to my studio and slammed the door. I tried to lock it, but the man was behind me and forced his way in. I held up my hands defensively and screamed, "Get away from me!"

Slam! He barreled into me and knocked me backward. My head banged against the wall, and my body crumbled from the shock and force of the blow. I was stunned but conscious and able to fight. I clawed at his face and felt the knitted fabric of a ski mask.

My cell phone crash-landed somewhere on the floor, and I could hear Leo's voice shouting through the speaker. He yelled at my attacker, identifying himself as Chicago PD and ordered him to cease the assault. Then he turned his attention back to me. "Evelyn? Evelyn, can you hear me?"

My screams drowned out Leo's voice.

The assailant grabbed my wrists with gloved hands and ended my attempt to scrape out his eyes. He shoved me to the ground and straddled my body. He pinned my wrists and breathed hard and pleasurably as he savored his power over me. He positioned himself between my legs. With his pants still on, he rubbed against me and groaned as my terror aroused him.

I bucked and snapped and found my strength as my fight-or-flight instincts took over. I wailed and kicked and fought with every ounce of strength I had, but his body was heavy and strong, and I was too weak to struggle free.

Tired of my resistance, he jammed his knee in my chest to keep me still. Once he rendered me helpless, he shoved a gag in my mouth and tightened it behind my head.

My throat burned, and I couldn't get enough air. Fear

brought on a rush of adrenaline when the realization hit me that he had planned this out, whatever his intentions were.

Gloves, a ski mask, bondage… is he going to rape me? Is he the same man who strangled the life out of Sydney? Am I going to die tonight?

My screams were reduced to a whimper as he secured my wrists with zip ties. Once I was subdued and unable to defend myself, he violently ripped open my button-down dress and exposed my breasts. With one hand, he slid up my bra, and with the other, he wrapped his fingers around my throat.

"I'll make it hurt if you fight me." He tossed me over his shoulder and carried me to the window at the back of my office. As I hung upside down, I spotted his creepy murder van parked in the alley below.

I writhed and kicked, but nothing I did deterred him.

He grunted a string of obscenities and shook me.

I dropped my head on his shoulder and tried to bite through the fabric of his thick coat. I kicked and thrashed to knock him off balance or bust the window glass, hoping someone outside would come to my rescue. If he shoved me into that van, my face would appear next to Sydney's on the victim list.

Where are you, Leo?

I was dizzy and nauseous and couldn't get enough air. Just before I lost hope and consciousness, sirens neared the building. My attacker cursed, angry the cops were closing in. While I struggled to fill my lungs with air, the brute dropped me to the ground in frustration.

"I'm coming back for you. Stay the fuck away from that dickhead, Evelyn." Before he fled the scene, my assailant stomped on my bound hands.

I cried in agony as my fingers throbbed from the intentional blow. Stars flashed before my eyes, and as I struggled to stay conscious, the tinny sound of footsteps bounded down the fire escape. An engine roared to life. Tires squealed down the alley.

Sirens blared in the distance for what felt like an eternity. I curled into a ball and tried to calm myself down so I could breathe. I pressed my hands against my chest to ease the throbbing pain of my injury.

As I lay stunned on my studio floor, a pair of men shouted, "Clear!" Heavy boots thundered up the stairs. A man yelled my name, but I couldn't answer because of the gag. I rolled on my side and inched my way toward the landing.

A flashlight shined down on me then a strong hand rolled me over and cradled my head.

"Hang on, Evelyn. I've got you."

POPPED—LEO

A COOL BLADE SLID BEHIND MY EAR, AND LEO REMOVED THE gag with one quick slice. As I gasped for air, he cut off the zip ties that bound my wrists and lifted me into a sitting position. I cradled my injured hand against my chest to soothe the throbbing pain.

Stars flashed before my eyes as a result of a blinding headache. Leo rubbed his warm hand on my back and whispered words of encouragement, assuring me that I would be alright as I trembled with fear. "I've got you, Evelyn. You're safe with me."

As my body tensed with shock and the fear of knowing I had narrowly escaped death, Leo removed his coat and wrapped it around my shoulders. Sirens neared the building. I clung to my hero while the reality of what had happened seeped into my bones.

If Leo and Parker had arrived a minute later, my abductor would've stolen me away down the fire escape and shoved me into the murder van. I whimpered in pain from my throbbing hand.

Leo sat beside me and held me in his strong embrace. "Do

you know who hurt you?"

"No. He was wearing a ski mask."

Leo stayed by my side as the crew checked my vitals and asked a series of rapid-fire questions.

"What is your name?... Where are you injured?... Are you allergic to any medications?…"

I wanted to give Leo more information, but as I answered their questions, the medics were preparing me for transport. But what I had to tell him couldn't wait. Leo needed to know about my encounter with Vaughn just before the attack. I needed to tell him about the phone calls and texts, the eerie feeling that someone had been following me, and that my drawings were stolen.

A round of vertigo made me nauseous as the crew lifted me onto a gurney. I squeezed my eyes and clutched the fabric of my dress to chase away the falling sensation. Once I was strapped in, a medic tried to place an oxygen mask over my nose and mouth, but I lifted it off with my uninjured hand and spoke to Leo. "He knows."

"We need to go, Detective," the paramedic said.

"I'm riding along," Leo responded, then turned his attention back to me. "How do you know?"

"My attacker is the one who stole my purse from the bar. After you left my apartment, I checked my sketchbook. My drawings from the vigil had been torn from the book. He saw me there, sketching, and wanted to see what I had drawn." I swallowed hard. "The drawings were of a young woman. I took pictures of the sketches and saved them on my phone."

The paramedic tried to place the mask again.

"Wait." I clutched Leo's forearm. "Vaughn confronted me at the coffee shop this evening. He knows I can see her."

The veins on the side of Leo's neck popped out. He was angry, possibly at himself. "We'll get him, Evelyn. I swear to God, he will never hurt you again."

THE WINDY CITY STALKER—LEO

THE REALITY OF HOW CLOSE EVELYN HAD COME TO BECOMING Victim Number Three lodged in my gut. Seeing her crumbled on the floor of her studio, bound and gagged, reeling from fear and pain, rocked me to the core. I was moments away from losing her forever.

When the paramedics loaded Evelyn onto the bus, I stayed by her side, whispered encouraging words, and assured her she was safe. While I meant every word, I was mentally cataloging everything I had witnessed so I could share the information with my team.

A vase of flowers at the scene from an anonymous sender, an ominous message written on a card with a hand-drawn heart, victim bound during assault...

The best way to ensure Evelyn's safety was to capture her stalker.

As far as suspects were concerned, all the men she dated from the agency were on the list. Twelve mega-rich businessmen, to be exact. I would have my team start looking at the surveillance photos from Sydney's vigil and see if any of the men Evelyn dated were in attendance.

There was a chance Evelyn and Sydney had dated the same guy. That gave me twelve men from the Armstrong Agency to check out, along with Vaughn and his brother, Braydon, who we had not ruled out as suspects.

Now that we'd uncovered the truth that Erin and Sydney were killed by the same man, we needed to review the list of suspects from both murder investigations. We needed to find a link between the first two victims—and now Evelyn.

Had all three women frequented the same place? Had they all hired Braydon to do repairs? Had they all dated the same man?

Parker and Talia were picking up the Reynolds brothers for questioning while I stayed with Evelyn. The timing of the disturbance at the coffee shop coincided with the time line of the attack. The rest of our team was trying to pinpoint a common thread between the victims that would lead us to their stalker.

Blackwater. Captiva. Halsted.

Evelyn's one-word epiphanies were all places. Captiva was on the nose. Evelyn knew Sydney had been married on the island. Halsted was another slam dunk for obvious reasons. I could dismiss those clues as lucky guesses. Anyone, with or without paranormal powers, could've come up with those clues.

Blackwater, however, I could not dismiss. My team had only made a connection between Erin and Blackwater after Evelyn had given me the tip. It was a crucial piece of evidence we may never have connected to Sydney's murder without Evelyn's insight.

It went against my beliefs, but I could no longer dismiss Evelyn's gift as a hoax. As the ambulance raced toward Cook County, I offered up a long overdue apology. "I believe you, Evelyn. You were right about everything. Sorry it took me so long."

Tears streamed down her cheeks for the first time since the attack, as if a dam building with pressure had finally burst. If it took me a lifetime, I would find a way to make it up to her, starting with hunting down and arresting the man who was terrorizing our city.

Now that the Violent Crimes Task Force had confirmed we were dealing with a serial killer in the making, the chief of police had called an emergency press conference to inform the public.

Evelyn was not identified as the killer's latest target. I'd kept her name off the radio. Still, the Chief had released information to the public that we believed the same man was responsible for the murders of Sydney Reynolds and Erin Messer, and a third victim had been targeted that evening who had survived the attack.

Once the press got a hold of the breaking news that a man was stalking and murdering women in our town, they gave the killer a nickname: the Windy City Stalker.

THE AFTERMATH—EVELYN

The next few hours passed in a blur of medical attention and police reports. From the moment Leo arrived on the scene, he never left my side. He held my hand on the way to the hospital and assured me I would be okay.

I had given him as much information as I could remember about my attacker, my confrontation with Vaughn in the coffee shop, and details of the phone harassment.

Leo stayed with me while the medical staff checked me out. I was banged up and traumatized but luckily had no serious physical injuries. My fingers were swollen and bruised, but I had only sustained a fracture on my ring finger.

I wouldn't be able to draw or paint for a few weeks, however, I was grateful the injury hadn't been more serious. I had a bump on my head and some contusions that would heal in a few days. After I had come so close to becoming the killer's latest victim, I considered myself lucky to be alive.

"Did your attacker sexually assault you?" a nurse in blue scrubs barged into the room and asked louder than necessary.

I cringed every time a doctor or nurse came in and asked the same questions while they went over my chart. While I'd answered the assault question a dozen times in front of Leo, he clenched his jaw every time I'd answered *no*. He's already bagged my clothing and logged it into evidence, hoping it had my attacker's vile DNA on it.

While the doctors insisted on keeping me overnight for observation, Leo planted himself at my bedside. In between escorting me to X-ray and checking the credentials of every health care worker who entered my room, Leo made sure I was comfortable—and, more importantly, safe.

He had told me that the chief of police had informed the public that there was a potential serial killer loose on the streets, and, luckily, I had not been named in the reports.

He was on the phone leading the Windy City Stalker investigation and taking notes as new information came in. There were no more secrets between us. He had my complete file from the Armstrong Agency, with my blessing, and my phone so he could read the harassing texts.

The worst part of the aftermath was describing what my stalker had done to me before Leo arrived on the scene. The sickening way he ground against me and got off on his position of power over me. The anger emanated from his body as he squeezed his hand around my throat. The sickening moans of pleasure that escaped his lips when he'd torn open my dress and exposed my breasts...

Someone knocked on the door, giving me respite from finishing my statement for Leo's official report. Parker had arrived with a coffee cup and a computer bag slung over his shoulder.

Leo gave him a nod to enter, and Parker padded slowly to my bedside. "How are you feeling, Evelyn?" His kindness was genuine, and although I was sure he was there to ask me some very personal questions about the men I dated, I never doubted his sincerity as he patiently awaited my response.

"I'm fine. Just a fracture and a bump on the head." I lifted my hand and showed him the splint on my finger.

He slid a chair beside my bed and gave me all his attention. His striking green eyes held my gaze as he set the cup on the table. "I thought you might like something warm." It was a small gesture that spoke volumes about his personality. He was a sensitive soul, and the pain of seeing me banged up weighed on his conscience.

"Thank you, Parker. I appreciate it." I inhaled the heavenly scent of a Pumpkin Spice Latte.

"Do you need anything? Can I call anyone for you? Has your family been notified?"

"I don't have a family. Leo already called Gibson and Luis, so they wouldn't freak out when they found the gallery had become a crime scene. Leo has been amazing." For the first time since giving my statement, I found the courage to look Leo in the eye.

Now, however, he couldn't look at me.

His expression burned with a mix of self-loathing, anger and remorse. I realized it was just as painful for him to hear the account of what my stalker had done to me as it was for me to relive the attack. I reached out and touched his shoulder. "I should've told you sooner. I knew something was wrong. I was going to tell you about the calls, but—"

Leo's cell buzzed repeatedly, stealing his attention. As he scrolled through his messages, the veins on the side of his neck stuck out. He got up from the chair beside me and nodded at Parker. The two of them moved across the room to confer about whatever information was coming in on his cell.

"Is everything alright?" I sat up in bed, nervous that two

detectives had dialed in on something significant. They ignored me and focused on the screen.

I squeezed the sheet with my good hand to relieve the anxiety building inside me. My body ached, and my head was throbbing, but I had a feeling whatever Detective Ricci had received on his phone was a million times worse than a fractured finger and a bump on the head.

SHE'S MINE—EVELYN

"Are you feeling up to this? What I have to show you isn't going to be pleasant."

I sat up with a start, fearing the worst. "Did he kill again? Is it someone I know? Did he send you a picture of the body?" The worst-case scenarios swirled around my brain as my creative mind conjured horrific images of what the detectives had received from the killer.

"There are no other victims at this point," Parker reassured me. He and Leo had come back to my bedside. They remained standing as if they were ready to spring into action.

Leo turned his phone toward me, so I could see the horrible image on the screen. It was a picture of me leaving work, walking alone down Michigan Avenue.

I recognized the picture had been taken last Saturday because that was the day I'd dressed all in black. My mouth went dry when I remembered where I was going. That was the night of Sydney's vigil.

Leo swiped to the next photo.

Me again. This time, a seemingly innocent photo of an

artist leaning against a brick wall with her eyes closed, sketching a genre scene in front of the Chicago Water Tower on a blustery day.

When Leo swiped to the next photo, I gasped. The image was of me with Sydney, taking a selfie outside my gallery on the day we closed. It was shocking to see the intimate photo of myself in the hands of a detective.

"Are you alright?" Parker asked.

The realization hit. "Yeah. I want to see all of them."

"The next photos are more intimate." Leo held his finger above the screen but hesitated before he swiped. It wasn't like him to be indecisive. He had already decided to show me. Whatever was in the photo must've been horrifying.

"Before I reveal the photo, I want you to know you're safe now. I'm not going to let this motherfucker anywhere near you ever again. You have my word, Evelyn." When Leo swiped to the next photo, my heart bottomed out. It was me —*asleep in my bed.*

"Oh god." I covered my mouth to stifle a scream. The killer must've climbed the fire escape and watched me through the window.

"I'm sorry, Evelyn," Parker said. "I can't imagine how horrifying this is for you. For your safety, we have arranged for you to go into protective custody as soon as you get your discharge papers."

"Wait. Protective custody? How… I can't live like a prisoner."

"The killer sent a message." Leo swiped one more time.

CALLER UNKNOWN: Stay away from her, dickhead.

The last photo was one that both of us recognized immediately. It was us leaving the bar together on the night my purse had been stolen. Leo was towering over me, serving as my bodyguard as he ushered me to his car to drive me home.

My heart raced as I took in the modifications the killer had made to the photo.

He had violently scratched out Leo's face with a sharp object. Then my stalker marked an "X" over my body with a red marker and wrote, *"She's mine."*

BODYGUARD—LEO

NOW IT WAS PERSONAL.

The killer hadn't made many mistakes. He had managed to abduct and murder two women without leaving a trail of evidence behind. He had stayed off our radar, and we hadn't yet connected a single suspect to both murders.

But once that coward targeted Evelyn, he had made his first mistake—fucking with the wrong guy. While Parker tapped away on his laptop and updated the team, I stayed beside Evelyn to comfort her. She had curled on her side and closed her eyes, silently processing her nightmare.

My gaze drifted to her injuries. From the bandages on her wrists where the zip ties cut into her skin. To the shadows that pooled under her eyes from the trauma. Then to the splint on her drawing hand.

What would've happened if we hadn't figured out it was her in the picture?

As grim as it sounded, I was relieved to see her in that hospital bed as the alternative outcome played out in my head. I imagined processing her crime scene and seeing her beautiful body dumped on a pile of trash. Her bruised neck.

Her bulging eyes. A photograph tucked into her busted-up hand...

I exhaled a deep sigh and paced the room, trying to chase the horrible images of Evelyn's death flashing before my eyes. The idea that I was minutes, maybe seconds, away from letting her abductor get away with another murder.

"Leo," Evelyn whispered. "I'm declining the offer for protective custody."

I shook my head, not believing the words out of her mouth. "He won't give up. He's going to try to take you again."

"I know." Evelyn's expression turned stoic. "That's how we're going to catch him."

I didn't like where her train of thought was headed. "I'm not sure where you're going with this, but as soon as the doctors let you go, I'm handing you over to protective custody."

"You need my help." She eyed the pad of paper and pencil on the rolling table next to her bed, longing to draw.

"You are not a detective, Evelyn. I don't have time to babysit you and catch a killer."

"He's not going to give up. Let me get back to my usual routine. If he tries to kidnap me again, your team will be ready to nab him."

"I'm not using you as bait to lure in a killer."

"Take me to the coffee shop right now. You know he'll be looking for me there."

"Evelyn." I held up my hands like a stop sign, commandeering the conversation. "I know you want to help, and you will."

She narrowed her eyes. "Would you ever back down from a case because it became too dangerous?"

"I'm a trained law enforcement officer. It's my job to protect the citizens of Chicago."

"For the first time since my accident, I have a chance to save lives." Tears welled in her eyes. "I was seconds away from being murdered, Leo. You were there to save me. Now it's my turn to return the favor to the next victim the killer targets. I won't slink away and hide when I have the skills to save another woman's life. I can't back down knowing what's at stake."

Parker had been quiet while Evelyn and I sparred. But he approached the bedside when it was time to offer his professional opinion. "It makes sense. The killer already believes the two of you are a couple. He will expect to see you together."

Parker held out his hands, asking for a chance to finish his thought. "Listen, I would never suggest we use Evelyn as bait." He shifted his gaze between us. "However, I'm ninety-nine percent positive she has met her attacker face to face at some point."

Evelyn nodded, agreeing with the statement.

"If you two keep up the pretense of dating, you can go places you don't normally go. If Evelyn recognizes someone while out of her element, our team can check that person out."

"What do you mean by *out of my element?*" Evelyn asked.

Parker picked up a pen and drew a visual. He marked a series of squares on the page and drew a circle around them. "Let's say this is your grid between your apartment and the gallery, Evelyn. The squares represent the coffee shop, yoga studio, bar, and the various places you visit most often."

"Okay," Evelyn said.

Then he flipped to a clean page and drew the same picture again. "And this is Detective Ricci's world. The places he goes and visits frequently. Let's say you see the same people in your everyday life. The same people at the coffee shop. Same people at the yoga studio. Those people, most likely, will not also be at Detective Ricci's favorite spots."

"I get it," she said. "If I saw someone from my world in Leo's world, that would be a red flag."

"Right. Your work is done if you spot someone who doesn't belong in Leo's world. We will check him out while you are safely out of harm's way."

I hated that Parker was right, but he made a good point. I carried a gun and wouldn't hesitate to use it. Creeps like our killer were cowards. He wouldn't make a move while Evelyn was under my protection.

Evelyn gave me a pleading look. "Please, Leo. We can do this. We have to catch him before he kills again."

Dammit. They were both right. "I will agree under three conditions. One, you are moving in with me until the killer is caught."

"Okay," Evelyn said.

"Two, I have the right to call it off at any time if I feel you are in danger."

"Agreed."

"Last, you don't go anywhere without me. Consider me your full-time bodyguard."

Evelyn offered a handshake to seal the deal. "Let's get to work, partner."

POLISHED—LEO

Evelyn was discharged from the hospital the next day. By late afternoon, we were at my place. She was exhausted, and I wanted to give her time to wind down from the trauma before we got to work.

No talking about the case

No interrogation about the men in her life.

No reminding her how close she came to dying—*again*.

All I had planned was to watch a movie and order a pizza for dinner. Evelyn's first order of business was to take a hot shower and change into clean clothes. I set her up in the guest bedroom and laid out a stack of my T-shirts and a pair of sweats.

One of my shirts was big enough to serve as a dress. Until we had a chance to go back to her apartment and pack a bag, Evelyn was appreciative of being able to clean up and have fresh clothes to change into. I worried she would get dizzy and fall in the shower.

"This is the least dangerous thing I will do today, Detective. I will not need your bodyguard services while I'm naked." For the first time since the attack, Evelyn managed a smile. I was relieved she had her snarky sense of humor back.

While she cleaned up, I went to the kitchen to make some appetizers. I had a couple ripe avocados and some tomatoes, so I whipped up some guac and chopped up some fresh veggies for dipping. I turned on some classic rock music to lighten the mood and opened the curtains to let in some natural light.

My job was intense, and as cold as it seemed, I had learned to turn off and tune out the horrors of work. There was a time and place to dial into murder, but this was not one of them. The human spirit needed time to recuperate and rest, if only for a few hours.

I sang along with Van Halen as I whirled up a batch of virgin margaritas made with fresh limes and frozen lemonade. When Evelyn came downstairs, I did a double take. She was wearing one of my XL Loyola University T-shirts and a pair of gray sweats, rolled at the waist to keep them from falling off.

Her hair was wet and wavy, and she wore it down to let it dry. Without a stitch of makeup, her skin glowed fresh from the steamy shower. I could get used to seeing her around my place. I imagined what it would be like if Evelyn spent time here more often—after the killer was caught.

We had solved the one problem keeping us apart. Even though Evelyn's gift defied logic, the evidence was too strong to ignore. I believed Evelyn could communicate with the dead. If that was the only thing stopping us from being together, it wasn't too late for a second chance.

"Don't stop singing on my account." As she entered the kitchen, I filled a plate and slid it her way. Then I poured us a round of nonalcoholic drinks.

She sipped the frozen margarita. "You went a little stingy on the tequila."

"No alcohol for you. Doctor's orders. Those pain meds should've knocked you out already."

"I didn't take them." She glanced down as if confessing a sin.

"Why not?"

"I didn't want to miss the party." She dipped a celery stick into the guac and gave it a taste. "Yum. I won the bodyguard lottery. Strong, highly trained, and knows how to whip up appetizers." As she chewed, I could tell she was in more pain than she was leading me to believe.

I didn't want to ruin the mood and bring her down with a round of questions, though. "Good. I don't want you to crash before I can treat you to the best dinner of your life." I slid her a grease-stained menu from my buddy's place down the street. I ordered delivery all the time when I had the guys over.

Evelyn grinned as she read the torn-up menu, marked up with stars and notes from my previous orders. "Everything looks amazing, especially the chicken parm hoagie and the double deluxe supreme with ricotta."

"Perfect. We have to get an order of deep-fried cauliflower with buffalo sauce and bleu cheese. I want you to have the whole Paulina's Hoagie House experience." I didn't know if she was being a good sport about the greasy food, but I had some healthy stuff in the fridge I could make her if she didn't like the local cuisine.

The point of the evening was to relax and enjoy some downtime. I reached into the fridge and popped the caps off a couple of Pabst Blue Ribbons. I passed one to Evelyn and she lifted her bottle to mine in salute. I turned up the music and led Evelyn to the living room, where we settled on my old comfy couch.

She curled her legs up and propped a pillow behind her back so she could face me. I could get used to seeing her wearing my shirts, drinking beer, and hanging out listening to music. She watched me as I grabbed the remotes and tossed the pillows on my side onto a chair.

I knew by now that her mind was always working, and it seemed like she was studying my domestic habits. She had never seen me relaxed, and it seemed she was taking note of my "off-duty" personality. She moved her gaze to my bookcase and eyed the photos of my friends and family lined up on the shelves.

There were ones of Santoni and me in our high school football uniforms. Me and my buddies on our annual camping trip. My family and friends at my detective promotion party at Navy Pier.

"You and Officer Santoni grew up together?"

"Best friends since birth."

Evelyn cracked a smile. "You look like your dad."

Since Evelyn brought him up, the time was right to tell her something that had been weighing on my mind.

"My dad used to take me fishing at the lake when I was a kid," I said. "Just me and him. We would rent a cabin and spend the weekend at Lake Michigan, drinking beer and grilling what we caught on an open fire."

Evelyn took a swig from the bottle and gave me all of her attention.

"We never spent a lot of time together outside of the lake. He worked crazy hours to support five kids, and I was always running around the neighborhood, screwing around with my buddies. The trips to the lake were the only time we really slowed down and had some deep heart-to-hearts."

I shared the memory of Dad and me cruising in his fishing boat and listening to his wild tales about the dumb shit he got away with when he was my age.

"Do you still go fishing with him?" Evelyn asked.

"As we got older, the trips became further spread out. A

couple times every summer turned into once a year, then once every few years... then we ran out of time." I took a sip of beer. "My dad passed away from cancer three years ago."

"I'm sorry," Evelyn said.

"On his deathbed, he put me in charge of the family. I was his only son, and he made it my responsibility to look after Mom, Nonna, and my four sisters. You know, I was a mess. The stubborn old man never even told me he was sick."

"I'm sorry you lost him." Evelyn set down her drink.

"The last thing he said to me before his heart stopped beating was, 'I'm going to the lake now, son. I'm going to catch us some *walleye*.'"

Evelyn sat up straight, her expression torn between guilt and sorrow. Before she had a chance to feel bad about saying the word, I assured her it brought me comfort.

"Here's the thing, Evelyn. At first, I was shocked. There was no way you could've unearthed walleye from any other source other than my dad. And after I had time to think about it, I realized that was his way of teaching me a lesson."

"Just so we're clear, your dad is not a ghost. The clairaudient messages come from a higher power. If anything, it proves your father is exactly where he should be—*the other side*."

"I know. I never doubted Dad's fate, and walleye validated that for me. When the shock wore off, I was relieved Dad was doing the thing he loved most."

"Fishing?"

"No. Proving me wrong."

Evelyn exhaled a sigh of relief and patted my shoulder. "I think I would've really liked your dad."

Dad would've loved to see me with a woman like you.

After I shared the truth about the walleye connection, the invisible barrier between us crumbled. We spent the evening watching classic sitcoms and noshing on greasy take-out food. We laughed for hours, and the conversation never lulled as we polished off an entire pie and chased it down with a couple more PBRs.

The only thing I didn't like about our evening at home was that it had to end. When we said good night and went to our separate bedrooms, I remembered some of Dad's classic wisdom:

"When you got something good, don't fuck it up."

I couldn't agree more, Dad.

BAD BOYFRIEND—EVELYN

Day one of our undercover mission started with me getting back to my usual routine—with my doting fake boyfriend along for the ride.

The Windy City Beat had made arrangements with Gibson for a second photo shoot. They wanted to run a follow-up article on social media about my process, and Gibson suggested they run a story on a work in progress.

In keeping with the spooky vibe of the fall season, my new collection—Haunted History—revolved around the city's historic landmarks. Highlighting my artistic interpretation of the earthbound spirits who still roam the city long after their death.

The photographer, Jeremy, suggested one of the city's iconic cemeteries for the shoot. Leo and I arrived ahead of schedule and strolled the grounds in the cemetery's historic section.

The fall breeze kicked up a pile of leaves, scattering them along the path around the memorial gardens. Leo and I strolled beside each other, seemingly enjoying the beautiful weather and scenic tour of the grounds.

Parker was stationed at the meeting point and asked us to act naturally so he could observe Jeremy's reaction. Apparently, every man in Chicago I had ever come into contact with was a person of interest.

A chilling thought, but according to our profiler, my attacker thought of me as his possession and would get insanely jealous to see me with another man. That was apparently a good thing for the investigation but not for me.

My attacker had obviously hated the *dickhead* I was spending time with. If Jeremy was my stalker, which seemed ridiculous, then Leo and Parker could assess his reaction to seeing us together.

But there was no way anyone could be jealous because Leo was a terrible actor.

He hadn't looked at me since we'd arrived. Leo was towering over me protectively in bodyguard mode, ready to throat punch anyone who came near me. The opposite of his fun and playful side last night, which, for the record, would go down in history as the best nondate in history.

"No one will believe you're my boyfriend," I whispered.

Leo shot me a smug look. "Because I'm too good-looking for you?"

I laughed as I shoved him on the shoulder, trying to loosen him up. His body was so strong and rigid, he didn't budge. "You know, *real* boyfriends show some affection to their girlfriends."

I felt the heat of his stare. "Are you asking me to kiss you, Evelyn?"

"I'm just saying, if *you-know-who* is watching, he'll know we're trying to set him up. A real boyfriend would hold his girlfriend's hand and *smile* when she's being playful. Have you ever been on a date before, Detective Ricci?"

"Once or twice. Enlighten me. What am I doing wrong?"

Behind his dry sense of humor, Leo's eyes were wild with amusement.

"Well, it's not just you who are doing everything wrong. I take half the blame."

"Thank you," Leo said. "That's very diplomatic of you."

"If I was your girlfriend for real, I'd snuggle up and keep warm against the heat of your strong body. And you—*my boyfriend*—would catch my hot-and-bothered vibe, steer me away from the sidewalk, and kiss me behind the mausoleum."

I waved my hand at the scenic resting places near the tree line. "Then, when we were both excited from our impromptu make-out session, you would whisper something naughty in my ear to see if I was in the mood for *you-know-what*."

He twisted his lips, amused by my imaginative fantasy, and gave me his undivided attention. "Would I try to make a move on you here? In front of all the dead people?"

"You might *try*, but I would swat at you playfully and guide you to a park bench. Then I'd lay my hand across your lap, slip my finger around your belt, and give the leather a little tug to let you know what to expect later." I laughed and turned away, embarrassed I'd said what I was thinking aloud.

I covered my face, willing the universe to swallow me whole. I was trying to lighten the mood, but my real-life fantasy about my sexy bodyguard crept into my funny story.

"Interesting, but you are the one who's got it all wrong," Leo said.

I met his gaze, eager for his opinion on how our imaginary date should play out.

"If I had a hot girl like you tugging on my belt, talking dirty to me out in public, we wouldn't be strolling around a cemetery on a beautiful fall day. I'd take you home, open all the windows, strip you naked, and keep you occupied in my bed all weekend."

My jaw dropped at his boldness. I tried to think of something naughty to say in return, but Leo had won that round.

Leo's phone vibrated, and he snuck a glance at the screen. "Keep up the good work, Evelyn," he said. "Your photographer is here. If he's our guy, he'll be pissed off to see you flirting with the *dickhead*. I guess I'm not such a bad boyfriend, after all."

I felt my cheeks warm and dropped my gaze to the ground. Leo was only doing his job by making me blush with his sexy banter. And I fell for it. It stung knowing that we almost had the chance to make our fake relationship a real one. Still, we had already decided we could never make it as a couple—unless his opinion has changed now that he believes my gift is real.

Leo picked up my hand and gave me a smug smile as we walked to the entrance to meet Jeremy. "Am I doing this right?"

"You could loosen your grip, big guy." I playfully knocked him on his shoulder.

When I spotted Jeremy at the meeting spot, I waved as we approached. His expression was tense, as if something was bothering him. *Is he jealous, seeing me with Leo?* "Hey, Jeremy. I hope you don't mind I brought my boyfriend."

"Hey, Evelyn." Jeremy popped his sunglasses on top of his head, ignoring Leo. "You're late." Jeremy was a tad socially awkward and focused more on getting the right shot rather than engaging with his subjects.

"Sorry to keep you waiting. I hope—"

"I was expecting you ten minutes ago." Jeremy's gaze shifted to Leo as if outing him as the source of my delay.

"Sorry. We were enjoying—"

"The sun is in a perfect position this time of day," Jeremy interrupted as he turned his attention back to me and pointed to the tree line. "If we hurry, I can get a gorgeous shot of you crossing the Stone Memorial Bridge while we have good light."

Jeremy grabbed a black duffel back and led the way to the bridge in his muddy boots. He must carry his extra lenses and equipment in there—or was it something else? Jeremy kept his gaze on the setting as if mentally staging the scene that captured the history and natural beauty of the iconic cemetery.

He ushered me to the old wooden walkway and told me to face the horizon, so my back was to him. Jeremy helped me out of my coat and tossed it to Leo as if my boyfriend had volunteered to be his assistant—his penance for making me late.

Leo eyed his bag as if trying to get a glimpse of the contents inside. He was curious about the bag, too. Knowing the detective, he probably thought my photographer had brought a murder kit to the park, hoping to catch me alone. But as I processed the thought, I realized it might be true.

Parker was certain I had seen my attacker's face before. I had seen Jeremy on multiple occasions. What if he was the man who had attacked me?

I rubbed my arms, chasing away the goose bumps.

Once Jeremy had positioned me in the perfect light, he swept my hair back so that it covered my back. I couldn't see Leo's reaction, but I doubted he liked the way my photographer was physically moving me. I didn't like it either, but I let it go.

"Now, keep your body facing forward and turn slightly to your right. Turn your shoulders. Keep your chin down and look up."

"Click... click... click..."

Jeremy wanted a different angle. He positioned my uninjured hand on the handrail, turned my shoulders then touched the top of my blouse to straighten it.

"Don't touch her." Leo moved to the bridge beside me and fired a death ray at Jeremy.

Undeterred, Jeremy didn't budge. "I'm not *touching* your girlfriend. I'm honoring the artist. An Evelyn Sinclair photograph must teeter on the edge of darkness and light. I can't capture her shadow without moving her into the light."

He pointed to our shadows stretching across the hallowed ground, indignant he had to explain the elements of photography to a nonartist. Jeremy turned his attention back to me. "Do I have your permission to adjust you for one last shot?"

I glanced down at our shadows, intermingling along the hallowed ground. I understood Leo's protective nature, but I also knew Jeremy was just doing his job, so I gave him my approval. Leo seemed annoyed but moved his big shadow out of the line of fire.

Jeremy swooped in and fingered the citrine pendant around my neck. He repositioned it so it was taut against my throat. He straightened the buttons on my blouse and lifted my chin toward the light. "Now you're perfect."

He snapped one final picture, staying true to his broody artist persona. The only thing that jumped out as unusual was that he didn't ask me what had happened to my hand. Maybe Gibson had given him a heads-up, or maybe he didn't care.

Once Jeremy took the last photo, Leo interlaced his fingers with mine and got me the hell away from him and out of the cemetery.

FAKE GIRLFRIEND—LEO

AFTER THE PHOTO SHOOT, WE WENT BACK TO MY PLACE TO GET back to work.

First, I reviewed her profile from the Armstrong Agency and asked her about the men she dated. "Have you broken any hearts? Ever been on a date with anyone more than once? How many wanted to see you again, but you turned them down?"

There was no love connection with any of the rich guys. She never went on a second date with any of them except for one—Tomas, that prick that made her feel uncomfortable on their dinner date at the gallery. After Evelyn had rejected him and gone home with me, the Brazilian billionaire never contacted her again—but he was on my radar.

My team had compiled a list of suspects from Erin and Sydney's case and wanted to see if Evelyn recognized any of the men. "Have you seen any of these guys at Marlins, hanging around the coffee shop, on your commute to work..."

As she studied the pictures, my phone buzzed with a string of texts bombarding it. After checking the first three or four, I realized I was in trouble. I had become the target of an explosive group text with my family over my noncommittal "maybe" response to the invitation to my nonna's birthday party.

I skimmed through the messages and set my phone on the table. When I looked up, Evelyn was watching me. My annoyance must've been evident because she seemed alarmed by my frustration.

"What's wrong? Did the killer strike again?"

I held up my hands apologetically, regretful my family drama had spilled over to my witness. "Nothing like that. Everything is fine. It's a family thing." Evelyn's concern was still evident in her body language, so I elaborated. "I have four sisters."

I figured that statement alone should've cleared up the confusion, but Evelyn's worry lines deepened. "Do they need you? Are they asking for your help? I can go to the guest room if you need privacy to call them back."

My sisters were always riding me about something. They never cut me slack when I had a tough case that required my undivided attention. Never let me off the hook when they decided I was neglecting my family duties. Never bought the excuse of "I'm working" when I failed to reply to their nonurgent texts.

I loved my sisters, but they needed to stand down and let me run my own life. I couldn't count the number of times I had to explain to my family that killers didn't give a shit about birthday parties. No killer had ever consulted my social calendar before committing murder.

I scratched the back of my neck and let out a sigh. "Actually, there is something you can do for me." I glanced at my phone as my sisters' texts scrolled across the screen.

Evelyn sat at the edge of her seat. "Anything. Name it."

Her eagerness to help was a relief, but she had no idea

what she was getting herself into. "I have a *thing* I have to go to this afternoon. I can't get out of it, so I need you to come with me."

"What? Like a funeral?"

I laughed at the idea that my reaction to my family's texts led her to believe that someone had died. "No. Nothing that bad. It's my nonna's seventieth birthday. My family is throwing a party for her at my mother's house."

Evelyn glared at me in astonishment. "That sounds amazing. Why are you acting like spending time with your family is some form of torture?"

To an outsider, I understood why she didn't get it. Unfortunately for her, she would soon figure out why I didn't want to involve her. "You're right. I'm blessed to have a big, loving family. It's just that—it's *complicated*."

Evelyn had pulled her hair up into a messy bun. A couple of her long wavy strands had fallen out, giving her a perfectly imperfect casual style. She'd had me twisted up since she shared her sexual fantasy with me at the cemetery. Since then, playing out her fantasy kept rising to the forefront of my mind.

"Detective?" Evelyn lifted an eyebrow, questioning why I was staring at her.

I caved and filled her in on the problem. "We're working undercover and need to keep up the pretense that we are a happy couple. I can't tell anyone, not even my family, the truth about our relationship. I don't want to disappoint my mother when I introduce you as my *girlfriend*."

"Oh." She lowered her gaze to the coffee table, then picked up an empty teacup and a plate of cookies she'd been noshing on and carried the dirty dishes into the kitchen.

Whatever she thought she had figured out was obviously troubling her. I followed her and watched her load the plates into the dishwasher. Her lips were drawn tight, and she seemed wounded by my remarks.

"What's wrong?"

She pulled the hair tie out and ran her fingers through her locks to fix her messy hair. "Nothing. I get it now. I'll stay here while you go to the party. I don't want to embarrass you in front of your family."

I lifted my hands incredulously. "What does that mean?"

"Obviously, I'm not your type."

I felt like a jerk for giving Evelyn the wrong impression. My family would love her. She was intelligent, funny, and successful, not to mention the most alluring woman I've ever met. If my mother met her, she'd never let me hear the end of it once we "broke up" after the investigation was over.

"That's what you think?"

She crossed her arms like a shield over her heart. "I've seen the type of girls you date." She nodded at the line of photos on the shelves. "I'm nothing like them. I'm not the false eyelashes, heavy makeup, big-haired, push-up bra kind of woman you normally find attractive."

"And you think that's a bad thing?" Damn, that felt like a punch in the gut. True. I did like a certain type, but Evelyn was unique in a way that was attractive on all cylinders.

Instead of calling her out for her shallow depiction of my character—or pointing out that the women in the photos were my sisters—I switched to offense.

"Speaking of wrong types, I'm not exactly your perfect match either." I crossed my arms and tossed her an accusatory glare, waiting for her to admit how she would never date a guy like me in the real world.

Evelyn gave me an incredulous scoff, eyeing me suspiciously as if I were joking. But when the sting of my accusation hit the mark, her jaw dropped when she understood what part of me I was referring to—my bank account.

"You think I dated the Armstrong guys because they're rich? Like, I'm some gold digger out to snag a billionaire. Recheck my file, Detective, I have plenty—" Once Evelyn started chewing me out, she caught herself and clamped her mouth shut.

The thing I noticed about Evelyn was that she was nonconfrontational. When she felt backed into a corner, she put up her walls and shut me out. Her family had never given her the benefit of the doubt and wrote her off as crazy.

Those wounds must've run deep, and Evelyn would take a sucker punch rather than try to defend herself. I didn't know what *Lauren* was like before the accident, but Evelyn was a lone wolf who steered away from conflict.

Even when she had faced the harassment of her stalker, she never reached out to anyone, including me, for help. Her dating profile showed that she wasn't looking for a workingman like me. Still, her huffy body language suggested I was way off the mark.

Before I could issue an apology, Evelyn stormed out of the kitchen. "Don't worry about me. I'll be fine here. You deserve a break from the case to celebrate with your family."

Instead of letting her run upstairs, thinking the worst, I placed a gentle hand on her shoulder, inviting her to hear me out. She turned to face me. When I met her wounded expression, I hated myself for putting her in a position where she had to defend herself.

"I'm sorry for jumping to the wrong conclusion. I shouldn't have gone there."

"It's okay."

"No, it's not."

"You're right," she said. "You're a complete jackass." Evelyn gave me a wry smile, giving me hope that I hadn't completely ruined my working relationship with my star witness.

"You wouldn't believe how many times I've heard that from the women I hang out with." After we shared a good-natured laugh, I owed it to Evelyn to tell her the truth. "I've never brought a woman home to meet my family. I've had a lot of relationships but never serious enough to take the next step."

Evelyn seemed surprised by my admission.

"Bringing you to the party says something, you know?"

"I totally get it. Like I said, I'm happy to stay—"

"It's not what you think," I assured her. "The problem is, my family will love you, Evelyn. And when the case is solved, and our fake relationship goes through its fake breakup, my family will never let me hear the end of it. They'll torment me for all of eternity for letting you go."

Evelyn's cheeks flushed, and she turned away to avoid my gaze. I had never been so forward on a personal level with a witness and needed to remember my job came first. But we were working undercover, and my job description did revolve around my fake relationship with the edgy and artistic Evelyn Sinclair.

I grabbed my phone, still vibrating with texts, and flipped the script on my annoying sisters. "Will you please go to the party with me? I'm in enough trouble already."

Evelyn laughed when I showed her the messages blowing up my phone. "Sure. Your family seems great. They only torment you because they love you."

"Good. Let's give them something to squawk about." I pulled Evelyn in for a hug and snapped a selfie just as I planted a kiss on her cheek. When we examined the picture, we busted out laughing. Just before I took the picture, when my lips touched her cheek, she scrunched her face and grimaced as if recoiling from my embrace.

Evelyn shoved me in the chest. "Do not send that! I wasn't ready. Your sisters will think I'm a prude."

"It's perfect. They'll appreciate your honesty." I sent the photo to the group text along with the message, "Evelyn and I will be there!"

Evelyn shot me a chastising look, but her lips were still curled into a grin. Although I wasn't thrilled about lying to my family, I was looking forward to spending some down-time with my fake girlfriend and loving family for a few hours.

DEVILISH—EVELYN

THUNDER RUMBLED, AND LIGHTNING LIT UP THE SKY ON THE way to the birthday party.

I loved the elemental energy of storms and the melodic sound of the windshield wipers clearing the rain. If it weren't for the fact that my life was in danger, I would've camped out at my studio and pulled an all-nighter.

Thunder awakened my creativity and served as a muse for my art. Rather than lamenting my injured hand, I focused on my budding feelings for Detective Ricci. The last few days had gone by at a dizzying pace, and I realized my feelings toward my handsome bodyguard were sliding into dangerous territory.

There was no denying the attraction between us. On the day we met, before I knew a single thing about him, I had found the sexy and mysterious man in the coffee shop incredibly attractive.

Once I'd tangled myself up in Detective Ricci's murder investigation, I pushed those feelings aside. Now that we had spent so much time together, I allowed myself to consider the what-ifs. Once the killer was caught, Leo and I would no longer be working together.

He'd rushed to judgment about my preference for rich guys. It wasn't money that I found attractive. The strong, driven, take-charge characteristic of successful alpha men lured me in.

That personality trait also described Leo, the domineering detective. I didn't need fancy wine and trendy dinners to sway my decision on whether or not there was a potential love connection. All the men I'd met through the agency were attractive and successful, but none of them made my heart pound like Leo did.

If I'd met him on one of my fancy dinner dates, the heat of our attraction would've burned the place down.

"Where did we meet?"

I snapped out of my lusty daydream and faced Leo. "What are you talking about?"

Leo lifted his eyebrows. "My family is going to want details about how we met. We need to get our stories straight. Are you planning on going with the coffee shop story?"

He was right. If we were going to pretend to be a couple, we had to be on the same page about the basics. "Sure. We met at the coffee shop."

Leo tipped his hand. "What happened at the coffee shop?"

"I was minding my own business, sipping my coffee, innocently sketching when you approached my table and interrogated me about my drawing."

Leo stared at me, unsure if I was making a joke or if that was my impression of our meeting. "Let's just say we met in line."

Back to all-business detective mode.

"What happened to your hand?"

I didn't know if Leo hailed from a long line of blue

bloods, but he was determined to grill me about the details of our relationship as if we were preparing to go in front of a jury.

"Uh, I got drunk and fell off a barstool?" I cracked up at my self-deprecating injury report.

"Classy. I have wonderful taste in women. My mother will be so proud."

I waved off my smart-ass answer and assured him I would devise a suitable accident that didn't involve alcohol, drugs, or bad guys. Then it was my turn to ask a question. "What *level* are we at in our relationship?"

"What level? You mean like on an intimacy scale?" Leo had that ornery grin I found so annoyingly sexy. "I seriously doubt our imaginary sex life will come up in conversation. Why do you ask?"

"It matters because I need to know how to behave around your family. Have we just started dating? Are we madly in love? Do I stay at your place, or do you stay at mine?"

"That depends. Are you going to flinch if I try to kiss you again?"

"I didn't flinch because you kissed me." I aimed my finger at him. "You startled me. Give me a heads-up next time instead of coming in hot like you did."

"A warning? You want me to tell you when I'm going to kiss you? That's lame, Evelyn. Maybe you should expect a kiss from your man. Shouldn't be such a surprise."

I twisted my lips and turned away to hide my embarrassment as we pulled into his mother's driveway. Leo put the car in park and turned off the engine. "Wait here."

I was accustomed to the idea that Leo wanted me to wait for him to come to my side before getting out of his car for safety reasons. When he came around and opened the door, he picked up my hand as I slid out of the Charger and then blocked me before allowing me to pass.

I glanced around, worried someone had followed us or Leo had spotted someone suspicious lurking around his house. But when his gaze was fixated on mine, my heart pounded—but not from impending danger.

Leo tugged on the belt of my coat and drew me toward him. He slid his finger along my jawline and lifted my chin. Never taking his eyes off mine.

My stomach fluttered with nervous excitement. No one was around to see us. His alluring gaze and seductive movements were of his own volition. He was making a move because he wanted to. Not because we were working undercover. He leaned in close. My lips parted in anticipation of his kiss.

When he was so close that I could feel his breath on my cheek, he whispered, "You've been warned, Evelyn." He tossed me a devilish grin as he placed his arm around me and escorted me up the stairs to his mother's front door.

I was thankful the air was chilly enough to cool me down from my almost kiss with Detective Ricci.

THE BUZZ—LEO

Evelyn kept her paranormal gift a secret and only admitted to seeing ghosts in her dreams. I knew that. I wasn't worried she would *sense a presence* and start drawing the spirit of my dearly departed father or any of my great aunts and uncles we'd lost over the years.

I also wasn't worried that she'd blurt out a word like *walleye* and question my family about what it meant. I was a seasoned interrogator, and I had to drag the information out of her. I wasn't worried about anything Evelyn would say. She was too considerate and self-aware to upset my family with her supernatural talent.

What concerned me were the questions my family would inevitably ask. *Where are you from? Do your parents live close by? Do you have any siblings?* Any mention of Evelyn's past or her estranged family had rattled her. I didn't want my family outing to turn into something that made her uncomfortable.

"You ready for this?" I squeezed Evelyn's hand as we pushed past the party streamers and balloons that decorated the front porch. There was a custom-designed happy birthday banner strewn across the doorway featuring a much younger picture of my grandmother as a teenager.

Celebrations were a big deal in my family. Evelyn's complexion glowed as she admired the thoughtful decorations in honor of our beloved nonna.

"You have nothing to worry about, Detective—I mean, *Leo*." She corrected herself, smiling at me as if we were sharing a private joke. "No ghost stories. I promise."

I figured she'd be nervous after I'd depicted my sisters as a coven of nosy witches. Still, Evelyn breezed into my mother's house with the confident stride of the cool and edgy artist that had taken my breath away in the coffee shop.

The living room was packed with our collective friends and family, handmade cards and gifts, and a pile of kids' shoes and winter coats dumped by the front door. The scent of freshly baked bread and Sunday gravy greeted us before all heads turned to me and my date.

"Put down your drugs and guns, guys! Chicago PD is in the house," my brother-in-law Nix yelled. He held up his hands in mock surrender, then laughed at his lame joke as he reeled me in for a hug.

"Hey, Nix. How's it going?"

"Can't complain." He slapped me on the back and then turned his attention to my date. "Hey, Evelyn, good to meet you. I thought my wife was bullshitting me when she said Leo had a girlfriend."

Evelyn laughed, enjoying Nix's boisterous sense of humor.

I made introductions to everyone within earshot. My sisters Etta and Tori bounded down the stairs like it was Christmas morning and greeted me like I'd just returned from a tour of duty on the moon. It had only been two weeks since I'd joined the last gathering, but I missed them too. I kissed their cheeks and wrapped them in a bear hug.

Etta was the more outgoing of the two and was the first to greet Evelyn. She gave her a once-over, starting from her tall leather boots, then moving up to her figure-flattering jeans, curve-hugging black top, and then to her artsy one-of-a-kind scarf.

"Love your scarf," Etta said.

Evelyn's latest design was a committee of vultures. The background was a rich emerald green that made the birds' purple, black, and gray colors pop. At first glance, the pattern appeared to be flowers. On closer inspection, the details of the harbingers of death were fantastically representative of Evelyn's macabre style.

Perfect choice for my grandmother's seventieth birthday party.

"Etta, Tori, this is Evelyn."

My sisters opened their arms and greeted my new girl-friend like family. I had pre-introduced her via text, sending photos of her gallery, media coverage, and her picture on the cover of the Windy City Beat.

Evelyn's social media personality shined with artsy street shots of pigeons taking flight at dawn, ghostly shadows of commuters cast on the sidewalk, and her trademark sketches like the one she had drawn of me at the coffee shop.

"It's so great to meet you both!" Evelyn smiled. "Leo never stops talking about you."

"Same," Tori said. "Your artwork is so cool. I can't wait for the Final Friday Gallery Walk."

Evelyn glanced up at me, surprised my sisters knew so much about her. "You're coming to the opening?"

"Of course," Tori said. "The whole family will be there."

"Wouldn't miss it." Etta knocked into my shoulder. "It's about time my brother did something cool other than work."

After the buzz of the introductions subsided, I steered Evelyn into the kitchen to meet the rest of the family. Mom was at the stove, stirring sauce, with her apron on and a dish towel slung over her shoulder. Her passion was cooking and feeding the people she loved and cared about in our tight-knit community.

Her salt-and-pepper hair was pinned back behind her ears, and she had on all her good jewelry that she kept in a drawer and only wore for special occasions.

When she glanced up and saw me with Evelyn on my arm, she set down her wooden spoon, dried her hands, and rushed over to welcome us. Whenever I came home, Mom's eyes glistened with relief. My job was dangerous, and it was hard on her knowing that every day I served my community, I might not make it to the end of my watch.

She needed to hear my voice every single day. No matter how exhausted or frustrated, or heartbroken I was after a rough day, I always made time to call my mom and tell her I loved her. As Mom came at me with her arms open, her gaze never left mine.

I would always be her baby. My badge, body armor, or a locker full of weapons would never change her vision of me as her little boy.

Mom planted a big one on my lips and clutched my shoulders as if she could hold me hostage and never let me out of her kitchen again. She spoke to me in Italian, thanking Mother Mary for bringing me home safely and calling me by my pet name, Patatino, which meant little potato.

I responded in kind, then cut the show of affection off and introduced her to Evelyn. Mom peeled her watery eyes away from mine and focused on the only woman I'd ever deemed special enough to bring into her house.

"Evelyn, this is my mom, Silvia." I turned my attention to Evelyn, who was drinking in the adoration and affection Mom was showering on me. It was unimaginable that Evelyn's once happy family had demonized her to the point she had to change her name, start over in a new city, and block them out of her life.

After knowing her situation, I hated that I was one of the people who hurt her the way her family had. I still didn't understand how the ghost of Sydney Reynolds was feeding her clues about the killer, but I was a detective. I would figure it out.

What I did know was that Evelyn wasn't crazy. She wasn't looking for attention by inserting herself into my investigation. She had stuck her neck out and ended up in the ER to help solve her friend's murder.

"It's a pleasure to meet you, Mrs. Ricci." Evelyn extended her non-busted-up hand to my mother and offered a polite handshake.

Mom opted for a greeting more her style and reeled Evelyn in for a hug, complete with kisses on both cheeks. We didn't do handshakes in my family. If you were a guest in my mother's house, you were special enough to skip the formalities.

"Where have you been, Evelyn? We've been waiting for you." Mom tossed me a wink. Her particular way of letting me know she approved of my girlfriend.

Evelyn may not have caught the subtleness of Mom's jab about me taking too long to find someone special. Still, I felt a tug of guilt that I would soon break Mom's heart when I had to tell her Evelyn and I were no longer together.

The more time I spent with Evelyn, the more I realized how hard it would be to let her go.

FALLING—EVELYN

It had been six years since I'd attended a family birthday party. I was Lauren then. The happy, overachieving high school senior with a bright future and a six-figure college tuition fund.

I didn't miss my family. The love I'd once felt for them was dead and gone. I did, however, miss having a family. And with Leo's outgoing, fun-loving, loud, and affectionate brood, Nonna's birthday party was the greatest gathering I had ever been blessed to be a part of.

Being together was effortless for the extended Ricci family.

There were folding tables in the living room to accommodate the growing number of guests. Leo's friend, Officer Santoni, was hanging out at one of the tables with a rowdy crew of cohorts heavily invested in a card game.

A stack of cash was pushed into the center of the table, along with beer cans and paper plates loaded with sandwiches, chips and dips. While playing poker, a few expletives were exchanged, followed by groans of defeat and boisterous laughter as Santoni cracked jokes aimed at his buddies.

Nonna, donning a glittery princess crown and a strand of pearls, was seated at the breakfast nook surrounded by Leo's other two sisters, Daniella and Audrey, and their young children.

While the kids were snacking from the trays of home-cooked food and drawing pictures for their beloved great-grandmother, the kitchen buzzed with conversation, good-natured teasing, and laughter.

Leo's family lovefest was on a level I had never experienced. Silvia's house was packed with multiple generations of kids, grandchildren, her mother and siblings, neighbors, friends from church, her book club besties, and more extended family members than I could keep straight.

Leo may have thought his sisters were annoying, but I would give anything to be a part of the unconditional love reverberating off the walls.

And that wasn't even the best part. I got to experience Nonna's special day cuddled in the handsome detective's strong arms. We were gathered around the kitchen island while Silvia and her helpers set out the appetizer course.

"Try these." Leo slid a plate of focaccia loaded with tomatoes, olives, and parmesan cheese toward me.

The scent of rosemary and savory spices made my mouth water before I sampled a slice. When I took a bite of the soft and crunchy appetizer, I let out an *mmm* of satisfaction. Leo tossed me a sultry smile as I swallowed and touched my hand when he asked if I wanted a beer to chase it down.

After he grabbed a couple of cold ones, he raised his glass and offered a salute. We clinked bottles and sipped. Leo wrapped his arm around my waist and rested his hand on my hip as Silvia asked the inevitable question, "Where did the two of you meet?" Her gaze shifted between us, not asking one of us in particular.

"You tell the story, sweetheart."

I caught a glimpse of his devilish grin as he sipped his beer. I would've rather had him tell the story for his family instead of me, but I wasn't about to back down from an opportunity to roast the good detective.

"We met by chance a few weeks ago. I was at my favorite coffee shop, sipping a cappuccino and sketching, the way I start every day. But this particular morning, I made the mistake of sketching the wrong guy. Apparently, not everyone appreciates having their picture drawn."

"Oh, yeah? Who was that?" Leo's brother-in-law teased, bringing a round of laughter from the room.

"What did he do when he caught you?" Silvia asked, clutching the heart-shaped locket around her neck. She waited anxiously, as if she were fully engaged in a TV crime drama.

"Well, uh..." I passed the torch to Leo, giving him the chance to finish the story.

He took a long swig of beer as his family egged him on. "So, I see this gorgeous woman sitting by herself. I checked the hand—no ring. I think maybe I should go talk to her. As I sat there coming up with a conversation starter, I saw my face sketched on her pad of paper. She gave me the perfect opening."

Silvia laughed as she beamed at her son. Nix popped the cap off another beer and handed it to his mother-in-law, ensuring she had a cold one while she enjoyed the story.

"What did you think when Leo approached you? What did he say when he asked you out?" Silvia asked.

Leo lifted an eyebrow and tossed the story back to me. "Well," I said. "Leo didn't actually ask me out."

"Loser!" Nix coughed.

"Well? What happened?" Silvia's gaze bounced between us.

"I asked *him* out." I covered my face with my scarf to hide my embarrassment.

"To an art show," Leo said. "*Her* art show."

"Did you go?" Leo's mom asked.

"Yeah. I went." Leo shot a smile my way, then turned to his mother. "Wait until you see her work, Mom. Evelyn is crazy talented."

My cheeks warmed with embarrassment as Leo pulled up my website on his phone and passed it to his mother. He wrapped his arm around me and slid his hand down my side, gliding down the curve of my hips.

The thought of being the object of Leo's desire excited me. The detective and I may not have agreed on much, but there was no denying the mutual attraction. Leo was too professional to act on his desires, and I didn't want to be just another one-night stand.

If there was a path for us to become more than just a passing fling, I would jump at the chance to spend more time with Leo, so we could spend time together under better, less life-endangering circumstances.

Saying goodbye when the murderer was behind bars would be difficult enough. If we let our desires cloud our judgment during this fake couple thing, it would only make the breakup more difficult. That didn't mean I couldn't play my part while we were working undercover and enjoy my role as his girlfriend.

With Leo's hand still on my waist, I curled into him and slid my finger around his belt loop. Leo met my gaze, questioning my motive. I gave the leather a little tug to let him know exactly what I was thinking.

Leo's eyes lit up, intrigued by my naughty gesture.

I laughed at our private joke, but Leo wouldn't let me off the hook. He bent down and gave me a peck on the lips. It was a sweet, spur-of-the-moment kiss, but the sensation of his lips on mine spread ripples of excitement through my core.

Leo tossed me a sweet smile he had never shown me before. His eyes were bright and playful, a stark contrast to the dark and broody demeanor he displayed when he was in detective mode. I mirrored his smile and rubbed the back of my hand against his cheek. "You didn't shave today, babe." I teased my fingers along his jawline. "You're going to give me beard burn," I whispered.

"You can handle it, gorgeous," he whispered back. He snaked his hand up my back and gently wove his fingers through my hair at the nape of my neck. In response, I lifted my chin and closed my eyes as Leo bent down and kissed me.

Lost in the moment, our kiss ranked a little sloppy in front of his mother. Leo's family chided him with a barrage of good-natured heckling. His mother swished the dish towel at us playfully as she laughed.

When Leo and I ended our impromptu kiss, he wrapped his arms around me from behind and squeezed me as we noshed and sipped our drinks. While I thought Leo and I were just playing our part, my feelings for him were no longer an act.

As much as I had tried to resist, I was falling for Leo.

AFTERGLOW—LEO

THE CONVERSATION NEVER MISSED A BEAT ON THE DRIVE HOME from Mom's. We talked about everything from music to dive bars to street art and everything in between. I couldn't remember a time I'd felt so happy and relaxed with a woman outside my family.

Evelyn asked if we could drop by her apartment to pick up a few things. I waited in the living room while she went to her bedroom to pack what she needed and took a moment to respond to the barrage of texts from my friends and family.

The Ricci inner circle verdict had been unanimous: *Everyone loves Evelyn.*

As I played back the day, holding Evelyn in my arms, laughing, joking around with my buddies, the impromptu kiss we shared in my mother's kitchen... what I was feeling for Evelyn wasn't a game. I was falling hard for the one person on this earth I couldn't figure out.

As I tapped on my phone, Evelyn's door creaked open, and she stepped into view. I glanced up and froze like a wild animal that had just heard a branch snap.

Holy hell.

Evelyn had changed into a silky nightgown with a sheer lace bustline. The moonlight from the window illuminated her silhouette, giving me a glimpse of her ample breasts, trim waistline, and the shapely curve of her hips.

She locked her gaze on mine and met me at the couch, standing before me like a goddess. "Leo." She took my hand and placed it on her hip. I ran my fingers along her curves and groaned from the excitement building inside.

God, the sensation of the silky nightgown gliding across her warm skin gave me an erotic rush of passion that lured me to her.

"Want to pretend to be my boyfriend in my bedroom?" Evelyn's lips curled into a sultry smile as she tugged on my arm, coaxing me off the couch. My gaze moved to her breasts and through the sheer fabric. I longed to smooth my hands over her soft skin and savor the sweetness of her femininity.

A thousand reasons why I should reject Evelyn raced through my mind. I'd made many mistakes in my life, but I wasn't about to add turning down a passionate evening with my dream woman to my list of regrets.

"I hope you have a lot of energy, babe. I can pretend all night." I wrapped her in my arms and pulled her close as I kissed her deeply. Her body melted into mine. She groaned with excitement as I squeezed her ass while she ground against me. Every kiss with Evelyn had been fantastic, but this time around, our passion had reached a new level.

Our intimate movements were in sync, as if our bodies were designed to fit together. Evelyn slid her hands up and tugged at my shirt. I stripped it off as if it was on fire and tossed it on the sofa. Her hardened nipples gliding against my bare chest sent a rush of blood down there.

I slid my tongue inside her mouth, inhaling her scent, then folded her into my arms and carried her into her bedroom. I laid her down on top of a leopard print throw blanket and slid the thin straps of her nightgown down her shoulders and exposed her breasts.

"God, Evelyn. Your body." I kicked off my shoes and slid down my pants. My cock sprung up, and Evelyn spread her legs seductively, inviting me to join her on the bed.

I pressed my body on top of hers and trailed my tongue down her neck. I rubbed her breasts as I brought each of them into my mouth, one at a time, and sucked and swirled my tongue around her nipples.

Evelyn arched her back and groaned with pleasure as I savored her full bosom and gave her youthful, gorgeous body all my attention. I slid my finger between her legs and massaged her slowly to excite her.

"Leo," she groaned. "What are you doing to me?" She swiveled her hips in sync with my touch, encouraging me to please her.

I removed her nightgown, slid my tongue down her toned abs, lifted her knees, and kissed her between the legs. I savored her sweetness as Evelyn ran her hands through my hair and pulled gently as we rocked in an erotic rhythm.

She panted with pleasure as I pleased her and ran her fingers through my hair as she reacted to my touch. Her taste, the scent of her body, her sexy moans had me rock hard and excited to bring her to climax.

I looked up at my gorgeous fake girlfriend and nearly blew when I saw her watching me as I pleased her. I lashed my tongue over the zone and massaged her until the intensity peaked, and I brought her to orgasm.

Evelyn groaned a throaty exhale as her body peaked with pleasure. I savored her sweet release until her arms dropped to the side as she recovered from her ecstasy.

"Dammit, Leo. God, you're amazing."

I had an insatiable appetite for foreplay, especially when

it came to oral pleasure. Her taste drove me wild, and I was ready to get inside her.

I was creative in the bedroom and had some ideas about all those fluffy pillows Evelyn surrounded herself with. Still, I needed to know what she was in the mood for.

I was a big guy in every sense of the word. If Evelyn wanted to take a smooth and sensual course our first time, I would take my time and make love to her, slow and easy. But if she wanted a wild and passionate ride, I was ready to give her that, too.

I grabbed one of the fluffy fur pillows Evelyn surrounded herself with and tucked it behind her head. I lay beside her and smoothed her hair out of her face, drinking in her sultry afterglow. Evelyn wrapped her fingers around my length and stroked me, kicking my anticipation of penetrating my creative lover into overdrive.

"Are you ready for me, Evelyn?"

She pulled me on top of her and wrapped her legs around me, giving me the answer I needed. Our bodies were ready for each other, and I wasted no time pushing inside her. Evelyn gasped from the sensation of my size, so I thrust slowly at first to let her body adjust.

"Are you alright?" I whispered.

"Yeah. I was just shocked." She scratched her nails down my back and moved her body in sync with mine.

"I can stop if you want me to," I said.

"No. I like it." She kissed me deeply as she moaned, enjoying my slow and sensual style of lovemaking. I slid in and out gently to get her wet and ready for the next round.

"I don't want this to be our only time, Evelyn."

She offered a gentle smile. "If you were my boyfriend, I would never let you out of bed."

Damn. She was the sexiest woman I had ever met. "Is that what you want? You want me to be your boyfriend?"

Evelyn's eyes lit up. "I would love to be your real girl-friend, Detective."

Finally, the words I wanted to hear. I was elated we got our second chance, plus I was so turned on by my new real girlfriend that my excitement was reaching the next level.

"Are you ready for a wild ride?"

When Evelyn answered with a smack on my ass, I grabbed the furry pillow and slid it under her hips, lifting her into the perfect position. I sat on my knees and lifted her legs as I prepared to take us there.

Her breasts bounced as I thrust harder and deeper. We were going at it so hard that her headboard banged against the wall. *To hell with her neighbors.* I grunted as our sweaty bodies slapped together as we headed to climax. Evelyn's back arched when she reached climax, moaning with plea-sure. Now that I had pleased her, I was ready to go. I held her hips and released into the condom.

My sweat dripped down on Evelyn as we savored the best sex of our lives. I slid out of her and crashed beside her on the bed. She rolled on her side and faced me. Her skin was damp, and her complexion glowed from our wild first time.

We cuddled as we came down from our sexual high. I took her hands and folded them into my heart. "I love you, Evelyn."

She rested her head on my shoulder. "I love you, too, Leo."

UNDERCOVER—LEO

My phone rang in the middle of the night.

That was never a good sign, especially in my line of work. When I got a call before dawn, it usually meant someone had been abducted or murdered. I lifted my phone off Evelyn's nightstand and answered the call.

It was Talia, calling to inform me our task force had uncovered a crucial connection between the Windy City Stalker's victims, Erin and Sydney. Both women had dined at Casa Italia.

Sydney and Vaughn had gone there on their first date, and Erin and her fiancé had gotten engaged there. "We need to find out if Evelyn has ever been to that restaurant," Talia said.

"Hang on." I put the phone on mute. Evelyn had fallen asleep on my chest. I touched her shoulder and rocked her gently. "Sweetheart, wake up."

"What?" She lifted her head and blinked in confusion.

"I'm going to put you on speaker with Talia."

Evelyn sat up, alarmed by the urgency of the call.

"Have you ever been to Casa Italia?" Talia asked. "That expensive place downtown that overlooks the lake."

"Uh, no. I've never been there. Why?"

We couldn't discuss the case details with Evelyn, but I had an idea of how she could help us draw out her stalker. "I'll call you back, Talia."

I ended the call and clicked on the light. Evelyn rolled out of bed and snagged a robe as I slid on my pants and jumped back into my detective mindset.

"Leo, what's going on? You're scaring me."

"My team uncovered some information that could lead us to the killer, and we need your help to lure him out of hiding —but it could be dangerous." I had no right to ask her to serve as a decoy, but I knew her well enough to know that was exactly what she'd want to do. She wanted the killer locked up as much as I did. He wouldn't get any more victims, especially not Evelyn.

"I'm in. Let's get that bastard behind bars."

Damn straight. "How would you like to go on an under-cover mission with me tonight? Just the two of us—and six highly trained agents and officers hiding in plain sight."

Evelyn seemed surprised at first, then when she realized I was dead serious, her lips curled into a smile. "Chez Italia?"

"Only the best for my girl—and star witness in my murder investigation."

"Let's get to work, partner."

While I was pleased Evelyn was willing to help, I didn't sleep another wink that night. The problem, my gut was telling me I was making a terrible mistake.

FRISKY—LEO

We arrived at Chez Italia in a borrowed classic red Ferrari like the one Tom Selleck drove in the *Magnum P.I.* series. The purr of an exotic sports car turned heads as I rolled up to the valet.

I was proud to be a working-class man in the city I loved, but I didn't mind playing the part of a rich guy with fancy toys for the night as long as Evelyn was along for the ride. When my knockout girlfriend stepped out of the car, all the attention shifted to her.

Her long hair was styled in big loose waves. She wore a nude sweater dress that skimmed her curves and landed just above her knees, not revealing too much or too little skin, but giving every man within a mile of The Loop something to fantasize about.

She had ditched her playful and artsy style and slid into dangerously sexy territory as she owned her role as the most desirable bachelorette in the city. Everything about Evelyn, from her smoky eye makeup to her soft-pink lips to her classy wardrobe, oozed sex appeal.

I rested my hand on the small of her back as we cruised

inside the hotel and took the elevator to the expensive and exclusive restaurant on the top floor. Heads turned as the maître d' escorted us through the dining room. We strolled past a solo violinist wearing a tux and into a next-level seating area complete with glowing candelabras, dimly lit pendant lights, and a built-in wine cellar that displayed the restaurant's collection of its most expensive vino.

Even though I was working undercover to catch a killer, I was incredibly turned on, gliding beside the sexy woman I was meant to protect. I tried to focus on the job at hand, but memories of last night replayed in my mind.

Her taste. Her touch. Her sultry voice when she panted my name.

I had to stay focused and professional. The killer could be in the room with us now, but I'd bet my pension Evelyn wasn't wearing panties under that dress. I tried to kick back the sexual beast inside me that longed to touch her bare skin, kiss her soft lips, and sink into her luscious body under the sheets, but hell—*I'm still a man.*

"As you requested, Mr. Ricci." The host swept his arm forward as if presenting a gift. "The most gorgeous view in the house for you and your lovely companion."

The table was set with a crisp white tablecloth, polished silver dinnerware, and decorated with a single white votive candle and a small collection of flowers and greenery in a clear glass vase. I'd been to nice restaurants before, but this place took opulence and excess to a new level.

"*Grazie. La vista e magnifica,*" I responded in Italian, acknowledging his effort.

Evelyn's gaze shot to mine. She licked her lips seductively as our host pulled out her chair and helped her into her seat.

Note to self: Speak in Italian next time I get her into bed.

After the attack, Evelyn had given the Armstrong Agency permission to turn over her file and a list of men she'd dated through the service. I read every word and knew the type of man she found attractive.

She wanted intelligent, physically strong men with healthy egos, and had specifically ranked Italian good looks as a bonus.

It went without saying that all the men who got an introduction to Evelyn were loaded. The minimum net worth to be considered by the agency was over a million. Still, since Evelyn was such a desirable candidate, her arranged dates had all reached billionaire status.

Once seated, the service staff poured bottled water and asked for our drink order.

I shifted my gaze to my date. "We'll start with a bottle of Cristal."

Evelyn smiled as if congratulating me on my excellent taste in champagne.

When the waiter left the table, Evelyn's gaze took a lap around my body. "You look amazing in that suit, Detective." Her voice was as soft and smooth as that fucking cashmere dress hugging her curves.

"Grazie, bella."

She tossed me a flirty grin, picked up her water glass, took a long drink then glanced around the room to check out our fellow diners.

Right. We have work to do.

I followed her lead and did the same. I didn't recognize anyone, but we had a lot of curious men and women stealing glances at both of us. Our fellow patrons varied demographically, but everyone in the place had something in common. They were all dressed to impress and rich enough to chug five-hundred-dollar bottles of champagne like water.

"Recognize anyone?" I asked.

"No."

The waiter returned with a bottle of shimmering gold

bubbly. He presented it to me and announced the name scrolled across the label. I gave him a nod, and he popped it open and then poured the first round.

I lifted my champagne flute to Evelyn and initiated a toast. *"Salute."*

She clinked my glass, her eyes locked and loaded on mine. *"Salute."* As she sipped, my gorgeous date snaked her bare foot up my leg.

Christ. I inhaled sharply. My body's reaction to her touch.

Had she recognized someone in the room and laid her sex appeal on thick to piss someone off? Or was this my girl-friend being frisky on our undercover mission?

Evelyn tossed me a grin, acknowledging her power and control over my body.

This woman is going to be the death of me.

PASS—EVELYN

Our romantic dinner had been fantastic, yet uneventful on the identifying a killer front. After the pasta course, I asked if it was okay to freshen up in the powder room.

"Of course. We've got you covered." Leo stood politely when I pushed my chair back. I knew Talia, Parker, and the rest of the team were watching, so I wasn't worried about the killer coming after me. Still, my nerves were jangling at the thought that someone might be watching.

On shaky legs, I headed to the bathroom and was met midway by a waitstaff member who offered an elbow and escorted me through the dining room. He was a polite older gentleman with an adorable smile and kind eyes—definitely not my murderous stalker.

I reapplied my lipstick inside the bathroom when Talia cruised over to serve as my stand-in bodyguard.

She blended in with the upscale clientele in a black satin suit with a low-cut gold tank, flashy jewelry, and strappy stilettos. She wore a jacket to conceal her weapon, no doubt. If I hadn't known she was part of the Violent Crimes Task

Force, I would've thought she was here to celebrate a special occasion.

Talia checked under the stalls, and once she confirmed we were alone, she aimed her cell phone at me. "Look who bellied up to the bar."

Oh, shit. "He's here now?" It was Tomas, the Brazilian businessman with grabby hands.

"He's been seething since he saw you come in with Detective Heartthrob. I don't think he likes your new boyfriend. You dated that creep?"

"Twice. Well, one and a half times. He's a pig."

"Safe to say you shot him down?" Talia asked.

"Point blank."

Talia's phone buzzed from an incoming text. "Huh, interesting."

"What?"

"Your buddy is hanging out in the hallway, waiting for you to come out."

"Shit. What do I do?"

"Do whatever you want. To hell with him. You've got nothing to worry about."

I felt safe with Talia. She would plant a swift kick in Tomas's groin if he tried anything, but I hated the idea that he was waiting to confront me while I was on a date. I was sure he recognized Leo—the guy who drove me home after I abruptly ended our dinner date.

Talia left the restroom first, while I trailed behind. Before I'd made it through the hallway, Tomas called out my name.

"Hello, Tomas." I was polite but didn't want to engage in a conversation, so I tried to pass him in the hallway.

Tomas stepped in front of me so I couldn't easily squeeze past him, an intimidating gesture. He bore his menacing gaze down on me as if I had committed a crime against him. "Was it your idea to come here, or did your boyfriend choose my restaurant?"

His restaurant? As in, he *owned* Chez Italia? Shit. He had mentioned over dinner that he dabbled as a restaurateur, but he had never explicitly dropped any names. Did Leo know he owned this place and failed to share that piece of information? "Your restaurant? I had no idea. Well, I have to give props to your chef. The cacio e pepe is heavenly."

Talia paused, pretending to check her phone. I was safe with her and knew the best thing for the investigation was to keep him talking. Maybe he would say something incriminating that would help the case.

"If you don't mind, I need to return to my date. Have a wonderful—"

"I know what you are doing. You want to make me jealous so I will take you back." His gaze drifted down my body and landed on my chest. "I like women who play hard to get. Makes things more exciting in the bedroom."

Tomas was delusional if he thought I wanted anything more to do with him. "Just so we're clear, I'm not apologizing, and I didn't come here to make you jealous." I tried to move around him, but he wouldn't let me pass.

He wagged his finger at me as if scolding a naughty puppy. "I like your fire, princess. We'll do it your way. I'll take you to a nice dinner and try again."

"Try *what* again?" I was losing patience with this prick.

Tomas sneered. "I'm trying to be a gentleman to appease your feminist side. You don't have to be such a bitch. You know what I meant. Play nice, Evelyn. You'll find I'm generous with my rewards."

My body trembled, and I fidgeted nervously as Tomas took satisfaction in making me uncomfortable. The last guy I ignored had put me in the hospital and busted up my drawing hand.

Since my attack, I had been running on adrenaline, working with Leo and the team to track down the killer. I hadn't had a moment to process what had happened, and the close call I'd had in the clutches of a serial killer.

But I was tired of being afraid. My stalker had systematically found subtle ways to frighten me for weeks. While I was still unnerved, my fear bubbled over into rage. What kind of man would intentionally scare me because I bruised his ego when I turned him down?

A fucking psycho murderer pig who got off on hurting women, that's who.

Whether Tomas was my stalker or not, I had reached my boiling point with men who meant to hurt and intimidate me. Still, in the presence of a man twice my size, fear took hold and all I could do at the moment was stay silent, not wanting to provoke him.

Tomas grinned, drinking in what he perceived as obedience. He was a dominant man and savored his control over me. I needed to find my voice.

Speak.

BUFFALO—LEO

My phone buzzed with an update from my partner.

PARKER: Evelyn confronted in hallway by Tomas. Bragging he slept with her to everyone in the bar. Stand down. Talia is with her. Let's see how this plays out.

A rush of rage boiled my blood. I trusted my team. I knew no one would lay a hand on Evelyn under our watch. Still, when that asshole confronted my girlfriend, I clocked off duty as a cop and jumped back into the skin of an Italian man with four sisters who never let anyone get away with talking shit to a woman.

I stood, straightened my jacket, and casually headed to the hallway to handle the situation myself. When I saw Evelyn in the shadow of a man using his size to intimidate her, my first reaction was to solve the problem for her by shoving him against the wall.

But I wasn't a Neanderthal and had years of training on how to use my brains over my body to defuse a situation. I came up behind the asshole and was ready to strike if the situation demanded force. But as I tuned in to the conversation, it appeared Evelyn had the situation under control.

"Let me make this crystal clear, Tomas. I don't want anything to do with you. Stay away from me. Don't talk to me ever again." She aimed her finger between his eyes. "Get out of my way." Evelyn held her ground and didn't show an ounce of fear.

The problem was, he wasn't following her order. I wanted to grab him by his shirt collar and drop him to the ground, but I wanted more for Evelyn to feel empowered by her actions.

Talia gave me the stink eye for interfering when they'd assured me the situation was handled. Clearly, if Evelyn were in trouble, Talia would've dropped him. I had no doubt in her ability, but for me, it was personal. If I didn't step in, I would look like a pussy in front of everyone in the room.

"I like your fire, kitty cat. Feisty women make the chase more satisfying." I knew that prick was dreaming up all the ways he wanted to punish her for challenging his authority. The adrenaline bubbling inside me was about to turn nuclear. I didn't know how Evelyn could let that disgusting human hold her hostage by refusing to move.

Legally, it was a crime to intimidate a person using the fear of physical force or treating a person in a way that suggested they meant to harm you. I had the authority to place him under arrest. But Evelyn was a part of this undercover operation, and more importantly, I trusted her judgment. I waited for her to give me a sign, but truly, she had no training, so ultimately it was my call to make.

I couldn't stomach another second of Evelyn trying to be brave for the sake of the investigation. I was doing the city a favor by getting this misogynistic creep off the streets, but as I reached for my badge, Evelyn shot me a death ray and shook her head.

Then she narrowed her eyes at Tomas and aimed her finger at his chest. "*Buffalo.*"

Evelyn may not have understood what the word meant, but I sure as fuck did—and so did Tomas Barbosa. When Evelyn fired that kill shot, the guy backed away like she'd pulled a 9mm and pressed it to his temple.

I'd checked out Tomas after seeing him at Evelyn's the other night. Turns out, three years ago, Tomas was involved in an auto accident that killed his girlfriend. He was driving late, veered off the road, and struck a pole. She died instantly. Tomas walked away without a scratch. He had been over the blood alcohol limit and charged with manslaughter, but his lawyer got him off the hook without a trial.

The accident took place in *Buffalo*, New York.

Once the shock wore off, Tomas eyed the splint on her injured hand and gave her a mock look of pity. "Hope your finger heals okay. Wouldn't want the world to miss out on your pretty pictures."

Tomas turned and sized me up as he passed by on his way back to the bar. His eyes were hazy, and his breath reeked of hard liquor and spicy bar mix. His defenses were down, and he hadn't realized I was lurking over his shoulder.

Talia trailed Tomas as he staggered back to the bar. Her cover hadn't been blown, and I knew she and Parker would observe and report his behavior after the humiliating incident with Evelyn. Hopefully, he would keep running his mouth at the bar and be drunk enough to say something incriminating. If he was our guy, the best move was to let him run his mouth.

Evelyn shot me a triumphant smile. I almost laughed. She knew she'd put him in his place. She didn't know that was the total loss of everything the bastard owned. Intentionally or not, she threatened a man who had everything to lose and all the resources money could buy to protect his lifestyle.

But I didn't laugh. Because little messes like Evelyn were easy for a powerful man to clean up, and that could be brutal.

Her clairaudient clues could end up getting her into a lot of trouble if spoken to the wrong people.

While my girlfriend beamed with pride at her victory, a disturbing thought crossed my mind—Evelyn's gift was more dangerous than she realized.

STRAIGHT UP—EVELYN

WHEN WE RETURNED TO MY PLACE, I WAS EXHAUSTED AND ready to unwind. I tossed my purse on the table, hung up my coat, and excused myself to change out of my evening attire.

"Freeze," Leo said.

I stopped dead in my tracks, worried Leo had noticed something out of place. What if my stalker had entered my apartment while we were at dinner? What if he was in the bedroom, waiting to strike when I least expected it?

I looked over my shoulder to read Leo's expression.

The sexy devil had tossed off his suit jacket and was loosening his tie as he prowled toward me with the hungry eyes of a predator. "Put your hands over your head."

Warm ripples of pleasure pulsed in my core as my sexy and domineering boyfriend came up behind me and wrapped his arms around my waist. He pushed my hair over my shoulder and kissed my neck. "I have to check for weapons, Miss Sinclair. Don't move."

I didn't know Leo was into role-playing, but I was excited to meet his creative side in the bedroom. I craved his authority. I wanted to please him in every way imaginable. If he was in the mood for sexy games, I was ready to see what my lover had in mind.

I bit my lip as Leo's hands glided over my cashmere sweater dress's soft and fuzzy fabric. He massaged my thighs as he pressed himself against my backside, letting me know he was hard and ready to play our erotic game.

He slid up my dress and pulled it over my head, leaving me in the living room wearing nude stockings, a tiger-print bra, and a mile-high pair of stilettos. I had been fantasizing about how Leo would take me after our date.

I had imagined a hurried *"I can't wait to get you into bed"* kind of need, but I loved the slow and sensual feel of his hands rubbing me in all the right places.

The inferno of attraction had been smoking between us all night. While I loved the playful way Leo was seducing me, sliding his hand between my thighs as he sucked on my neck and whispering naughty thoughts as he unhooked my bra, my desire to have all of him was intense, and my body ached for the next round.

I tried to turn around so I could strip off his clothes, but Leo held me firmly, not ready to relinquish control. I panted with excitement as Leo guided me to the couch and bent me over the soft side of the sofa. While I was in the vulnerable position, he removed my shoes and slid my silk stockings down my legs, taking his time as he caressed my skin.

Once he stripped me naked, he brought me up to a standing position and wrapped his arms around me. He still had his pants on, but I could feel his rock-hard erection poking me in the back. "Do you like surprises, beautiful?"

His hands slid from my waist up my abs, then he cupped my breasts as he massaged me, teasing his thumbs over my nipples.

"I like the sexy kind of surprises. Are you going to put me in handcuffs, Detective?"

"When I decide to restrain you, I won't give you a warning, Miss Sinclair."

The hum of a vibrator purred in his hand as he rubbed the toy between my legs.

"Oh, wow. What are you doing to me?" The sensation of the pulses gave me an instant rush of pleasure as my body tingled excitedly.

"Oh my god. *Damn.* It feels so good." My back arched as Leo toyed with me, sliding the bullet-shaped, rubbery plaything over my wet and ready body. Leo had complete control over me. My legs stiffened as he quickened his pace, bringing me closer to orgasm.

As I panted on the way to ecstasy, Leo increased the pressure and held the vibrator in place as I came undone. As I climaxed, I leaned my head back and arched my back against his chest, wrecked from the pleasure my boyfriend had given me.

Leo was a fantastic lover, and I wanted to give him as much as he gave me. I was inexperienced, but I knew how to make a man feel good. I slid my hand down and touched him below the belt. His body tensed, and he groaned as I massaged him through the fabric of his pants.

"These need to come off." I tugged on his belt and then removed his pants. Once I had him naked, I dropped to my knees, stroked his length, and teased him with my tongue.

"Fucking hell, Evelyn. What are you doing to me, babe?"

Leo groaned, glided his fingers through my hair, and held me in place as I pleased him, rocking me gently as I brought him inside my mouth. The oral sensation of my warm and wet mouth pleasuring him brought his erection to rock-hard status.

"Evelyn…" He panted my name as I brought him out of my mouth and lashed my tongue across his head. His body tensed, and I thought he was going to blow, but instead, my sexy lover lifted me off my feet, cradled me in his arms, and carried me to my bedroom.

He laid me down on top of my covers, tossed the pillows onto the floor, and pressed his strong body on top of mine. I wrapped my legs around him, letting him know I was ready for another hot round of lovemaking.

He slid inside of me and pushed slowly as my body adjusted to the sensation of my hot Italian lover. I moved my hips and grabbed his ass, encouraging him not to hold back. Our foreplay had been mind blowing, but nothing compared to being wrapped in Leo's embrace, sweat rolling over our bodies as we synced into an erotic rhythm.

Thanks to Leo's surprise, I had already had one orgasm, and I felt another one coming. This time, from a different place deep inside me. I kneaded the muscles on Leo's back. My breathing had gotten faster, and Leo must've recognized the signs.

"Give it to me, sweetheart." Leo sat on his knees, placed a furry pillow underneath me, and grabbed my ankles. He lifted my legs and rocked me forward, moving me into an exciting new position.

I didn't think it was possible, but Leo pushed deeper inside me and thrust harder and faster as I panted his name. My breasts shook, and the headboard banged against the wall as Leo held my gaze in anticipation of my climax.

"Let go, babe. I'm coming with you."

My body tensed as I exhaled with pleasure. Leo was still going strong, thrusting as he panted on his way to orgasm. His grip tightened around my ankles, and his body stiffened as he grunted with pleasure.

After our energetic lovemaking, Leo rolled off me and ran his fingers through his sweat-soaked hair as he recovered. I lay on my back, wonderfully exhausted from our sexual high. I had never imagined my life would include a man like Leo, who accepted me and my gift.

Leo rolled on his side and met my gaze. "How are you feeling, beautiful?"

"Perfect," I said. "I love you—*and the sex*. You're incredible." I bit my lip, embarrassed I had said what I was thinking out loud.

Leo pulled me into his arms and snuggled me against his chest. "You mean everything to me, Evelyn. I love you."

As we settled in for the night, I thought about what our new normal would look like. He would still be a detective. I would still be a medium. Where were we going to land once things got back to normal?

"What is the first thing you want to do when we're free?" I asked.

"Take you out in the neighborhood. Introduce you to the people I grew up with."

"Love it," I said. "And I thought we could do something like a long weekend on the beach somewhere tropical. Frozen cocktails, hitting the waves, hanging out poolside without having to run a background check on everyone at the resort—"

"I can't really plan vacations with my work schedule, but it sounds nice. Maybe we could spend the night in a nice hotel with a pool and a tropical-themed bar when summer comes around."

That sounded tragic. Had Leo never taken a vacation? Would he never be able to have someone cover for him so he could take a couple consecutive days off? I knew he was dedicated to his badge, but he needed downtime other than drinking with his buddies for a few hours.

"Sounds nice," I said, not wanting to make a problem. Maybe he was just tense because of the situation we were facing. He didn't mean he could never have time off.

Being in Leo's arms was the most incredible feeling I had ever known. My strong and sexy man stroked me gently as I closed my eyes, grateful we had vanquished our demons and fought to make our relationship work. As I drifted to sleep, I thanked the universe for bringing us together.

GHOSTLY—EVELYN

IN MY DREAM, I MOVED TO THE WINDOW TO INVESTIGATE THE source of the taps.

I drew back the curtains, stared into the glass, and Sydney appeared over my own reflection, merging our forms into one blurred vision.

The ghost of my sweet and beautiful friend banged on the glass in a rage, ticked off at me, it seemed, for not trying harder to bring her killer to justice.

"We're trying to find out who killed you, Sydney. Give me a clue?"

Her ghostly image stared into my soul and repeated the word she'd said repeatedly since her death.

"Captiva...Captiva...Captiva..."

I touched my finger to the glass and spelled out the word in the condensation that fogged the glass. C-A-P-T-I-V-A.

"I hear you, Sydney, but I don't understand why we need to know this word. Can you help me out with another clue?"

Sydney's ghost lifted her fists in desperation and pounded on the glass. Her ghostly expression was not filled with rage, and although her features were distorted, she appeared to be pleading for help.

Something was happening in real time. If Sydney had been following her killer, perhaps she knew he was about to strike again. "Who needs help, Sydney? Give me a name?"

Sydney's mouth opened wide as she screeched the answer: *"Vaughn!"*

The clairaudient scream was so loud, she woke me from my dream. I bolted upright in bed and panted to catch my breath.

Leo grasped my shoulders and stared into my eyes. "Evelyn? Are you alright? You were having a nightmare and wouldn't wake up."

"Sydney," I panted. "She's upset." I hopped out of bed and slid on a robe, but before I could make it to the living room to grab my sketchbook, my cell vibrated on the nightstand.

I glanced at the clock: 3:07 a.m.

Leo slid out of bed and stood beside me as I checked the screen.

VAUGHN REYNOLDS: I'm going to kill again.

I gasped when I read the message, stunned by Vaughn's message. I looked at Leo to gauge his reaction, then shot my gaze back to the screen as a string of texts bombarded my phone.

VAUGHN REYNOLDS: I can't live with the guilt. I'm going to end this.

VAUGHN REYNOLDS: There are two different versions of me. One is the true me, and the other is a monster. I can't control him. He takes what he wants and leaves me to clean up his messes. Sydney found out. She had to die.

While I was too stunned to react, Leo grabbed my phone and responded to Vaughn as me.

EVELYN SINCLAIR: Did you murder Sydney? How many other women have you killed?

My heart pounded as the dots bounced for what seemed like a lifetime...

Dr. Vaughn responded with photos of his victims—before and after he killed them. The horror of seeing the bodies of two innocent women brought acid up my throat. I didn't want to see the images, but I was so shocked and horrified, I couldn't look away.

The last photos that landed on his phone were my stolen sketches. The ones I had drawn at Sydney's memorial. My body was shaking, and the information was coming in so quickly that I could hardly process what was happening.

Dr. Vaughn lived a Jekyll and Hyde type of existence and had fooled everyone with his charismatic persona and successful image. I had a sinking feeling Sydney figured out her new handsome and loving husband had a split personality—and he killed her to keep her quiet.

VAUGHN REYNOLDS: Once the drugs stop my heart, I will find you. You're the only woman who will ever understand me. I'll haunt you forever, Evelyn. I'll screw you while you're sleeping. I'll wrap my hands around your throat until you feel my wrath—

Leo snatched the phone out of my hand to spare me the rest of the message. He grabbed his phone and called dispatch to report the emergency and send officers to the home of Dr. Vaughn Reynolds.

Detective Ricci rattled off a mouthful of cop jargon and codes I didn't understand. However, the intent was clear. Dr. Vaughn Reynolds was about to be arrested for murder—if he survived his apparent suicide attempt.

As Leo got dressed, I paced the room, trying to make sense of what was happening. Sydney had been trying to tell me Vaughn was in trouble, but why was she trying to help him if he had killed her? Sydney wasn't angry—she was desperate.

Whatever was happening with Vaughn, he was in mortal danger. As Leo rushed out the door, promising to call me as soon as he could, I grabbed my sketchbook and moved to the living room.

The only way to find out the truth was through my art. I peeled off the Velcro splint on my finger, grabbed a pencil, and held the tip to the page. I inhaled a series of cleansing breaths to calm my mind and body.

While Leo was doing his job, I would do mine.

Once I found myself in a relaxed state, my hand began to move across the page.

I worked through the pain of a fractured finger, and by the time I finished, I had completed four drawings. The sketches were all of jars. Tall mason jars, each filled with scraps of paper, trinkets, barrettes, candy, playing cards, locks of hair... mementos of murder.

These jars were trophies to memorialize the Windy City Stalker's victims. I examined the pictures and recognized Sydney's mega-carat, oval-shaped wedding ring along with a pair of diamond studded hoop earrings she had worn on the day we closed on the gallery.

I studied the other pictures and didn't recognize the objects in the second or third jars, but the killer's unholy treasure trove of personal items rattled me. What level of humankind could take a life and savor the memories of the kill?

The first three jars had their lids attached, but the fourth jar was still open—until he killed his next victim. The images inside that jar were blurry, and I couldn't tell what object had been stashed inside. I didn't know how the jars related to

Vaughn's suicide attempt, but one thing became shockingly clear.

The killer was going to strike again.

WRECKING BALL—EVELYN

THE BREAKING NEWS OF DR. VAUGHN'S SUICIDE ATTEMPT AND murder confession blanketed the local news stations. Crews and swarms of reporters had camped out in front of his townhome, at the police station, and at Cook County Hospital, where Vaughn was in a coma, clinging to life.

According to the news anchor, he was unresponsive when the first responders arrived, but medics performed CPR and resuscitated him.

By the time Leo returned to my apartment, it was late afternoon, and I was downing coffee to keep my eyes open. Even though Leo couldn't discuss the case, I'd learned from the news that law enforcement believed they had solved the crime.

But I had paranormal intel that suggested they had the wrong man.

Leo was exhausted but relieved to see me. He hugged me tight and assured me our nightmare was over. I hated breaking the news to him that he was wrong, but I had to share my drawings along with the ghost story Leo needed to hear.

"There's been a development in the case on my end," I said. "Sydney is adamant that Vaughn didn't kill her." I paused, giving Leo time to process the news.

Leo remained silent as I went on to explain my interaction with Sydney and how I was certain she wanted us to help Vaughn. I knew from his rigid body language and tight lips that he wasn't receptive to my otherworldly update.

"I've been at the crime scene the last few hours. I can't give you details, but I'm convinced Vaughn is our guy."

"But what about Captiva? Sydney was adamant—"

"I don't know, Evelyn," Leo said sharply. "Right now, I need to focus on *real* evidence that I can hand over to the prosecution. I can't enter opinions from the dead to prove my case," Leo said. "What I have right now is solid. A confession, a suicide attempt, and enough tangible evidence at the scene to convince a jury of his guilt."

I was floored by his dismissal. I had opened up to him and shared things I had been too afraid to say to anyone else. I trusted him with my life, and this was the ultimate betrayal. Reflexively, I shoved him off me to put distance between us.

"Now my gift doesn't matter anymore?"

"Evelyn, that's not what I meant." Leo was fully charged in detective mode while his loving and compassionate side had been bottled up and stashed away for when it suited him.

"Can you consider for a minute that you have the wrong guy?"

I picked up the envelope that held my latest drawings. If the killer had one jar for each of his victims, there were three closed *Soul Jars*, meaning there was one more victim yet to be identified, and one open jar that represented a victim he had yet to claim.

"I drew these after you left." I fanned out the papers so he could quickly tell I was on to something. "The killer keeps mementos of his victims. There are three, not two, and another one—"

"We're searching his property now. I'm sure those items will turn up." He glanced at his phone and sighed. "We'll talk about your drawings later. Right now, I need to focus on the case. I just stepped away to check on you. I'll keep an officer stationed outside the door until I get back."

He kissed my cheek and was on his way out before I had a chance to respond.

Are you serious?

I resented the idea that he thought I was messing around when there were lives on the line. When Leo reached for the door, I decided it would be for the last time. "Don't come back. You solved the case. I'm no longer in danger. There's no need to pretend to be a couple anymore."

He turned and shook his head, annoyed I wasn't backing down. "Evelyn, you need to understand—"

"Linwood." I spoke the clairaudient word that popped into my head.

Leo sighed, frustrated by my ill-timed message. "I know it's shocking to believe Vaughn killed his wife, but you have to trust me—"

"Because you're a detective and I'm not? Whenever I asked you to trust me, you waved me off as crazy. You never believed anything I told you until your evidence proved I was right."

"In this case, you're wrong." Leo argued. "I get it that you see ghosts. I understand you are interpreting your information differently than what my team has discovered, but I can't change the facts to fit your story."

"My *story*? Now you think I'm making this up?" My heart raced as our argument headed down a path we may never come back from.

"I can't do this, Evelyn." Leo rubbed his unshaven face and

lifted his gaze to the ceiling as if summoning the gods to keep the words from escaping his lips. "Is this how our relationship is going to be? Butting heads every time I have a murder investigation and your paranormal gift contradicts my evidence?"

Leo exhaled in frustration. "If this is how our life is going to be, we need to think this through. I can't compete with your ghosts."

When his words settled into my soul, my breath left my body as if I had been blindsided by a wrecking ball. If Leo wanted out of our relationship because he couldn't accept ghosts were a part of my life, I was more than willing to let him off the hook.

Feeling the sting of rejection, I dropped my gaze to my feet, pointed to the door, and choked out a response. "Leave." I moved to my bookshelf and buried my sketches between two heavy art history books.

I kept my back to him and waited for the sound of the door opening and closing before I melted down. I held my breath and bottled up my tears, not wanting to crumble in his presence. A warm hand touched my shoulder.

"I'm sorry. I shouldn't have said that. Can we talk?" Leo tried to turn me around to face him, but our relationship had crashed and burned the moment he dismissed me. He would never change. His badge would always carry more weight than my gift, and I refused to live a life where my feelings were less important than his job.

I wouldn't change either. I liked the person I'd become after the accident. My gift will always be a part of my life, my art, and my soul. If Leo wanted an answer about where our relationship was headed, it was an easy one. "Goodbye, Leo."

LINWOOD—LEO

VAUGHN WAS OUR GUY. NO GHOST STORY, NO MATTER HOW imaginative, would change that.

Dr. Reynolds hadn't yet regained consciousness after ingesting a lethal dose of sedatives, and possibly never would. The doctors gave him a fifty-fifty chance of survival. We had guards at the hospital, and I gave orders to inform me if Vaughn showed signs of coming out of the coma.

Now that we had apprehended the Windy City Stalker, Evelyn was no longer in danger. That was the good news. The bad news was she wouldn't speak to me. Her only reply to my calls was a text message informing me not to contact her again.

She said if there was official police business that required her involvement, she would only speak to Talia or Parker. I understood why she was angry, but I hoped, for her sake, she would concede and accept that the case was closed.

We found personal items that had belonged to Erin Messer in his home office. Vaughn had over fifty photos of Erin he'd printed from a cheap portable device, along with pictures of Sydney taken when she was unaware her husband was watching her.

My theory had been correct about the connection between the women—they had known each other. There were several photos of Sydney at Erin's bakery. There was an eerie photo of Sydney and Erin smiling at each other at the counter as Erin handed Sydney a box of pastries.

Vaughn also had a stack of photos of Sydney and Evelyn on Halsted and at Sydney's office. The most terrifying images were of Evelyn sitting in the coffee shop, sipping her coffee the way I'd seen her do a dozen times. Sketching and enjoying her morning sweet treats, unaware she was being stalked.

While I was relieved Evelyn was safe, I hated how things ended. I couldn't tell her about the evidence we'd discovered at his home because it was classified. Once I could divulge our findings, I would ask Parker to deliver the news.

Eventually, I hoped she would learn not to hate me for doing my job. While our romantic relationship seemed irreparable, I hoped distance would give her time to heal, and we could at least get back to speaking terms.

It wouldn't be easy getting over Evelyn. Still, it was better to make a clean break instead of repeating a history of hurting each other every time a ghost from one of my homicide victims appeared in our bedroom.

I wanted Evelyn to accept the truth about Vaughn. That was the first step in healing from the trauma. But as much as I believed my team had it right, I couldn't get Evelyn's one-word epiphany out of my head.

Linwood.

Every word she'd said was dead on as it related to the Windy City Stalker case—or to me personally. But when Evelyn sniped me with a clairaudient clue in the heat of our argument, my gut told me this murder investigation wasn't over.

FINAL FRIDAY—EVELYN

MAYBE I GOT IT WRONG.

It was hard to accept that Vaughn was living a double life as a well-respected doctor by day, serial killer by night. But when Parker assured me they had recovered damning evidence to prove their case, I had to believe Leo and his team were right—Dr. Vaughn Reynolds was a killer.

Three days had passed since Vaughn's alleged suicide attempt, and I had not spoken to Detective Ricci since he'd left my apartment.

Sydney hadn't contacted me either. I hoped that once Vaughn had been outed as her killer, she had found peace and moved on to eternal bliss on the other side. It was time for me to move on from the case and my whirlwind romance with Leo.

"You are not a detective, Evelyn." I would heed Leo's words and move on with my life as an artist—not an amateur sleuth. While I was heartbroken by how our romance ended, it was best to make a clean break instead of drawing out a doomed relationship.

I tucked myself back into my armor, put up a firewall

around me to protect my feelings, and shut down the prospect of ever finding love. Trust was a dangerous virtue. To live a normal life, I had to lie about my gift.

I was naive when I believed Leo would learn to accept my gift, but I didn't regret my flash romance with Leo. At least I would have our intimate memories to hang on to.

What hurt the most was the heartache that stemmed from my false belief that I was special. That was my mistake. Leo would have no trouble moving on with someone new—a woman with less baggage and a more agreeable personality.

"Enough about death and hot guys. Let's talk art galleries." Sydney's words of wisdom rang true. I couldn't have agreed more.

The day Gibson, Luis, and I had planned for all these months was here. The Final Friday Gallery Walk. We had poured our souls into marketing for the big day, and I wouldn't let anything stand in the way of our monumental accomplishments.

Now that I was out of mortal danger, I focused all my attention where it belonged—*Halsted*. The Halloween-themed decorations had been hung. The goody bags had been stuffed with *The Death of Me* merchandise. The media kits had been delivered to every press outlet in town.

We had been setting up and preparing all day, and the three of us had all run home to freshen up before the doors opened to the public. I stood in the shower and inhaled the steam as I cleaned my body with a refreshing salt scrub.

Pangs of regret churned in my gut, knowing Leo wouldn't be coming to the opening. I had been elated at the idea of him and his loving family supporting me on my big night, but I had lost them, too.

Meeting his family was one of my life's highlights, given that I was estranged from my parents. The idea that the man I was falling in love with came with the bonus of a supportive family and friends was more than I could've ever hoped for.

I splashed warm water on my face to wash away my tears as I wondered what Leo had told his family about our breakup. *Yeah, Evelyn was alright, but she wasn't my type... too needy... too weird... too delusional... too fucked up for a guy like me...*

I stepped out of the shower, tied on a robe, and checked my phone for messages.

GIBSON: I gave Jeremy from the Windy City Beat your address. He is stopping by to drop off proofs. They are running a special edition tonight and want to put your picture from the cemetery on their home page!

GIBSON: Sorry to give out your info. I'm not at the gallery. They need your approval to run on the website ASAP. Hope you're not mad!

While I was thrilled about the promo, I was not happy Gibson had given out my home address. After all I'd been through, I would've thought she would be more sensitive to my privacy. Before I could text back, there was a knock on my door.

Shit. Someone must've let Jeremy into the building.

I tossed on some clothes and rushed to answer the door. I kept the chain on to ensure it was him, then slid the lock and invited him in. Jeremy held a large envelope in one hand and a coffee carrier with a pair of iced caramel macchiatos in the other.

"Hey, Evelyn. I was at the coffee shop when I texted Gibson. Thought you might need some caffeine to get you through tonight." He set the carrier on the kitchen counter and handed me a drink. It was my usual afternoon go-to treat. I ordered it every day. A rush of paranoia washed over me that Jeremy had known my order.

Reading my wary look, he elaborated. "You don't like

caramel macchiatos? Gibson asked me to grab one for you when I told her where I was. I swear that's what she texted. I was already in line, so I got the same." He started flipping through his texts like he was going to show me proof.

Stop being a paranoid disaster, Evelyn.

I shook my head to chase away my ungrateful response. "I love them. Thanks." I sipped as Jeremy pulled out the photos from our shoot in the cemetery. The shots were spooky and atmospheric, lending the perfect setting to my artistic style.

But as he went through the stack, I got a weird vibe when he showed me some extra pics of Leo and me as we strolled the grounds before he arrived.

There were a series of shots of us holding hands, with me beaming at my heroic protector like a cooing lovebird. Some focused on Leo, gazing down at me as a fiery attraction burned between us. Jeremy's photos immortalized our sexual energy, which was hot enough to scorch the hallowed ground we trod on.

"Why did you take pictures of Leo and me?" My words came out a little slurry. A bout of dizziness brought on a head rush, and I reached out to steady myself against the couch. The muscles in my legs wobbled like jelly.

"Are you alright?" Jeremy put his arm around me to steady me. I winced at his boldness. Leo was right. I shouldn't let him put his hands on me. I tried to shrug him off, but he squeezed tighter.

"I have more pictures you need to see."

My body felt heavy. I blinked away the stars flashing before my eyes.

Jeremy flipped to the next picture of me sitting alone in the coffee shop, sipping my drink as I gazed out the window. "You were lonely. I could see it in your eyes. That was the day I chose you, Evelyn."

What the hell?

Then he flipped to the next photo of Leo joining me at the table. I recognized the scene as the first day we'd met. He flipped to the next shot of us smiling at each other, with Leo's green smoothie cup littered with the remains of my drawing. Jeremy had snapped a flirtatious photo of the moment the flame of attraction had ignited between us.

When he revealed the next photo, my body shook with fear. It was a photo of Leo and I walking up the sidewalk that led to his mother's porch. The birthday banner for Nonna was strung across the porch.

Jeremy had followed us to Leo's mother's house.

The next photo was taken through the window of my apartment. I was standing over Leo in my living room, tempting him in my sheer nightgown.

Oh, God. He has been stalking me after the attack, while I was with Leo.

"I hate that fucking *dickhead* cop. He ruined everything. I told you to stay away from him, Evelyn." Jeremy's anger bubbled over into a punishing grip on my forearm. "I hate him so fucking much. I will make him suffer for taking you away from me."

I squealed from the pain as Jeremy flipped to the next photo. It was the same picture of us from the coffee shop, only our faces had been violently scratched out. Just like the photo Sydney had desperately tried to show me on the night she was killed.

My heart raced as a rush of fear washed over me. My head was spinning. I felt numb.

Oh, God. Jeremy drugged me. "What did you put in my drink?"

"I told you I'd come back for you." He moved closer and grasped my upper arms to keep me from falling. His leering gaze moved from my eyes to my pounding chest.

With his eyes filled with lust, he squeezed my biceps and

pulled me toward him. I stumbled as he backed me against the wall and tore open my blouse, exposing my lacy bra underneath. I fought to push him off me, but my efforts were in vain.

Jeremy. The quiet and broody photographer who flew under the radar. The nice guy who was always around with his camera in front of his face, never drawing attention to himself. As I stared at his plain clothes, generic haircut, and basic face, I realized that he was the one person I had seen at different places, of all the potential suspects.

The gallery. The coffee shop. The cemetery.

I never suspected him because the photo shoots had been arranged through the magazine, and we had invited him to the media events. He was a freelance photographer, hiding in plain sight. Although I had never seen him at the coffee shop, he always had a cup in hand bearing Taboo's logo. I never considered him a threat. All along, the truth was there.

"Why are you doing this?"

"Because I can." A sickening grin crept over his face as I struggled to free myself from a killer's embrace. He enjoyed the hunt and now the euphoria of closing in on another kill. I scanned the room for a weapon I could use against him.

I pounded my bare feet on the floor and banged on the wall to alert my neighbors, but my body was so weak that my effort was in vain. If I could manage to struggle free or reach a book from the shelf, I could knock him over the head and try to escape or lock myself in my bedroom.

My energy was fading. I blinked to chase away the stars flashing before my eyes, but I lost my battle to stay conscious. I slumped over. Jeremy lifted my body and cradled me in his arms. "Let's get you to bed, Evelyn. I want your last night to be perfect."

My body went limp. Everything fell dark.

MERCY—LEO

<small>Vaughn had regained consciousness.</small>

The doctors said it was a miracle he was alive, but they weren't confident he would still pull through. He was weak but talking, so Parker and I needed to rush to his bedside to get a confession about the killings on camera.

According to the officer stationed in his room, the only word Dr. Vaughn had spoken since he'd opened his eyes was *"Captiva."*

While I raced to Cook County Hospital, Parker and I reviewed our game plan. Vaughn had confessed via text, but a defense attorney could allege that someone else had sent the message. That was why it was crucial to record the confession.

"After we read him his rights, we need to—"

My phone buzzed when a text came in. I glanced at the screen and found a selfie of a woman from the neck down, wearing a lacy bra and matching panties. Shit. The message was from Evelyn.

"Oh, wow," Parker blushed, then set his gaze out the window. "I thought you broke up."

My phone was charging in the center console of my car, face up, making the screen visible to both of us.

"We did." We were at a red light, giving me a moment to check my messages. As I examined the picture, another selfie came in. Evelyn slid off her bra and covered her breasts with her long hair. A message followed:

EVELYN: Come over, Detective. I need you.

I held the screen away from Parker's view. It pained me that she wanted my attention, and instead of talking things out, she was sexting and inviting me over to sleep with her.

But that isn't her style.

The Evelyn I knew wouldn't resort to desperate measures. The only way she exposed her true self was through her art. Something wasn't right about this. I set my phone back down when the light turned green.

Parker glanced at the screen when another round of photos appeared and lifted his eyebrows in surprise. "Are you going to respond?"

I shook my head as a round of pity punched me in the gut. Evelyn was clearly talented and thriving in the art world. Whatever she'd gone through had seriously messed her up in the head. The last time I'd seen her, she was so upset I had doubted she would ever speak to me again—much less sleep with me.

EVELYN: You're a fuckup. You could've saved her. How many more people have to die?

My phone buzzed with a string of incoming pictures.

Erin Messer's body behind a row of trash cans.

Sydney Reynolds's corpse in a dumpster.

Vaughn crashed on the floor of his office, clinging to life.

Parker and I exchanged glances. Wherever Evelyn got this information, it wasn't from a ghost or some cosmic resource beyond the grave. These were photographs. She had guilty knowledge about each of the victims.

"Have a uniform pick up Ms. Sinclair for questioning," I snapped at Parker. "I want her at the station by the time I—"

My phone buzzed with another text.

EVELYN: This is your fault.

Another round of photos appeared on my phone.

The first image was Evelyn in the nude, stretched out on her bed. Flower petals covered her body, and her hands were crossed over her chest in an artsy-type nude photograph. My pulse quickened when Evelyn's hands were visible in the photos, which meant she was not taking selfies.

Someone else was the photographer.

In the next photo, Evelyn was face down on the bed. A blanket covered her from the waist down, exposing her bare back. The picture revealed a line drawing in blue ink on her skin that appeared to be a portrait of Evelyn, marked with a pen. The artist had drawn her hair as long squiggly lines and exaggerated the size and shape of her eyes. They were wide open with an "X" over each eye—the universal symbol of death.

In the next photo, she was in a different position. Her hair was brushed out of her face, and a teddy bear holding a red satin heart had been tucked at the crook of her neck.

Her eyes were rolled back, and her left wrist was draped dramatically over her forehead. The yeti scarf she'd worn on the day we'd met at the coffee shop was wrapped taut around her neck.

My heart raced when I realized what was happening. Not only were we wrong about Vaughn being the killer, but I had also left Evelyn alone and at the mercy of a killer. The Windy City Stalker had taken her and was taunting me with photos of her corpse.

"Fucking hell!" I pounded the roof of my car. A rush of anger and adrenaline pulsed through my veins as I processed what was happening. Evelyn had gotten too close to the investigation and drawn the killer's attention. Instead of protecting her, I shoved her into the path of a killer.

I could hate myself later for all of this, but time was ticking away. "Call dispatch!" I barked at my partner. "Send field officers to her apartment. If she doesn't answer, tell them they have probable cause to bust down the door. She could still be alive."

I steered the Charger down a cross street and sped off toward the art district. I tapped Evelyn's number. It was a long shot, but as her phone rang, I prayed she would pick up and curse me for not believing her when she was right.

"Dammit!" I lay on the horn when a confused driver was slow to get the message that my blaring horn meant to get the fuck out of the way.

Within minutes, uniforms reached her apartment and went inside. Parker took the call. "She's not there," he said to me, then instructed the officers at the scene to mark Evelyn's apartment as a crime scene.

The fact that Evelyn wasn't at her apartment gave me hope that she might still be alive. The previous two victims had been taken to a second location before they were murdered. If the killer had taken her to Location *B*, we had to find her fast, before Evelyn suffered the same fate.

My heart dropped out of my chest when Parker instructed the officers to also search the dumpsters in the alley behind her apartment. "I should've fucking listened to her." I imagined Evelyn at the hands of her killer, thinking the same goddamn thing.

"If you would've trusted me, I'd still be alive."

I slammed my hand on the dash and cursed. Then I remembered Evelyn had permitted me to track her phone while she was under my protection. I had never turned it off.

I handed my phone to Parker and told him to track it. I

strangled the steering wheel and was ready to steer the car in any direction the information led me.

"Her phone is near her gallery."

"We're five minutes away. Get the exact location."

Parker zeroed in on the map. His expression tanked when he discovered the precise location.

"Where is it, Parker?"

"In the alley behind her building. It appears to be in a dumpster."

While the worst-case scenario stared me dead in the eye, Evelyn was still a missing person. Unless my team recovered a body, we still had a chance to save her.

UNHOLY—LEO

When I got to the scene, Santoni was outside the door of Evelyn's apartment, standing guard. I tried to steamroll past him, but he blocked me before I could get inside.

"Get the fuck out of my way." I tried to push past him, but my best friend of twenty-seven-plus years backed me against the wall and held me in place.

"Listen to me, Leo. I'm going to let you in, but I need you to enter the scene as a detective, not a boyfriend, got it?" Santoni held me back as he awaited my response. "I'll be straight with you. It's disturbing. If you don't want to do this—"

"I'm going in."

Santoni backed away and led me inside.

Before I stepped over the threshold, I slipped on a pair of boot covers and rubber gloves to avoid tainting the crime scene.

The first thing I zeroed in on was a torn button-down shirt and a lacy bra strewn across the floor. My heart pounded when I recognized the soft-pink floral pattern of her lingerie. I'd stripped that bra off her the night she seduced me after the party at my mother's house.

I exhaled sharply as the thought of some psychopath undressing Evelyn raced through my mind. *I have to get through this. I'm Evelyn's best chance...*

Santoni led me to the living room and pointed to a set of photos scattered across the table. Acid came up my throat when I realized the photos were of us from the shoot at the cemetery. They were taken before the photographer, Jeremy, arrived.

The killer had been watching us the whole time.

Using tweezers, I moved the photos so I could see them all. Pictures of us at the coffee shop. The killer had targeted Evelyn before we had met. He had been stalking Sydney, which meant he had most likely seen the two friends together. Once Sydney was dead, he moved on to Evelyn.

"Are you alright, buddy?" Santoni clutched my shoulder. His tortured expression mirrored my own, and I was grateful he was here to help me keep it together.

"Show me the bedroom." Time was ticking away, and I needed to find Evelyn fast. All the women who had fallen victim had been killed within six to eight hours of their abductions.

When my gaze landed on Evelyn's warm and cozy bed, my breath caught in my throat. The soft gray-striped comforter had been torn off, and a fresh round of blood splatter stained her silky white sheets. Nausea flooded my gut at the sight of her fuzzy animal print pillow tossed on the floor, covered with shards of blood-stained glass.

That was the same pillow I'd made love to her on only a few days ago. Seeing the pillow and her bed where we had laughed and teased each other and had the best sex of our lives rocked me with guilt and regret.

"Hey, Leo. Are you alright?" Santoni grabbed my arm to get my attention.

The idea that some fucking psycho had taken the love of my life filled me with an unholy amount of rage. I could feel sick about this later, but I had to save Evelyn first.

But to save her, I had to find out who had taken her. The only witness who could out the killer's identity was one of his surviving victims—Dr. Vaughn Reynolds.

UNLEASHED—LEO

Vaughn was hooked up with plastic tubing attached to beeping machines, an IV drip, an oxygen tank, and a pair of handcuffs attached to his wrist and the bed frame. His skin was pale and blotchy, and I hardly recognized him with all the swelling around his eyes.

When I entered the room, I introduced myself to a nurse at his bedside and asked for privacy. The middle-aged brunette gave me a nod of acknowledgment.

"He's been asking for you, Detective Ricci. He may not remain conscious for long." The nurse tapped her patient's shoulder to wake him.

When Vaughn opened his eyes and found me at his bedside, he got agitated and tried to sit up. With the restraints and his weakened condition, all he could do was lift his head slightly off the pillow. "Where's Evelyn? Is she safe?"

I shook my head and placed my hand on his shoulder. "No, Evelyn is in mortal danger. Do you know who took her?"

Vaughn nodded as he struggled to keep his eyes open.

"The photographer from our wedding. Sydney met him in Chicago and then paid his expenses to travel to Captiva for the ceremony."

Vaughn dropped his head back on the pillow and blinked his eyes to stay awake. His energy was fading, and I needed more information before he lost consciousness again.

"How do you know this?"

"He called me and said he had extra photos from our wedding that he wanted to give me. He was sorry about what had happened to Sydney. I let him inside our home. He drugged me with an overdose of my sleeping pills and took my phone. He said he was going to get Evelyn so he could *keep his girls together.*"

Tears rolled down Vaughn's cheek as he recalled the horrific memory. "He killed Sydney. The man she hired to take our wedding pictures murdered my wife."

As a sense of urgency coursed through my veins, the word "Captiva" churned in my gut. The word Evelyn insisted Sydney wanted me to know from the start was dangling in front of my face like a swaying noose.

I would make it up to Evelyn later for not giving her the credit she deserved, but first, I had to save her life. Dr. Vaughn closed his eyes, clinging to consciousness. I tapped his chest to wake him and asked him one last question. "What's the photographer's name?"

His lips trembled, and he opened his eyes. "Jeremy Nash."

Jeremy Nash. The fucking photographer who had arranged Evelyn's photo shoot in the cemetery. I was there. The killer was within my grasp. "Thank you, Vaughn. I'm going to go track down that son of a bitch. You better be alive the next time I see you."

"Don't let him win, Detective. Save Evelyn."

As I left the room, I ordered the officer on duty to unlock the handcuffs, stating that Vaughn was an innocent victim—

not a criminal—and was to be treated as a hero. Now that I had a name, I unleashed every resource the Windy City had to offer.

Once my team leaped into action, my top priority was to figure out the meaning of the word *"Linwood."* Whatever it meant, it was the key to finding Evelyn.

PINNED—EVELYN

I FELT THE WARM SENSATION OF SOMEONE HOLDING MY HAND.

I lifted my head and fluttered my eyes to see who it was. Everything was a blur. My back ached. My body felt weak and dehydrated. I had no idea where I was.

I couldn't make out the face of the person beside me, only the shadow of a man. I tried to sit up, but strong hands pinned my shoulders on the bed.

"Who are you?" I whispered.

No answer.

A door opened and closed.

I drifted in and out of consciousness and remembered bits and pieces of background noise. Bottles clinking. Jazz music. Silky sheets covering my body. A warm bath and someone lathering my hair with shampoo.

My body felt heavy and cumbersome, and as much as I wanted to get out of bed, I didn't have enough strength to roll over.

I got a whiff of roses and scanned the room for flowers, only to find the scent was coming from me. I sniffed my arm and detected a fragrant floral lotion had been massaged into my skin.

I don't have any rose-scented lotion.

Once my body awakened, the horrible memory of what had happened sparked an adrenaline rush. I sat up and tried to run, but my wrists and ankles were bound to the posts of an antique wooden bed. I twisted and struggled against my restraints, but I was so weak from the drugs that my attempt to free myself was as unlikely as my chances of surviving this nightmare.

I checked around the room for signs of my captor, but I was alone, at least for the moment. Not only was I glad the psycho wasn't around while I was helpless to protect myself, but I also needed time to devise a plan to outsmart that monster.

I opened my eyes and blinked to make out my surroundings. I was tucked into a bed, covered with blankets, in a small bedroom. I fought the urge to scream until I could grasp my situation.

Jeremy wasn't in the room, and I needed to be ready for him when he returned. I pulled myself to a sitting position and discovered he had dressed me in a raunchy red teddy and slid on a pair of silk stockings. The same type of outfit Sydney was found wearing.

I checked the security of my restraints, but there was no way I could get free unless Jeremy released me. Crows were cawing outside the window, and a strong breeze rustled the fall leaves still clinging to life on their withered branches.

Where am I?

I was woozy from the drugs and dehydration, but I was determined to fight off the killer who aimed to make me his latest victim. I scanned the room for anything I could use to my advantage.

A teddy bear with plastic eyes was tucked next to me in

the bed. A pack of cigarettes with a lighter, an industrial-sized flashlight on the dresser, a scented candle in a hurricane glass, and a large thermos on the nightstand.

With the items in the room, I could break the window with either the flashlight or the thermos and yell for help. If there even was anyone around to hear my cries.

Using the same tools, I could hurl them at him and slow him down long enough to escape the confines of the house. None of those options would work unless I convinced Jeremy to untie me. If he had killed his previous victims in the same manner, I was sure they were thinking the same thing as they were strapped to the bed.

It pained me to imagine their last moments, but they undoubtedly had tried and failed to fight him off. If there was no way to convince him to release me, then my only option was to buy time in hopes Leo and his team were trying to track me down.

That would depend on someone reporting me missing.

I did not remember what had happened once the drugs knocked me out. It felt like I had been asleep for hours, maybe an entire day, but I had no way to be sure.

I had missed the gallery opening event by now. Yes! Gibson would've called Leo. She would've told him she'd given Jeremy my home address. I had a momentary burst of confidence, knowing Leo was trying to track me down. Still, a fresh round of fear shook me when I considered I might be dead by the time he came to my rescue.

Find me, Leo.

The realization that I would never see him again added another layer of fear and panic to my terror. Leo would blame himself for my murder. Would he be the one who pulled my corpse out of a dumpster?

I imagined my face plastered on a MISSING poster hanging in shop windows around the city. A happy photo of smiling Evelyn Sinclair, the artist obsessed with death. The Windy City Art Beat with a follow-up article about the charismatic artist whom Death had tracked down.

I thought of everything I would say to Leo if I had the chance. I wished someone like me, a fellow medium, could stand with him as he stared at the postmortem photographs of my dead body pinned to the corkboard in his office.

"Evelyn says she loves you, Leo. She wishes you would've saved her. If you had listened to her instead of dismissing her gift, you could've lived a happy life together. She's with you now. Does the word 'Linwood' mean anything to you, Detective?"

Linwood. The last clue I'd given Leo. He had been so cavalier about the message. Would he remember the one word that could lead him to me? I wasn't sure what it meant yet, but I knew that word would save my life.

I struggled against my restraints, to no avail. Jeremy would be coming back soon. I had to mentally prepare. I was done feeling sorry for myself and needed to come up with a plan to outsmart him.

Tears fueled by anger and rage ran down my cheeks as I realized he would do the same thing to me as he had to the other victims. When my friends realized something was wrong, I would already be dead.

How long had I been unconscious?

Where the hell was the killer?

Footsteps. The doorknob twisted.

Shit. He was here, and I had no plan.

MEMENTOS—EVELYN

THE LIGHT FROM THE HALLWAY ILLUMINATED JEREMY'S BULKY silhouette. He was dressed in all black and had his professional camera in hand. As he entered the darkened room, bright flashes of light blinded me as he moved toward me, snapping pictures as I recoiled in horror.

He sat beside me on the bed and grasped my chin to force me to look at him. "Quiet, Evelyn. You're disturbing them." He covered my mouth with his hand and stared into my eyes.

Now that Jeremy had entered the room, I felt the presence of *the others*—his victims. My gaze shot from the window to the walls to the ceiling…

Shadows swirled around the room like a frenzy of sharks. The dizzying movement nauseated me, but I forced myself to try to make out the figures. I had never seen ghosts before outside of a dream. This was something new. I concentrated on one of the forms. The tortured face of Sydney Reynolds became painfully clear.

I tore my gaze from hers and focused on another shadow. Her eyes were open wide, and there was a dent in her shadowy head as if it had been bludgeoned to death with a blunt object—Erin Messer. I focused on a third shadow, but it was moving too swiftly for me to make out a face.

Jeremy smiled when he noticed my horrified reaction. "You see them, don't you? I knew you would, Evelyn. I've known about your gift since I took your sketches." He laughed as he picked up the lighter and lit a series of candles around the room.

"I told you, girls. I told you!" Jeremy pointed his finger at the room's shadows as if he'd won an imaginary game only he was playing. His sickening bravado brought acid up my throat.

I couldn't fathom how the ghosts of Sydney and Erin could coexist with their killer. *Will I join them? Is it possible I will be so angry about my murder that I remain earthbound to seek justice?*

Once the candles were lit, I noticed they were set up next to mason jars. As the flickering flames of the candles illuminated the room, I discovered the walls and ceiling were plastered with photographs and magazine clippings.

The first face I recognized was Erin's. She was behind the bakery counter that showcased her cupcake selection. There were pictures of her decorating cupcakes and biting into one of her creations and a newspaper article about her new business.

Next to the professional shots were a series of photos of her walking to work alone, getting into a car, hanging out with her friends…

Then my gaze drifted to Sydney. There were dozens of photos of her from her wedding. A portrait of her veil-covered face. A candid shot of her holding her bouquet. An intimate moment in her mother's embrace. Her feet were in the sand while the tide tickled her toes.

"You were Sydney's fucking wedding photographer?" I could no longer hold back the horror creeping over my skin. How a person as deranged as Jeremy could skate through life without drawing attention to himself was a mystery.

No one suspects him. He is invisible. A loner no one thinks twice about.

I turned back to Erin's photos, and a fresh round of rage overtook me. He had done a professional photo shoot of Erin baking cupcakes for her social media campaign. And as I scanned the room, searching for familiar faces, I found another one—mine.

He had taken photos of me when I had no idea he'd been watching. Me petting my neighbor's dog. Me watering the flowers outside the gallery. Me drinking margaritas with Tess. Me at Sydney's vigil. The drawings he had stolen from my sketchbook…

Like the other victims, I had invited Jeremy into my life. He worked for the Windy City Beat and was a welcomed member of the media.

As my gaze bounced around the walls and ceiling, taking in the shrine, Jeremy studied me curiously when I focused my attention on one of the jars. The room was dimly lit, but I could make out material and scraps of paper.

"Curious to find out what's inside?" Jeremy lifted one of the jars and brought it to me for closer inspection. "This is yours." He carefully lifted a memento from the jar and picked out a trinket.

"Your lighter. Black nail polish. Hair ties. Lip balm…" He pulled out a biodegradable spoon from Taboo. There was a hint of vanilla icing on it, probably lifted from the trash.

"All my girls have their favorite things." A sickening smile curled up on his lips. "Erin loves board games. I brought her dice and some cards so she could play with the others."

My body trembled as the horror of his collection revealed my captor's twisted mind.

"Sydney likes to watch the birds outside her window. I collect feathers for her. It makes her happy." He turned his attention to me and lifted a strand of my hair. "I almost forgot something."

He pulled a knife from his pocket and flipped it open. I screamed when he lifted a lock of my hair and sliced off a long strand.

He looped one of my hair ties around my hair to keep it together. Then he sniffed it as if it were a cork from a bottle of French wine. As he digested my scent, his expression turned sinister. "That fucking dickhead detective thinks you're dead. He knows you're mine now. I hate him so fucking much. I hope he blows his brains out from the guilt of what he did to you."

His body trembled with rage as he slid under the covers next to me and wrapped one hand around my neck. He caressed my body as his hand squeezed my throat in a sickening rhythm. I feared this was the moment I would die. I struggled against his grasp, but there was no way to escape his wrath.

I closed my eyes, not wanting to see his face as he stole my life.

"Don't worry, Evelyn. I'll keep you safe with the rest of my girls. You'll never be alone again."

Bang... Bang... Bang...

I opened my eyes and saw Sydney's fists clenched with rage as her ghost pounded on the window. Erin appeared at my bedside and vexed Jeremy with a primal scream as if trying to prevent my murder. While I believed their efforts were in vain because I was the only one who could hear them, I was blindsided when the glass mason jars began to shake, startling my captor.

Jeremy lowered his hands while he shot his gaze around the room, trying to determine the source of the noise. "They're here, aren't they? They're happy to see you. I promised I would keep all of you together."

I scanned the shadows in search of the third ghost I had yet to identify. I zeroed in on her features, but I didn't recognize her. At that moment, I lost hope. I was going to die in this old haunted house.

The third ghost appeared behind Jeremy's back as I struggled to breathe. Her eyes fixated on him as if she could control him with her mind, and she was willing him to stop. She shot her gaze to mine, and a word popped into my head —"*Scarlet.*"

The mysterious Red Ghost.

I had one chance. One sliver of hope to change my fate. I screamed the word as if it was my last saving grace. Jeremy stared at me, stunned, as if the word was laced with a drug. His lips curled into a sickening smile, and his eyes widened with an unholy sense of satisfaction.

Jeremy's entire demeanor had changed, and his expression resembled a greedy child set free in a candy shop. My memories boomeranged to the drawing of a teenage girl with a teddy bear tucked beside her corpse and the shadow of her killer stretching across the room.

The shadow was Jeremy. Now the drawings were starting to make sense. Scarlet was his first kill. She was special. I could use this information to get out of this haunted house. "Scarlet wants to speak to you, Jeremy. Take me to Linwood."

Jeremy hurriedly removed my restraints. He lifted me off the bed, tossed me over his shoulder, and carried me outside. He had taken me to a secluded location in the woods. There were no other homes in sight. Just his ramshackle house.

My head was spinning from the sensation of being upside down and the dizzying effect of the drugs he'd given me. He stopped. I got a head rush when he dropped me to my feet. A heavy van door slid open, and Jeremy pulled me inside the vehicle.

Oh. God. I'm inside the murder van.

SCARLET—LEO

Now that we had confirmed the identity of the Windy City Stalker, the breaking news lit up the airwaves like fireworks. Evelyn and Jeremy's pictures landed side by side on every news outlet in the city and all over the web.

While the manhunt was on, I assembled my team. I had every resource available from the FBI and Chicago PD on the killer's trail. If we had any chance of saving Evelyn's life, we needed to find her in the next few hours.

To do that, I needed to divulge Evelyn's clairaudient clues and drawings for the experts to analyze. Evelyn was drawn to death, and I was certain there was a body out there that would lead us to Linwood. It was up to me to find it.

"If there is anyone here who does not have an open mind about paranormal phenomena, leave this room now." I scanned the faces of the twenty-plus team members of the best and brightest talent the FBI and state law enforcement had to offer.

Not a single person flinched.

"We have unconventional evidence from our victim, Evelyn Sinclair, that involves automatic drawings, clairaudient messages, and clues from restless ghosts who deliver information through dreams."

I ticked off the clairaudient clues first. "Captiva. Blackwater. Halsted. Linwood." Then I brought up the photos of Sydney Reynolds, Erin Messer, and Evelyn Sinclair on the monitors and detailed what we knew about the victims to the sharpest tools in the criminology vault.

"We have associated each one of Evelyn's clairaudient clues to a place. The last clue Evelyn gave me was Linwood. We need to find out the significance of this location. I believe this is the clue that will lead us to our victim."

I rubbed my jaw to ease the tension and pulled up all the sketches Evelyn had produced. The ones I felt were the most significant were the drawings from the vigil—the ones the killer had stolen from her purse. The flashback-style grainy ones of a young woman we had yet to identify.

I displayed the photos of the drawings Evelyn had saved on her phone. The innocent teen walking along a path with a long shadow lurking behind her. The victim innocently stood naked in a bedroom, unaware someone was violating her privacy. The girl's body with a teddy bear tucked beside her corpse with the omnipresent shadow covering her body.

Then I showed Evelyn's painting of the young woman in the red dress that appeared to be a stylized version of the sketch. *Does the color red mean anything to you?* I remembered Evelyn had asked me that question on the night her purse had been stolen. "The color red might be significant," I said to the room.

Parker stepped in and took the reins. "Childhood trauma is a common trait among serial killers. We need to dig into Jeremy Nash's past and find out who the woman is and where this crime occurred. This information, I believe, will lead us to Linwood."

While our team tapped on their laptops, searching

records, I stepped aside to breathe as the dire state of the crisis settled into my bones. Evelyn was at the mercy of a killer, and it was my fault. I'd let my quick temper and stubborn ego get ahead of my feelings, which could cost Evelyn her life.

Once she was safe, I prayed Evelyn would give me a chance to tell her how wrong I was about putting my job ahead of her. I would never make the same mistake again if she gave me a chance. I loved her. She was more important to me than anything else on earth.

"Detective Ricci?" Parker handed the floor back to me.

I moved to the evidence we recovered from her apartment—the automatic drawings I had been too stubborn to look at when I had the chance. "Evelyn titled this series, *Soul Jars*." I pinned up the originals on a corkboard.

"Sydney Reynolds communicates with Evelyn through her dreams. In the early morning hours when Dr. Vaughn Reynolds was attacked—"

"Got it!" One of the agents lifted her hand, signaling she had vital information to share. "Jeremy Nash's stepsister disappeared twelve years ago. The report was filed by a concerned neighbor who believed the girl was a victim of foul play. Abusive stepfather. Mother was an addict. The girl is in the system as a missing person."

"What's the name?" I moved to her workstation to see the report.

"Scarlet Drake," the agent said.

Scarlet. The color red Evelyn had seen when she lit the candles. Evelyn had that one right, too. Now I was more convinced than ever that finding Linwood was the critical next step.

"Locate the parents and the neighbor who reported Scarlet missing," I said to the room. "Find out where the crime occurred and how it connects to Linwood."

"The place could be a street name, a business, a school, a boat, a motel..." Parker stepped in to clarify and lead the team while I caught my breath. My heart pounded as horrible images raced through my mind. I had to keep it together. Time was ticking away...

Hang on, Evelyn. I'm coming for you.

LINWOOD—EVELYN

My captor gagged me, dropped me on a pile of musty blankets, and cuffed me to a long chain attached to the van's roof. Maybe he didn't bother to blindfold me because he had already decided that he was going to kill me.

The interior was littered with trash and dirty clothes. He had been living in there, at least part time. There were stacks of dirty magazines, photographs of the women he stalked, and photo albums piled up in the corners.

I felt queasy as the van rocked, and horrible images of his victims swirled in my head. Jeremy had packed the "soul jars" and placed them in the back of the van. They rattled angrily as Jeremy drove toward some unholy mystery place called Linwood.

Find me, Leo. I gave you all the clues.

The van bounced as the terrain turned onto an off-road path. The windows were covered, so I couldn't see where we were going. Still, I recognized the sound of low-hanging branches scraping against the exterior.

I imagined we were headed to a makeshift grave where Scarlet's body had been buried and never recovered. I tried to stay calm as Jeremy drove, running through the steps I needed to take to survive my nightmare.

Step one: Remove the restraints.

Step two: Run or kill.

Step three: Escape.

The first step seemed the easiest part of the plan. I had a direct line to the dead. I'd tell Jeremy that to communicate with them, I had to draw. If Jeremy wanted to converse with the ghost of his first victim, he would have to unlock my cuffs.

The rest of the plan would depend on my fight-or-flight instincts. Would I take my chances and try to outrun my captor? Or find a weapon and fight to the death? Mentally, I was prepared to go either way and would evaluate my surroundings first, then execute my plan.

I would have to be decisive. Once I chose a path, I had to commit to my decision.

There are no second chances.

The van stopped. I jerked forward from the motion. Jeremy turned off the ignition. He stomped back to where I was chained up and unlocked the cuffs from the top. "This is as far as we go. We need to walk the rest of the way."

Instead of unlocking the handcuff from my wrist, he used the chain length as a leash to keep me tethered to his side. Although it was not what I had anticipated, I still considered getting the fuck out of the murder van a win.

It was freezing outside, and Jeremy tossed me a stack of my own clothing he had stolen from my apartment. I dressed in jeans and a sweater and looped my yeti scarf around my neck before stepping into my tall boots.

The negative energy bouncing off the cold gray walls made me think maybe the murders had all taken place back there. I had a sickening feeling that the woman had already been murdered when he got them to the creepy room where he had held me captive.

I sensed the bedroom was where he violated the victims postmortem. Then he took his time with them, fixing their hair and applying makeup before dumping their bodies. How a human being could inflict such atrocities on another human was beyond my comprehension.

I must stop him before he kills again.

He slung a backpack over his shoulder and carried an industrial flashlight. He pulled me along like a dog, leading me to a secluded location in the woods. The sun was going down, and the bright-orange harvest moon was setting on the horizon. We probably only had about an hour of daylight left.

Jeremy had parked the van under a canopy of trees and marched me through a densely wooded area on a well-worn dirt path. He seemed to know where he was going. This bastard was going to kill me when we reached Scarlet's grave. I was convinced of that.

The frigid air cooled my clammy skin, and I was grateful Jeremy had given me clothes to wear over the skimpy lingerie on our impromptu hiking trip. As Jeremy led the way, I memorized the path and searched for markers to guide me back to civilization once I escaped.

When the trail wound around the bend, a wooden sign welcomed us to *The Linwood Lodge*. Like the other clairaudient clues, Linwood was a place. If Leo was looking for me and had remembered the word I'd told him, I had faith he would figure out a way to find me here.

I must've shown a twinge of optimism that caught Jeremy's attention. He frowned as if trying to figure out what I was thinking.

"She's here," I said. "Scarlet is waiting for us."

Jeremy pursed his lips and nodded. He was moving so quickly that I panted as I tried to keep up with his pace. After trekking another mile through the woods, Jeremy pulled off the path and led me through a thick section of woods. Branches slapped me in the face and body as he pushed toward a creek.

We followed the muddy path until we reached a clearing large enough to make camp. I stayed silent as my captor unpacked his survival gear and spread a large blanket over the slippery fall leaves. I was shocked when Jeremy pulled my favorite three-wick candle out of his backpack. He must've taken it from my apartment.

Jeremy set out the soul jars and placed pillar candles next to each one. There was four total. Including the one he had made for me. By the way he was setting up his ritual, I sensed I hadn't much time left.

"Dad and I buried Scarlet under that pile of rocks." He pointed to the left.

Jeremy's dad was involved. My god, he helped his son dispose of Scarlet's body. I reasoned that Scarlet was Jeremy's first kill, and each victim since was committed as if he were reenacting the original murder, killing the same person over and over and over…

I mentally called out to Sydney. I had no way of knowing if she could hear me, but if there was anything she could do to create a diversion, now would be the time for one.

The wind around our camp picked up, swirling leaves like a tornado around us. I took that as a good sign. Jeremy had heard Sydney pounding on the glass and Erin's banshee cries. Scarlet had only leered at him, but even mentioning her name evoked a disturbing reaction.

"The spirits are with us, Jeremy. I need my sketch pad if you want me to communicate."

He obliged and hovered over me, waiting for me to start drawing.

"You have to uncuff me."

He ran his fingers through his greasy black hair. "If you try to run, I'll kill you fast. I won't give you a nice ceremony like I did for the others."

I shuddered from the visual image and then turned my fear into adrenaline. I wasn't strong enough to fight him. I had to take him by surprise and make an offensive strike before the killer had his hands around my throat again.

He unchained my hand. I placed the tip of the pencil on the page.

"Arrange the jars and candles in a circle," I said with authority. "I need the elemental energy of fire to hear their voices." I rolled the pencil in my fingers as if it were a necessary ritual, buying time as I scanned the woods for a weapon. Once the Soul Jars and candles were in place, I entered the circle and stepped into the moonlight like an actress taking center stage.

I stretched out my arms, aimed my face toward the heavens, and spun slowly, reciting the victims' names. I needed Jeremy to believe I had the power to summon the spirits of the dead and deliver messages from beyond the grave.

While I did have a gift, I had never held a conversation with a ghost in my life. I had received clairaudient clues, and my drawings spoke volumes. Still, I needed to take control of the situation and con Jeremy to help me with the ritual. He was only keeping me alive because he believed I could channel the ghosts of his victims.

I had to keep up the pretense long enough to make my move. I would have the advantage if I could convince him to get on the ground. Once I had him in a vulnerable position, I would grab a weapon and strike—then run like the devil was on my heels.

"Sydney... Erin... Scarlet... join the circle..."

As I mock summoned the dead, a strong gust of wind

blew through the trees, releasing the dead leaves from the nearly naked tree limbs. Negative energy radiated around the circle. It seemed my ritual worked—this was no longer a game.

Sweat beads cropped up on my forehead. The gathering ghosts were not icy and frigid. They were burning with unholy rage. The heat of their energy pulsed through my blood, fueling my fight-or-flight instincts.

Holy shit.

I had never experienced anything like this before—nor had I attempted to summon the dead. The restless spirits banded together and manifested into some sort of supernatural being. The dead were no longer defenseless victims; Erin, Sydney, and Scarlet had combined efforts and assembled to seek revenge on their killer.

I had a deeper connection to Sydney than I had ever experienced before.

"We're going to kill him."

Sydney's voice was as clear as my own thoughts.

BLOW—EVELYN

I FLINCHED AT THE INTIMATE AND HORRIFYING MESSAGE. SHE was right. I was a heartbeat away from death and never questioned her motive. I would kill to save my life. I would fight to the death and drag this psychopath to hell if it meant ridding the earth of his despicable soul.

I lured Jeremy into the circle. "They're all here, Jeremy. All your girls. Join us." I waved my arm in a *come-hither* motion and pointed to the spot where I wanted him.

He did as I commanded.

"Give me the lighter. Scarlet wants me to light the candles."

Jeremy handed me the lighter and then hovered over me in anticipation of what was next.

As I lit all four flames, I continued the game as I pocketed the lighter. "Sit on the hallowed ground. Take off your shoes."

I spotted a large rock in my peripheral vision as I selected a sharpened graphite pencil from the case. I held the tip to the page and pretended to wait for the spirit to move me while I came up with my plan of attack. I sketched Scarlet's features from memory to pique Jeremy's interest.

"Is she saying anything? You said she had a message for me."

Right.

"Scarlet has held a secret for a very long time. She's been waiting for someone like me to deliver it to you. It's about—" As I scrambled to conjure up an imaginary tale, I felt the presence of Scarlet around me. I concentrated on her energy as a vision played out in my head…

A beautiful teenage girl with long glossy hair stands before a mirror in her bedroom, applying lipstick. She wears only a towel as she gets ready and has a lacy bra and panty set spread out on the bed.

As she slides off the towel and stands naked before a mirror, her phone beeps with an incoming text. She giggles at the message, then lifts a stuffed animal off her bed, shields her naked body with the fuzzy plush bear, and snaps a sexy selfie.

As she sends the message, she hears a noise.

Click… click… click…

She turns toward the door and sees it's open a crack, and someone is snapping Polaroid pictures of her as she stands naked in her bedroom. "Jeremy!" she screams. "What are you doing?"

Scarlet opens the door and tries to grab the camera, but Jeremy holds it out of her reach. "Give it to me, pervert. I'm telling your dad!"

Teenage Jeremy's face reddens with rage. His expression burns with lust as his gaze slips to her breasts and then trails down her body. His eyes turn cold as he stares at his stepsister's panicked face.

He drops the camera, grabs Scarlet's wrists, and wrestles her to the bed. She tries in vain to hold him off, cursing and snapping at him as he wraps his hands around her throat to silence her screams. "He doesn't deserve you, Scarlet. You belong with me."

When Scarlet lost her battle to stay alive, Jeremy retrieved his Polaroid and snapped pictures of her corpse. He moved her into different positions and tucked her favorite teddy bear at the crook of her broken neck...

Jeremy knocked me in the shoulder, bringing me back to center as the vision faded. "What is her secret, Evelyn? What did Scarlet tell you?"

I inhaled a sharp breath and flushed the horrific scene from my mind. I had to prepare for my next move before facing the same fate as the others. "Scarlet wants me to tell you, but you must come closer. The secret is personal, and she says I have to whisper it in your ear."

Jeremy leaned closer. His eyes wild with anticipation.

I tightened my grip on the pencil.

"Scarlet wants you to know—"

Whack! I stabbed the pencil into his eye. Blood rushed from the socket as Jeremy wailed in agony and flung his arms, desperate to grab me before I escaped. I hadn't immobilized him but had done enough damage to get a head start. I grabbed the rock and hurled it at his head, but I missed.

Instead, I smashed the top of Erin's jar. The moonlight reflected off the glass and illuminated her cherished Blackwater mood ring, glowing a deep shade of purple.

Erin is giving me a sign.

I grabbed the ring and placed it on my finger. With renewed energy, I grabbed the jagged base of the jar and launched it at his head. The glass grazed his cheek, sending a fresh round of blood oozing from his skin.

While he was down, I picked up another rock and bashed him in the head. That time, I nailed him in the forehead. Jeremy stumbled back, dazed by the blow, still standing and hurling insults and death threats as he groaned in pain.

The sun had set. The woods were pitch black. I ran for the trail, fearing I would never find my way back to the main road.

Desperate to get away, I fumbled through the darkness

until an eerie blue light appeared ahead. A gust of wind blew a trail of leaves toward the path.

"*Follow me, Evelyn. I'll show you the way.*"

I'm right behind you, Sydney.

OBSESSION—EVELYN

I RACED UP THE HILL, TRUSTING SYDNEY'S LIGHT WOULD LEAD me in the right direction.

Nearing exhaustion, I knew that if I made it to the van, I would find my way back to the main road where I would flag down help. With the end of my nightmare in sight, I cringed when Jeremy cursed my name from only a few yards behind me.

"You won't get away from me, Evelyn!"

Oh, God. He's gaining on me.

Even if I could outrun him through the woods, I had nowhere to go once I reached the van. I didn't have the keys to his precious rolling murder den and was reaching my limit of physical exertion. I would have to knock him unconscious to get the keys, but getting too close while he was fueled with rage would get me killed.

To survive the night, I needed help.

If Leo had figured out where Jeremy had taken me, he would've been here by now. Maybe Jeremy was right: *Leo thinks I'm already dead.* The woods were silent. No flashing lights ahead. No sirens. No search dogs barking in the distance.

I had to make a commotion if I had any hope of being rescued. No one—except Jeremy—would hear me if I screamed. I needed a flare, a car horn, or something loud to draw the attention of passing cars on the distant road ahead.

As my brain searched for answers, I was at a loss. Jeremy was bigger and stronger than me, but I had something he didn't have—three pissed-off ghosts on my side who would scorch the earth to wreak vengeance upon him.

Come on, ladies. I can't do this without you.

The mood ring turned purple. I caught a whiff of the energizing scent of lavender. The world around me was bathed in red.

"Fight, Evelyn." My tribe lifted my spirits and gave me the strength to keep moving.

"Stop running, Evelyn! I'm going to piss in your jar and leave you out for the coyotes. I fucking hate you. You're not coming with us!" I checked behind me. Jeremy was gaining ground. He had the flashlight and was able to navigate the trail.

The ghostly blue lights circled above the van, signaling me to follow. I bolted for Jeremy's vehicle when I reached the top of the path. I grabbed the door handle and tried to get inside, but the door was locked.

The light from Jeremy's flashlight was getting closer.

A helicopter sounded in the distance. Had Leo figured out the Linwood clue and tracked me down? I was hidden under the canopy of trees and couldn't risk going out in the open with Jeremy so close behind. If he caught up with me, I would be dead before the helicopter could land.

But I had to make my way out into the open for the search team to find me.

I needed to create a distraction—*like a fire.*

I reached my hand into my pocket and retrieved the lighter. While the trees and earth were too wet to catch fire, I had a gas tank loaded with fuel and a lighter that would blow that rolling murder den back to the gates of hell.

I yanked off my gauzy scarf, flipped open the gas cap, and stuffed the flammable material into the base. The beam from the flashlight was getting closer as I flicked the lighter to set the material on fire. After a few tries, the flame took hold and ignited the cloth. The fire spread and grew stronger. I needed to take cover.

Sirens screamed in the distance. Help was on the way. *Hurry, Leo.*

After all that had happened, I realized how stubborn I had been. We had a big fight, but Leo immediately apologized and wanted to talk it out. I let past feelings of heartache and mistrust seep into my new life, causing me to lose the only man I had ever loved.

I'm sorry, Leo. I hope I get the chance to make things right.

As the smoke rose, I took off down the gravel road and broke into a sprint to take cover. As I ran, I slid on the slippery rocks, twisting my ankle on the way down. I heard a pop. Pain shot through my leg, and I knew it was broken. I was only a few feet from the burning van. I could no longer run and was defenseless if Jeremy reached me before the rescue team found me.

I turned and spotted Jeremy closing in on me. Black toxic smoke lifted from the rusty old van and the fumes were so noxious that the scent of burned rubber burned my eyes. I watched in horror as Jeremy shifted his gaze between me and the burning van. Deciding whether he should kill me first or save the contents of the van before taking my life.

Jeremy flung off his shirt and waved it at the fire, desperate to smother the flames. But to no avail. When he realized the van was too far gone, he set his murderous sights on me.

"You are fucking dead, Evelyn!" Jeremy stormed toward me, limping as he pressed his hand to his gouged-out eye. The sirens were too far away. The search team wouldn't reach me in time. Black smoke lifted from the burning van, and the fumes were so noxious that I fell into a coughing fit.

I lay flat to get some air and watched in horror as Jeremy stomped toward me. I had exhausted every bit of strength to stop him, but it was too late to save myself. When Leo's team eventually found me, I would already be dead.

I won't go down without a fight.

I grabbed fistfuls of gravel to throw in his face. If dying in these godforsaken woods was my fate, I would fight to my last breath. Jeremy's big body lumbered toward me—then stopped abruptly.

A red light darted across his face. His eyes were wide and past me.

"Freeze! Put your hands up where I can see them."

BLOWN AWAY—EVELYN

Leo positioned himself between the killer and me. He was dressed in all-black gear and night-vision goggles and held some vicious-looking rifle that looked like it was from a high-tech spy thriller.

"I said put your hands up where I can see them," he ordered again.

As the flames spread, Jeremy sidestepped toward the burning van. The heat alone was enough to melt human flesh, but the sweltering temperature and toxic smoke didn't deter him.

"You fucking prick! You'll never take me away from them. You can have Evelyn, but the others are mine."

Leo issued one last warning, but Jeremy ignored him and dove at the flaming van, sliding open the door and screaming the names of his victims as he rushed inside to save his precious mementos. Leo let him do it. Jeremy had made his choice.

Flames engulfed the van. Black smoke lifted into the heavens. My thoughts turned to Jeremy inside the van, clawing at his morbid treasures in a desperate attempt to save his precious trophies. I imagined flames consuming his flesh while he was burned alive by his selfish desires.

I pictured the intrusive photos of his victims, burning to a crisp. The photos of his artistically staged corpses. The profoundly personal mementos he'd stolen from his victims, Erin, Sydney, and Scarlet. His twisted obsession with unrequited love had gone up in flames.

Soon, Jeremy's screams were reduced to nothing.

The monster was dead.

As I covered my mouth to block the fumes, a pair of strong hands lifted me off the ground. "Hang on, Evelyn." Leo cradled me in his arms and ran down the gravel path. A moment later, an earth-shattering explosion rocked trees. The blast was so intense that it knocked Leo off his feet, slamming us both to the ground.

Stars flashed before my eyes as I lay on the gravel path and watched clouds of black smoke billow from the van. I covered my nose and mouth with my hands to filter out the toxic fumes. Leo picked me up again and ordered me to keep breathing. "Hang on, partner. I'm taking you on a helicopter ride. The view of the city at this time of night is amazing. You don't want to miss it."

Overcome with exhaustion, I was too weak to keep my eyes open.

"Evelyn." Leo tapped my cheek. "Stay with me, sweetheart. I'm sorry for everything. If I live a thousand years, I'll never stop trying to make it up to you. Can you hear me? Talk to me…"

I lost my battle to stay awake and drifted into a deep sleep.

I DREAMED of a bright tunnel swirling as Sydney, Erin, and Scarlet hovered at the entrance, basking in glory. They were no longer orbs radiating an eerie shade of blue. The morbid signs of death had been replaced by their natural beauty and a glowing aura of eternal peace.

Erin and Scarlet ascended upward into the light, but Sydney paused and focused her energy on me. She waved her hand and a golden swirl of light radiated around me. The sky lit up in a magnificent colorway of pastels and jewel tones the natural world had never known.

Angels blanketed the sky and soared over the heavens, welcoming Sydney's beautiful spirit into their heavenly home. The angels were huge and magnificent, and each was unique in appearance. As I studied them individually, I noticed a pattern.

Each one had imperfections. Some had scars on their faces and bodies, while others wore torn clothes. One had a soldier's uniform.

These are not Michelangelo's cherubs or Raphael's angels.

This ragtag team seemed more like an angelic motley crew of kick-ass warriors on a mission—serve and protect. As I scanned the sky, I understood the nature of their being.

Guardian angels.

Heavenly bodies took flight over the trees, singing a beautiful melody that filled my soul with a rush of joy and gratitude. As my friend moved on to eternal bliss, a single word popped into my head:

"Bridgemont."

ANGELS OF THE WINDY CITY— EVELYN

Six months later...

The gallery buzzed with excitement as our invited guests mixed and mingled at our private sneak preview event. While Chicago's famous tulips popped up around the city, gracing us with their simple beauty, the city had been reborn with new energy as springtime was upon us.

Luis, Gibson, and I had come up with a theme for our latest collection that embodied the season's vibe. After all the hell we'd been through last fall, we rebranded and kicked off the gallery with a fresh new vibe.

We added a few new artists to round out our pack. My fashion designer friend Tess joined our gallery, along with a graphic design team. With the new additions, the studio space felt more fun and energetic. The DOM was growing to her full potential.

I breezed through the crowd and welcomed our guests with my biggest fan by my side. Leo and I held hands as we sipped champagne and mingled with our friends. Everyone was excited to support my bold new art style, inspired by my second survival story.

"Hey there, Evie! Still breathing, huh?" Santoni swooped in for a hug, along with a good-natured tease. I was a part of the Ricci family circle now, and Santoni and I had become fast friends. He always had a joke or a story to brighten my day, and I loved the fun-loving energy he brought to every occasion.

Now that Leo and I were officially dating—for real—he had introduced me to every cop in the city. I had become a celebrity around the precinct because of my gift. I earned my street cred when the chief of police credited me with ending the Windy City Stalker's reign of terror.

I deserved partial credit, but my *partner* and I couldn't have done it without each other. Leo was able to pinpoint my location thanks to the fire that signaled the rescue team. Once he spotted me from the helicopter, he dropped a ladder and rappelled down to the road, not wanting to waste one second to reach me.

Our love for each other proved to be the most powerful tool in our arsenal.

Leo's sister and brother-in-law volunteered to serve as models for Luis's latest tattoo collection featuring edgy angels clad in leather and lace, reigning over the Windy City. Etta wore leather shorts with a set of heavenly bodies riding up her thighs.

Not to be upstaged, Leo's brother-in-law Nix had a full sleeve of vintage pinup tats with a posing calendar girl on each arm. He strutted around the gallery shirtless, flexing his guns and six-pack abs, even though the temporary ink was only on his arms.

Leo's mom and nonna noshed on apps. They sipped pink champagne as our jazz trio played a syncopated version of Led Zeppelin's "Stairway to Heaven." Gibson took the mic and welcomed the crowd when the mood was set.

I glanced around the room and felt a rush of happiness

that had evaded me for so long. I no longer had to hide. I no longer had to pretend to be someone else. I no longer had to live inside my protective shell.

With Leo, I got everything. Unconditional love, friendships, a doting family, and the sexiest and most open-minded detective in the city of Chicago.

While I was recovering from my nightmare, Leo never left my side. He took an extended leave of absence from work, moved me into his home, and helped me navigate the media storm while I carved out a life in my new-normal creative space. Once my ankle healed and I could ditch the cast, my sexy boyfriend surprised me with a tropical vacation in the Bahamas.

Leo was everything to me. Trust was the cornerstone of our relationship, and Leo and I had spent months building our bond so it would never break again.

Gibson dimmed the lights and began the introductions.

Leo reeled me in for a quick hug before I took the stage. "You are wicked talented, babe. Your fans are going to love your new collection." He planted a kiss on my lips and gave my backside a little squeeze.

"I hope there's more where that came from after the party." Under the cover of darkness, I slid my finger through his belt loop and gave it a gentle tug. I pulled away to make my entrance, but Leo drew me back. I thought I would get another smooch, but his expression turned serious.

"He's here," Leo whispered. "In the back of the gallery by Gibson."

As I stepped onstage, I searched the crowd until I found Dr. Vaughn. Our eyes met, and he gave me a nod of encouragement that fueled my confidence.

I lifted the mic and gazed into the crowd. "Have you ever been alone and sensed someone watching you? Have you heard someone whisper your name, only to turn around and find no one there? What if I told you we're never alone? Want to know the truth about angels?"

The audience hummed a collective yes.

"They're everywhere."

I lifted my arm and waved my hand over hundreds of twinkling string lights hanging above the gallery. "Roaming the city streets, standing guard over our households, keeping us safe from hazards unknown. Soaring over the lake, towering above skyscrapers, shielding pedestrians on their blustery commutes..."

No one spoke, mesmerized by my words. "It is my pleasure to present *Angels of the Windy City*."

As the audience applauded, I met Leo's gaze. I felt an overwhelming rush of gratitude that we had survived not only a killer but our own fears and doubts.

Gibson raised the lights and unveiled my collection of paintings of angelic beings reigning over the city. While the angels had never appeared to me again in my dreams, I used my wicked imagination. I took some artistic liberties with my battle-ready army of angels.

One of the guardians wore a Scottish-style kilt and posed with a gargoyle at the top of one of our city's iconic Gothic buildings. Another angel was dressed in tribal clothing and held a sharpened spear at the ready as he hovered over the city's beloved library lion statues.

I loved adding the city's history into my art and shining a spotlight on the artists that brought their visions to life decades before I was born. While this round of paintings was devoid of my stylized ghosts, I was proud to stretch my creative wings and incorporate a lighter style to balance my dark side.

As the crowd reacted to my new style, I stepped off the stage and met Vaughn by the door. He looked like a different person now. He'd grown his hair and styled it in a carefree, tousled wave. Instead of a sharp suit, he wore jeans and a soft gray T-shirt with loafers.

"Thank you for coming," I greeted him with a hug. We had become friends because of our shared story of survival. I wished I had the power to erase the horrors of his past, but he was a survivor, and I had no doubt he would continue his life path of helping others.

"I'm here to say goodbye, Evelyn. I'm leaving in the morning."

I was surprised to hear the news, but understood why he needed to make a change. "Where are you going?"

"A small town in Indiana. Bridgemont."

"Bridgemont?" I recognized the clairaudient word that popped into my head while Sydney crossed over. It was the one time I had held back a clairaudient clue. I sensed Vaughn needed to find his own path and would eventually find his way to where he needed to be. "We'll miss you, but I know you'll be happy there."

The light on Gibson's desk flickered, stealing our attention. Vaughn and I exchanged knowing glances. Heavenly signs from our loved ones appeared when we least expected them—we just needed to learn to recognize the signs.

SERVE AND PROTECT—LEO

I'D BEEN LYING TO EVELYN FOR WEEKS, AND I WAS AFRAID SHE had caught on.

Sneaking out after dinner to follow up on a lead... leaving the house an hour early in the mornings... stepping away to take calls I had said were work related...

Evelyn had been staying at my place since she'd gotten released from the hospital. She never wanted to step foot in her old apartment again—for good reason—and I was happy to let her stay with me until she found a new home.

I knew my place wasn't her style, so I'd offered to help her find a new apartment near her studio. I'd gone with her to check places out, but I always came up with reasons why she should keep looking. I wanted what was best for her, but the truth was, I didn't want her to move out.

I had made some life-altering decisions after I'd almost lost Evelyn. I was still devoted to my job and dove in head-first into every one of our cases. However, I learned to balance work and life by prioritizing my family and friends while trusting my team to take the reins on my off days.

I wanted to spend every moment with Evelyn, so I put my

detective skills to good use and figured out a solution: Lie to my girlfriend's face, sneak around behind her back, and shock the hell out of her by making a life-changing decision without her input.

In short, I would find a place near her gallery where we could live *together*.

While we had agreed to always be honest, this type of lie fell more into the "surprise" category, so I ran with it for the sake of the greater good of our relationship.

I tracked down a newly remodeled apartment less than a mile from the gallery. Big windows with a view of the tree-lined streets, wood floors, and freshly painted walls.

Finding a nice place was only part of the plan; I was an all-in type of guy and wanted everything to be perfect before the big reveal. So, I picked out some new furniture and set it up with the help of a couple of my fellow blue-bloods on our off days. I got a comfy couch, a coffee table, a small dining table, a king-size bed loaded with pillows, and those snuggly throw blankets she loved.

I added a few finishing touches, then drove to pick Evelyn up from work. I was singing along with the radio, totally pleased with myself. Dinner was ready to go into the oven, wine was on the table, the lights were dimmed, and romantic music playing.

I'd clicked on about a half dozen battery-operated candles that mimic the real thing. Evelyn loved her fire, but I hoped we could compromise on special occasions and keep the summoning of spirits to a minimum on date nights.

I'd even taken a large box of salt and poured a line across the threshold of our door, then poured another line across all the windowsills and an extra-large pour at the entrance of our bedroom. I'd been researching all things paranormal and discovered salt was supposed to chase away the dead.

I mean, ghosts interfering in our lives was our new normal, but they needed to learn their boundaries.

When I picked Evelyn up from the gallery, she looked nervous as she slid into the Charger. She put on a good game face, but I could tell she was keeping something from me—which wasn't like her. Since we had become a couple, we'd promised never to keep secrets.

If a clairaudient word popped into her head, she told me. No more hiding clues. When it came to my work, she understood I was obligated to keep some things from her because of my job, but I never shut her out regarding our personal life.

"How was work?" I asked.

"Fine. Interesting. I started sketching something new today." Her cheeks warmed as if something I'd said had embarrassed her.

"An automatic drawing or one of your own?"

"I'm not sure. It felt different."

I was an inquisitive guy and wanted to know more, but I didn't want to turn our special night into an interrogation, so I dropped it. Evelyn seemed in good spirits, and I didn't want to kill the mood. If I needed to know something, she would've told me. I turned the ignition and was about to pull into traffic, but Evelyn touched my hand and stopped me.

"Come up to my studio. I need to share something with you."

She probably wanted to show me what she'd been working on. I wanted to ask her if it could wait, but I felt whatever she had drawn made her nervous.

As she led the way to her studio, her anxiety bounced off the walls. When she'd finished the remodeling job, she kept the entire third floor for herself. She added an efficiency-style apartment wing with a mini kitchen, full bathroom, and a pull-out sofa bed for those times she wanted to work through the night.

I had my buddies down at the FBI help me design and install the most reliable security system known to mankind. I promised no one would ever hurt her again, and I did everything within my power to stay true to my word.

So, what had her so anxious?

Evelyn pulled out her key and slid it into the lock. When she opened the door, she held back a smile as she took my hand and guided me to her private space. She had bought some room-separating bookcases and set up a row of billowy curtains over the entryway to her makeshift lounge area.

She pulled me into her room, illuminated with rows of string lights and paper lanterns. I was pleasantly surprised to see Evelyn had done some redecorating in her space. The sofa bed was opened and covered with silky sheets and furry pillows and bolsters from the XXX shop, which aided lovers who explored different positions.

A small table next to the bed held a collection of erotic lotions and oils that I couldn't wait to rub all over her gorgeous body. The sexual beast inside me growled with excitement when I zeroed in on a couple of vibrating toys my smoking-hot girlfriend wanted me to add to our playtime.

Damn. She knows how to turn me on.

I had no idea what had inspired our new love nest in her studio, but I didn't need an explanation. I scooped my sexy girlfriend into my arms and carried her to the bed. I stripped her naked, tossed off my clothes, and pressed my body on top of hers. I grabbed one of the fluffy fur pillows and tucked it beside her. I rolled her onto her stomach and guided her onto the pillow.

I brushed her hair aside and ran my tongue down her bare back. I grabbed a bottle of oil, squirted it on her skin, and massaged the slick oil all over her body. I groaned with anticipation as I fantasized about penetrating her warm and wet femininity.

"How do you want me, Evelyn?" I whispered.

She was quiet for a moment as she contemplated her answer. "I want you to be in charge. I'm up for anything."

I liked her answer. I wanted to dominate her, but I needed to be sure she was ready for what I wanted to give. I rubbed oil over one of the vibrators and teased her between the thighs. The pulsing sensation brought her to orgasm quickly. We loved our toys, and I experienced incredible erotic satisfaction from bringing her all levels of pleasure.

I kissed her lips and trailed kisses down her body. I tossed the toy aside, rolled her onto her back, and rubbed my cock over her *V* to get her wet and excited for a hard and fast ride. I made a big mess on the bed as I squirted oil over her breasts and massaged her as my erection soared to rock-hard status.

Evelyn let out an erotic moan when I slid inside her. I moved slowly at first, easing in and out under the soft glow of the mood lighting. "You're full of surprises, babe." I kissed her deeply as I gave her a good, deep thrust.

She wrapped her legs around me and lifted her hips until she found that special erogenous zone deep inside that never failed to drive me wild. "Give it to me hard. I want to feel your strength. Take me there, Leo. I'm ready to give it to you."

Evelyn must've been playing out a fantasy. She didn't usually talk dirty to me, but I loved her sexual energy. If my girlfriend wanted The Beast, I would take whatever she was willing to give.

I coaxed Evelyn onto her stomach and slid the furry tiger-striped pillow underneath her. I wrapped my arms around her waist and pulled her to her knees so her back was against my chest.

I sucked on her neck and massaged her breasts as all the

blood in my body went south. "I'm going to give you the most intense orgasm of your life."

Evelyn purred her approval as I guided her onto all fours. Once I had her in the perfect position, I slid back inside her V and gave her a few gentle thrusts. The slightest movement between us in this position felt like a sexual explosion of pleasure.

I wouldn't last long, but we would climax together if I timed it right.

Evelyn swiveled her hips and groaned, enjoying the deep erotic sensation of our new position. I was dominant by nature and found it gratifying to bring Evelyn pleasure in ways she had never experienced.

"What are you doing to me? God, Leo. You're making me so wet."

Damn. "You're so fucking sexy." I pushed deeper inside her, grunting as I headed to climax. Evelyn panted and moaned as I grasped her hips and thrust harder and faster until our passion peaked together.

As we came down from our sexual high, I snuggled beside her on my new favorite bed. I wiped Evelyn's hair out of her eyes and cradled her head under my arm. "What brought this sexual fantasy on?"

"Uh, just something that came to me."

"I love your imagination, babe. I have a surprise for you later, too."

"Great. Can't wait." Evelyn's answers were short and to the point, and her eyes kept drifting to her purse. Something in there was making her nervous. The only things she kept in her bag besides her wallet and shades were her sketchbook and phone.

Had she drawn something she needed to share?

Received harassing phone calls?

After Evelyn's close call with a killer, I needed the truth.

"Is there something you need to tell me, Evelyn?"

She nodded as she slipped on a silky white robe and retrieved her sketchbook. She returned to the bed and issued a warning before flipping it open. "Promise me you won't freak out. This started yesterday, but I didn't understand what was happening until we got here."

Evelyn flipped open the book and showed me a sketch of a building—the new apartment I'd picked out, complete with the balloons and a welcome banner my sisters insisted Evelyn would love.

I shot my gaze to hers. "You drew this *yesterday?*"

She nodded as she flipped to the next drawing of the exact dining table I'd bought, set with flowers, wine, and the new dishes my mother had passed down to me. The next drawing was of the houseplants with the sun shining through the blinds and a line of confetti on the counter.

Evelyn had drawn our apartment's interior before I showed it to her.

I was about to rattle off a string of questions, starting with, "When the hell did you become psychic?" but nearly choked on my tongue when she flipped to the next collection of sketches.

No fucking way...

Evelyn had drawn us in our new studio bedroom, making love in different positions on the fold-out bed. The erotic pictures were sensual, raw, and jaw-droppingly sexy.

As I silently assessed her work, Evelyn's expression had gone flat. After all the heartache her drawings had caused her, it seemed she was worried about how this would affect us. If I had learned anything from past mistakes, it was to never doubt Evelyn's gift. Ever.

"Tell me what you're thinking, Leo."

Life would never be dull with Evelyn, and I was ready to take that wild ride with her.

"I think we need to get some picture frames. I'm plastering these bad boys all over the new place. You like it, right? Your *almost* surprise?"

Evelyn laughed as I pulled her in for a hug. "I love it. And I love *you*."

"I'm sure glad that's me in those pictures, babe," I teased. Evelyn melted in my arms, relieved I didn't freak out. "Anything else I need to know?"

She smiled and pointed to a painting covered with a drop cloth. Evelyn pulled me out of bed, tossed me a matching robe, and pulled off the tarp.

Holy shit. It was a painted version of us having sex in her studio. Our skin glistening with oil. Me behind her, grasping her hips as I thrust inside her. Our bodies tight and toned, perfectly molded together. Our faces frozen in ecstasy.

My gaze drifted to the brass plate attached to the frame:

SERVE AND PROTECT
By Evelyn Sinclair

Evelyn squeezed my hand to bring me back to center. "I've been thinking about a theme for the summer collection. Something like *Sex in the Windy City*? You won't mind if I put our erotic collection on display for the entire city to devour?"

"Well, you've captured my best look." I pointed to my erotic expression. Evelyn had immortalized the moment we had climaxed together. "I'd be honored, babe."

As we laughed and Evelyn tossed her sketchbook on the unmade bed, I had a gut feeling her new ability would wind up getting her into trouble. Ghosts seeking her out to solve their murders was bad enough, but it seemed Evelyn was seeing premonitions that could predict the future?

Her new skill was dangerous, and I didn't like the idea of her new talent falling into the wrong hands. But no matter what the future holds, Evelyn and I would get through it together.

We were partners in crime and in life. I would protect and serve the good citizens of the Windy City and the beautiful and talented woman who had captured my heart for all of eternity—which, according to Evelyn—was a damn wonderful place.

WANT TO READ MORE?

Start a new series from Kat Shehata!

Love mafia romance? The complete Russian Tattoos Trilogy is available now. Falling in love isn't a crime, but falling in love with a Russian mob boss could be deadly.

ENJOYED DRAWN TO DEATH?

If you enjoyed this story, please consider leaving a review. Even a short review might encourage a new reader to take a chance on my book. I would love to introduce Evelyn and Leo to as many readers as possible. To leave a quick review, please visit:

    Amazon
    Spread the book love on Goodreads here:
    Goodreads

WANT MORE EVELYN AND LEO?

Don't miss the next release in the Evelyn Sinclair series! DRAWN TO THE MAFIA, will be released later in 2023. Stay up to date by signing up for my newsletter: www.katshe hata.com/newsletter

ACKNOWLEDGMENTS

As with any book, there are so many people to thank. The first shoutout goes to my incredibly supportive husband. It has taken me years to work out the world and characters for this story, and he has cheered me on from the beginning.

He has read many drafts and versions of this story and always delivered constructive feedback to help me work through the process. We often discussed details about the book on our date nights over a bottle of wine and spoke of my fictional characters as if they were part of our family. I am blessed to have this wonderful man in my life.

High-fives to my kids for always believing in me and supporting my dreams. Fist-bumps to my friends who are especially eager to read the steamy scenes of my books and grill me about all the delicious details. Thanks to my editor Deborah for helping my story reach its greatest potential and the behind-the-scenes experts crucial to my team.

Most of all, I want to thank the readers! I have an artist's soul, and the most important part of my career is delivering books readers will love. Thank you to every single person who has supported my writer's journey. Bloggers, reviewers, and readers, I appreciate your support more than words can express. Group hugs to all the book lovers out there.

Being an author is the best job in the world, and I enjoy interacting with readers on social media and in my Facebook reader group. Let's chat! Visit my website for all the details. *www.katshehata.com*

ABOUT THE AUTHOR

Kat is a New York Times Bestselling author—with the help of a psychic. After teaming up with world-renowned psychic Sylvia Browne, Kat co-wrote and published Animals on the Other Side. The book was a hit and landed on the New York Times Bestseller list.

Kat's writing career took a romantic turn when a love story about a mob boss and a troubled young woman wouldn't get out of her head. After spending years writing The Russian Tattoos Trilogy, a new couple, Evelyn and Leo, the main characters of Drawn to Death, demanded her attention.

When Kat is not reading or writing romantic suspense, ghost thrillers, or murder mysteries, she enjoys long walks and traveling with her husband. She splits her time between Cincinnati, Ohio, and Boca Raton, Florida.

She holds a bachelor's degree in theatre from Wilmington College, a professional writing certificate from the University of Cincinnati, and a master's degree in creative writing from Spalding University.

Russian Tattoos: Obsession

A Russian billionaire becomes obsessed with a small-town American woman. Vladimir has been stalking Carter from Russia for years and moves to Ohio to meet her. He works his way into her life, and Carter is drawn to the sexy and mysterious businessman with a delicious Russian accent.

Vladimir is a dangerous man who earned every tattoo inked on his skin. He's a bad guy in some respects, but he's not all bad.

He is a powerful man who gets what he wants, and after stalking the gorgeous tennis player for years—Vladimir wants Carter. A little charm melts her heart, and behind the scenes, he orders his henchman to track her every move.

When Carter falls for Vladimir's charms and gets in too deep with the Russian mafia, she must fight for her freedom before the attraction turns fatal.

Russian Tattoos: Prisoner

Carter Cook is being held prisoner by the Russian mafia.

Carter is the obsession of mob boss Vladimir Ivanov, a man she once loved. Now a mafia war has erupted on his home turf, and Vladimir's enemies have put a bounty on her head to force him to surrender.

If she is captured, his rivals will deliver a deadly ultimatum—his life in exchange for hers. The price for Carter's freedom is Vladimir's blood.

Vladimir vows to get her home and never interfere in her life again.

Giving up the woman he loves is the only way to protect her from the bad guys—including himself.

Russian Tattoos: Criminal

Russian mob boss Vladimir Ivanov has many enemies; one just kidnapped the woman he loves.

A mafia war has erupted in London, and Vladimir's enemies know his one weakness is his deep passion for his loyal and headstrong soulmate, Carter. When rival mob boss Maksim kidnaps her, Vladimir is willing to pay the ransom with his blood.

But Maksim's plans go deeper than that. Vladimir's blood may not be enough.

Maksim wants Carter for himself.

Made in United States
North Haven, CT
06 June 2023